The 1

"Between four and five o'clock I saw the *Greenwich* board a disabled Dutch ship
which had fallen among our ships. The *Greenwich* took her and carried her away."
The Journal of John Narborough, Lieutenant and Captain of the Prince, *May 28th 1672.*

To Georgeanna and Nyx, with love.

The Lion of Sole Bay

Julia Jones

Illustrated by Claudia Myatt

GOLDEN DUCK

First published in 2013 by Golden Duck (UK) Ltd.,
Sokens,
Green Street,
Pleshey, near Chelmsford,
Essex.
CM3 1HT
www.golden-duck.co.uk

ISBN 978-1-899262-18-2

Image of the Stavoren © National Maritime Museum, Greenwich, UK
All other illustrations © Claudia Myatt
www.claudiamyatt.co.uk

Design by Megan Trudell
www.emdash.me.uk

Title font
Old Rubber Stamp © Rebecca Simpson Design

Solebay Lectures font
Grandjean © Intellecta Design

e-book conversion by Matti Gardner
matti@grammaticus.co.uk

Printed and bound in the UK by Berforts Information Press

Strong Winds series

Contents

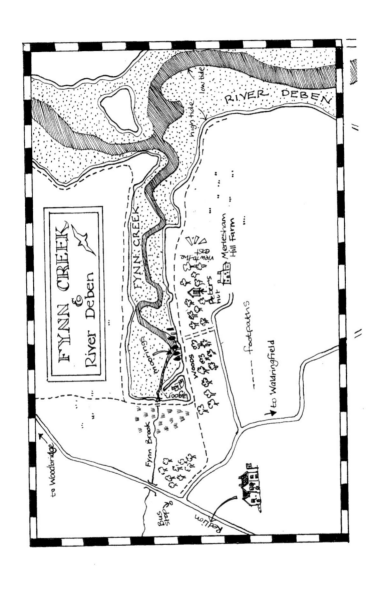

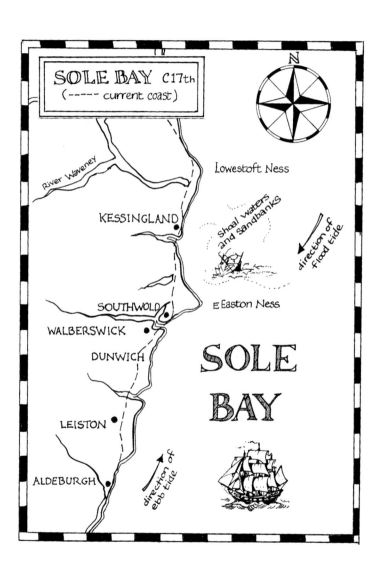

AUTHOR'S NOTE

Luke, who is the hero of this story, has already appeared in other titles in the *Strong Winds* series. This, however, is his own adventure and there's no need for you to have read any of the previous books before you set out with him through the woods to the creek on the night of Halloween.

Luke has lived in Suffolk all his life but, at the beginning of this story, he knows almost nothing about the Battle of Sole Bay which took place off the Suffolk coast in 1672. If you know as little as Luke (or as little as I did before I began my research) you might like to read the series of lectures contributed by our mutual friend Mr M.W. Vandervelde. They are at the back of this book and can be read at any time – or not at all. Mr Vandervelde is so full of enthusiasm for his subject that he admits he's often given his talks to a row of chairs in an empty hall or even to his wife's collection of garden gnomes.

Suffolk people will notice that many of the places in this story are using older, alternative names. The tide times, stages of the moon and the weather in this story are correct (+ 24 hours) for October/November 2010.

Julia Jones, Essex 2013

CHAPTER ONE

Halloween I

Friday 31 October, moon entering the last quarter

Luke, Angel

Luke waited until he was certain he couldn't hear the car any more. Then he waited a little longer. It was a quiet car. So quiet the engineers had to fix a noise to tell people the engine was on. What if Lottie or Anna remembered one more thing and came back? He needed to know they were completely gone.

Then he let himself through the wicket gate and into the magic wood. He wasn't going down the asphalt track or through the cleared picnic area. He was living in the Land of Legends now. He was on a Quest.

Luke crouched low as he traversed the top hedge. It was brambly and bristling. There were nettles in the grass.

His backpack was no trouble. In his mind he'd taken out the t-shirts, pyjamas, boots and spare jeans and refilled it with imaginary weapons and a magic cloak. The extra blanket, sleeping bag and buoyancy aid were awkward because they were bulky and the supermarket carrier – loaded with all the provisions Lottie seemed to think he'd need for a week – was a complete pain. Its handles were too small to fit over his shoulders and, because Luke was still quite short for his age, it dragged through the damp grass. When he tried to lift it higher, it banged against his ankles. He might get jumped at any moment.

How could he use his sword arm while carrying stuff like this?

For a moment Luke considered running down the track to the moorings and leaving his luggage on his dad's boat. Coming up and starting his Quest again.

That would be one life lost before he'd properly begun.

Luke paused and glanced round, checking for danger. Then he put down the buoyancy aid, the sleeping bag, the blanket and the food carrier and slipped the backpack off his shoulders. He opened it and rummaged inside. In a game all this would be his inventory. He pulled out the scarf Lottie had forced him to pack.

"It's nearly November," she'd said. "There's no heating on *Lowestoft Lass* and you'll be out of doors most of the time – except in the mornings on the kayak course. People who work outside need to dress sensibly. Even Bill would agree with me about that."

Lottie was his step-mum. He mainly liked her quite a lot. He wasn't certain that he always liked the way she talked about his dad. Lottie was getting banished from his life this week along with all the rest of them – especially her daughter Anna, his know-everything step-sister.

Luke's dad was Bill Whiting. He worked part-time in a boat-yard. Bill was Liam's dad as well, and Vicky's. Liam and Vicky had chosen to go to Italy with Lottie and Anna. They'd all be on the main road to the airport by now.

Lottie was a singer. Her career had gone quiet after she'd had Vicky but now she was making a comeback and she had a recording date at a studio in Milan. Anna was going because she sort of managed her mother and Vicky would go anywhere as long as she didn't get left behind.

Liam was going – almost out of his head with excitement

– because Anna had booked tickets to a Champions' League football match with Manchester United and AC Milan in the San Siro stadium. She said it was his Christmas and birthday in advance. Probably for ever.

Luke didn't like football and had managed to make out he wasn't that bothered about seeing the recording studio or going on an aeroplane. He hadn't never in his whole life spent time alone with his dad. There'd been his mum when he was a baby. And then, later, there'd been Lottie. Then his dad had gone away and Lottie had gone too and all of them – him, Liam, Vicky and Anna – had been taken into care.

They'd met Donny and Gold Dragon and *Strong Winds*. And Xanthe and Maggi and Skye. The bad days were like a done dream. No more shouting or worry about money. They could be what they liked now.

Bill had been paid out for some salvage and he'd bought an old wooden fishing boat called *Lowestoft Lass* which he was beginning to restore. He and Luke were going to live on *Lowestoft Lass* all week and Bill had said he could do with some practical help.

No-one had ever described Luke as practical. Practical was mainly Liam. Luke, they said, was dreamy.

Now Luke was ready to enter the wood above the water. He wasn't going to come out the same person as the Luke who lived at home with the rest of them at Bawdsey. Nor the Luke who went to school neither. If he got through this wood safely, then he was going to come out someone new for this week: someone who would make his dad feel proud of him.

He looked at his bags and bundles – all that for one half-term holiday!

He hooked the scarf through one arm of the buoyancy aid and through both handles of the food carrier. He wrapped the next bit around the blanket and tied some knots, but then it wasn't long enough so he extended it with a pair of thermal leggings. Another of Lottie's orders. You wouldn't think she was as bossy as Anna but she was. He'd had to pack a full set of waterproofs as well!

The sleeping bag got shoved into the carrier on top of the eggs and bread, then he fastened the loose end of the leggings to his backpack. Hitched the backpack over his shoulders so that he was pulling everything else behind him. It wasn't exactly how it would work in a game but it left both his arms free for attack and defence plus it would brush out his tracks if there were sniffer monsters on the trail.

Luke fitted an imaginary arrow to his imaginary bow and carried on to the place where the trees grew close together and he could begin his descent to the river unseen by mortal eyes.

The supermarket carrier twisted and bumped. It must have brushed out his tracks pretty well on the grass as he made it into the wood without being jumped once. But then it started snagging against undergrowth and fallen twigs. It was possibly worse in the few places where it did run free as it collected a whole bow-wave of leaves which fanned out behind him. He was leaving a track like a motorway.

Jabberjays flew shrieking from the branches. Ivy snaked up and down the tree trunks while grey-brown roots lay across his path like old, gnarled knucklebones. The next section of the wood floor was littered with small, greeny-brown balls. They were totally spiny. They looked explosive.

Luke stopped and took off the backpack. Then he tried to untie the bundles but the knots were strained too tight. He stood up slowly and rotated 360 degrees, imaginary bowstring pulled taut against his ear, squinting intently along his imaginary arrow. Nothing dared move but he knew that they were waiting. A dark-green holly loomed twenty feet high. He'd never seen a bush so tall. It was a wood giant, robed and sinister among the brown and gold of the autumn leaves. He wondered how soon it would transform.

Luke wasn't used to being on his own. They'd all been in the car, cases packed and changes of clothes ready, when Lottie picked him and Anna up from school. She'd brought snacks but there wasn't hardly time to eat anything as she drove round the head of the creek and along the narrow road to the gate at the beginning of the track. They'd been carrying on the row about them dropping him at the top and not coming all the way through the wood to the boat.

"Bill won't be back from work yet and I really need to know you're safe."

"What's different about being safe at the top of a track and safe at the bottom end? I'm twelve now. I can take myself down. I've gotta do things for myself sometimes. You even said so."

"Ring me then. As soon as you get there."

"But you'll be driving."

"Okay. Ring Anna."

"Might not have reception." He could see they were about to gang up and insist. "Okay, okay, I'll text you when I can."

These days were short. Luke remembered it was Halloween and looked back at the wood giant. Was there something stirring in its twisted leaves? He needed to check out the area. Create a forcefield maybe. He couldn't do that carrying a backpack and a blanket and a buoyancy aid and a supermarket bag. He propped them together and used the first of his invisibility philtres. He hadn't got many, even playing by imaginary rules.

Then he was off, darting from tree to tree, leading his pursuers away from his inventory and away from the moorings as well. He was planning to reach Fynn Creek further down. There was a path between the riverbank and the trees that would bring him round and back to the houseboats. He needed to arrive at *Lowestoft Lass* from an unsuspected direction. He'd only got a week. He had to start it special.

＋　＋　＋

Halloween. Trick or treat. Most of the other Year Eights were going round each other's houses. No-one had invited Angel and, even if they had, her parents would have fussed. They'd have wanted phone numbers. Find out who was organising. Ring the other parents. Check she wouldn't be exposed to flashing lights or eating the wrong food or over-excited.

To be fair they'd had some bad experiences in the days when everyone got asked to everyone else's parties. Angel's mum and dad had invariably been called within the first half hour to come and take their daughter away.

She wasn't a kid any more. She wasn't going to go home and bob apples. So she told her parents she might have an after-school rehearsal for a Christmas show. That seemed far enough away to be safe.

She didn't have any idea what she was going to do – except she was going to do something. If she hung around until it was nearly dark she might find a group of other people in her year and they might not notice it was her. Rules changed on Halloween. She'd bought a mask.

Her parents were so pleased it was embarrassing. Her mum got out her diary to pencil in the date and her dad wanted to ring the school straight away for tickets. Angel had to switch her story fast.

"It's not like that. Not for parents. It's just a tutor group thing. We might be doing a dance for end-of-term assembly."

Well, they might have been doing a dance for end-of-term assembly. Except they weren't. And she wouldn't have been in it if they were.

Angel didn't feel comfortable with telling lies and making plans so she did the whole day in school. Thought she'd go crazy. Didn't even bunk at lunchtime. Couldn't believe how boring it was. And people did this all the time?

Her phone was confiscated second period to stop her messing about. She was sent out in third period and by fourth she was in isolation. She'd never last in school till she was sixteen. Today she was doing it for her mum and dad. This once.

Angel was straight down the skate-park as soon as the clock hit half-past. Didn't wait for the bell or get her phone back. Grabbed her bag and punched the exit knob, then jumped down the steps of isolation, dodged through the cars and the bikes and the buses and ran.

Angel was quick and she had brilliant balance. She'd gone out over the roof at one of her primary schools. At some places they'd thought she might be an athlete or a gymnast so her mum and dad had tried taking her to all sorts of different coaching sessions. They still hadn't completely given up. Every half-term and holiday they paid out and persuaded her along. The clubs they chose all felt like school – people talking at you all the time and waiting ages for your turn. Angel was a rubbish listener and she hated standing still. The other kids would get annoyed and start picking on her. Then there'd be a fight.

She'd got her tracksuit in her bag. It was black, with a hood. Wicked! As soon as she reached the public conveniences she changed into it and shoved her skirt and blazer in the bag instead.

Angel gave a skip of relief. She hated skirts. You could wear trousers to secondary school but they hadn't known that when she joined and her mum and dad said they weren't going to buy trousers until she'd grown out of the skirt. Basically they'd got fed up with buying her new uniforms cos she got thrown out of schools so often.

Angel hadn't got thrown out of Fitzgerald (so far) but she hadn't grown either. She'd always been small and she'd learned that if you were the smallest in the class you needed to be tough. That was partly why she'd dyed her hair red at the beginning of the second year. She gelled it to make it spring out from her head like a mane – warning people to back off. Her mum and dad hated it of course. It was no good trying to explain why she'd done it.

The skate-park was good. If she had a bike or a board of her own she'd be down here all the time. She'd given up asking her parents. It was partly the kit was expensive but mainly they were worried she would hurt herself. There wasn't no-one responsible at the skate-park.

Angel knew that it was mainly the pills she had to take that made them fuss. And she wasn't any good at thinking about risk. They'd offered to buy her a scooter for her birthday if she'd completed a whole page of the frigging Behaviour Modification star charts that Extended Learning kept giving her.

And she had! But then the scooter was one of them stupid little folding ones. Her mum had bought it and it was pink …

Angel had run out of the house and down to the railway line and taken herself off to Ipswich and hadn't come back all day. When she did come home she knew her mum had been crying and her dad was in a grump. She'd tried to say sorry but she just couldn't see why they couldn't see it. She'd asked if she was adopted but that made her mum cry some more and anyway they said that she wasn't. She must have been swapped at the hospital.

There was a gang of hard-lads at the skate-park. They were older than Angel and they didn't do school. They did cigarettes and beers and other stuff and then they started shouting or got silly. When they were hanging-out the other kids soon went home.

They had all the kit though – stunt-bikes and skate-decks – and Angel knew they were as bored as she was. If she played up to them a bit, they'd usually let her use a deck or a bike. Then she could practise the wheelies and the flips, the grinds and the three-sixties that made them watch her and tell her she was a dude. She'd be buzzing and scared enough to concentrate.

If she got scared too much…that was different.

It didn't work out so well today. The lads had been there a while already and they were getting restless. It wasn't long before they took back the kit they'd lent her. Then they headed for the train station and the river wall. It wasn't worth her splitting and going back up the town cos it wasn't dark yet. Angel balanced across the railway bridge and did hand-flips on the flat top of the covered seating. The lads passed a bike up for her to try some stunts but then a couple of passers-by shouted that they were calling the police so they took it back and slouched on towards the boatyard.

Angel had been in school all day. Her body fizzed and crackled with unused energy. Maybe she could climb the crane. She'd leave if they started swearing at anyone or doing damage.

They were over the No Admittance gate – bikes and all – and into the Phoenix Yard. There were a load of boats standing out of the water on the stones. Some of them were on trailers but there were others propped up on telegraph poles or metal legs. The surface was pebbles so it wasn't any good for boarding but the lads had a couple of well-small bikes and soon they were daring each other to ride in and out of the props, close under the boats. You had to duck right down to do it.

Angel was the best obviously because she was the smallest but the others couldn't be beat by her because she was a girl. So they got stupider and louder and started showing off more and taking more risks.

They none of them noticed that the boatyard wasn't empty. There was still a bloke there, black woolly hat and a donkey jacket, clearing up before he left.

If people were on their own they didn't normally tangle with the hard-lads. They shouted from a safe distance or got out their phones. But this bloke stopped what he was doing and came walking over towards them as if he had something to say, something to explain maybe.

Whatever it was they didn't get to hear it.

Angel had found the lowest boat of all. Little yellow one – *Gingerbread Man* – she liked that name. "You can't catch me!" she'd yelled and she'd gone under really fast. Her head right down, crouched flat to the handlebars. She'd felt the underneath of *Gingerbread Man* brushing the back of her hoodie.

One of the big lads was right behind her. Tanking it. Then he saw he wasn't going to make it under and he bottled. Spun his bike hard round and hit the first of the three telegraph poles that were chocked against the boat for legs. Hit it straight out.

Gingerbread Man lurched sideways.

The lads shoved Angel off the bike. They grabbed it and then they ran. Over the gate and across the railway line and…gone.

Angel saw the second leg begin to slide and she double-somersaulted backwards. The bloke in the donkey jacket couldn't have looked properly. He was running towards the boat with his arms out as if he thought he could stop the fall. She might have blanked for a minute, or maybe she just shut her eyes.

The man caught the boat all right. It came right down on top of him. Would have squashed him completely if the poles hadn't still been there. They were lying flat but they were thick and solid. They kept *Gingerbread Man* just that last bit off of the ground.

It wasn't a big boat but big enough. The man was stuck under the part towards the back where it started curving up again.

Angel could only see his top half.

"Guys!" she screeched. "Come back!"

But the lads were gone and the bloke on the ground wasn't saying anything and it was, finally, getting dark.

"Help, somebody help!"

There wasn't anyone and she didn't have her phone. She forced herself to crawl over to the man. She could see that he was totally trapped. She couldn't see whether he was alive.

"Hey!" she said, not loud. "Hey, mister?"

But he didn't answer. He was breathing which was something. There wasn't much more. His face was sort of whitey-green and his eyes didn't open. Not even when she leaned right close.

Angel tried to get her hands in his pockets case he had a phone on him. Knew it was urgent for an ambulance. Couldn't reach though. Bloody boat was in the way.

She stood up and screamed for help again. She sort of sensed that the lads hadn't all gone. That a couple of them might've stopped and turned back, needing to see what they'd done.

"Call an ambulance," she shouted into the shadows. "If you won't use your own phones, get into their office and use that. He's hurt really bad. You've got to or he might not make it. And tell them they need lifting gear. I don't know you. You don't know me neither."

She guessed they'd do it. Specially now it was dark and they could break into the office. They wouldn't have used their own phones – too scared to get caught.

It might be ages before the ambulance came. You turned their head didn't you? Case they were sick.

His head was heavy and the ground was lumpy with pebbles.

Angel sort of propped his head on her leg while she pulled off her sport-sack and got her blazer out. Made him a pillow with it. Kept his face off the damp.

She couldn't think what else. There was one of his hands available so she hung on to that.

Then Angel tried to say sorry. Tried to tell him it was going to be okay.

+   +   +

Luke's Quest got put on pause once he'd crossed the gangway onto *Lowestoft Lass* and stepped down onto her scuffed grey deck. She felt safe. Like home, even though she wasn't.

The tide had lifted her out of the mud and he could see more than halfway down Fynn Creek. It was almost high water. The shallows were hidden and only the positioning of the red and green marker buoys revealed what a winding channel you had to follow if you wanted to reach the River Deben beyond.

Bill had had to bring *Lowestoft Lass* into the creek on the top of a spring flood to manoeuvre her safely into her berth. Luke wondered, fleetingly, how the long Dutch barge next door had managed to get in at all. She was from Amsterdam: Hooge 52 tonnes. That meant weight, he supposed. Her name was *Drie Vrouwen*.

It was a good spot where the moorings were. Right at the top of the navigable creek before the Fynn became non-tidal and changed its name from Fynn Creek to Fynn Brook. Luke and Liam had chased each other across the flood bank at the west end. Then they'd dared each other to climb down to check out the metal sluice that controlled the water flowing in from the brook to the creek. It was just a trickle at low tide but when the tide was high or there'd been a lot of rain it came surging through. You could see why there were DANGER notices.

Fynn Brook arrived through reed beds with lots of different streams joining together. There was plenty of exploring to be done. Adventures, probably.

The high, sloping wood on the south side sheltered the moorings from the prevailing wind. There was a clutter of miscellaneous vessels secured to stakes and jetties. All sorts but mainly small. The people who came here a lot called themselves the creekies. They seemed a cheery bunch. There'd been barbecues in the summer.

Bill mainly liked Fynn Creek because it was cheap and you could get on with your work without being disturbed. If he'd kept *Lass* in Phoenix Yard there'd always have been people wanting him to help with all their jobs and his dad didn't seem to know how to say no. It was typical he wasn't back yet. He'd still be clearing up after everyone else had left to start the weekend.

His dad spent most of his free time on *Lowestoft Lass*. Didn't seem to want to come home to the rest of them in the big house at Bawdsey. Not unfriendly. More out of place.

Same with the holiday. It had been organised by Anna, who wasn't anything to do with Bill. She was paying but Luke was sure she'd asked Bill if he'd like to come. Asked as if she meant it. But his dad had said no.

Didn't matter. He hadn't gone to Italy either. They were going to have dads'n'lads this half-term. He'd never slept on *Lowestoft Lass* before. Been visiting on board and playing about with Liam but not slept. He could imagine the days when she'd been buffeting out in the stormy seas. Away from home for weeks at a time, seeking her finny fortune.

Bill had been a fisherman before any of them had been born. And his family before him. When he bought *Lowestoft Lass*, he'd also bought a solid, flat, plastic dinghy and then he'd got some nets as well and he'd gone fishing in the summer evenings in the warm shallow water at the edge of the river.

Luke had been there when he'd caught a half dozen tiny sea bass. They were twisting and struggling in the net. Gills opening and shutting, desperate, like tiny wings that couldn't fly. His dad had tipped them all back. Said it was because of their size but it could've been because he saw Luke couldn't cope.

Luke was going to have to man up this week. Try not to think too much. Forget Land of Legends, maybe. All that stuff with heroes and monsters.

He got out his mobile to text Lottie:

Safe. Love u xx

But it wouldn't send.

He decided to make him and his dad some tea. Wasted loads of matches trying to light the gas before he realised it was off at the cylinder. Then he remembered he'd left all his bags at the top of that slope, including milk and stuff. If he ran up there to fetch them, using the asphalt track this time, his phone would get reception. His message to Lottie would ping off from the top and he'd be back with all the food and luggage before Bill could begin to wonder where he'd got to. They might meet. He wasn't sure which way his dad came home.

Luke shivered suddenly – violently – though he wasn't cold.

He'd told Liam that if you shivered like that it meant someone walked over your grave. But Anna had got cross and said that was superstitious rubbish. An involuntary muscular reflex was all it was, she said.

It was a good thing, Luke thought, that his step-sister was always right. He couldn't see anyone as he left *Lowestoft Lass* and it was starting to get dark. There were birds flapping in the trees like trapped spirits; branches cracking like crushed bone. If he emptied his mind and forgot Halloween and didn't think of graves and ran until he was onto the asphalt path, he probably wouldn't shiver again.

It was like trying to make yourself stop having hiccups just by holding your breath. It didn't entirely work.

✦   ✦   ✦

Angel was holding the man's cold hand and talking to him and listening out for the ambulance and trying to see which bits of him the boat was squashing. And she was sort of praying – which was something she'd never done before – and she was feeling the pebbles sticking into the side of her leg and the other foot getting pins and needles and wondering how long this was going to be and whether the man would die and if she could move without making things worse and what her mum and dad were going to say and hoping they would never find out.

She was thinking angry thoughts about the lads who had run off and envious thoughts wishing she'd run off with them.

Her whole body was starting to jump and to fidget like it did at Sunday lunch or in assemblies but she knew that this time she was going to sit still and she was going to channel all those tickly feelings into one bright stream. And that bright stream was gold and scarlet and warm and it was going to run together out of every bit of her and across into the man's cold hand. Then it was going to flow up and along his limp arm like molten metal until it brought the life back into his heart and brain. She wasn't going to allow this crushed man to freeze away.

Angel's foot wanted to kick something. There was an itch nibbling at the middle of her back. Her shoulder twitched. Mentally she grabbed the whole lot of them and pulled them into line. They were to go down her arm and into the man's hand. No argument.

She carried on talking to him. Made it louder and more definite. Promised him he was going to be all right.

His breathing was weird and it was too dark for her to see his face any more. She felt that he was growing colder.

Angel was small but she was supple. Without disarranging her hand for a moment or stopping her flow of words she wriggled her whole body close to his body, pulled her skirt out of the bag and draped it lightly over his chest. Then she held him without hardly touching. Angel had funny feelings about touching. Her mum was normally the only person who got near her. Except in a fight.

"You're going to be okay," she told him over and over. "You're totally, definitely going to be okay. Take it from me. OK. Gold Star Promise. That's the ones I really keep."

She was concentrating harder than she'd ever concentrated. Every bit of energy she had she was giving. She was concentrating so hard that it was a huge shock when she heard the ambulance sounding its way across the railway line and into the yard. Its headlamps dazzled her as they swung round and settled on the pale hull of the fallen boat.

The flashing blue light was doing something funny to her head.

No! Not here!

Angel jumped to her feet, her arm shielding her face. Then she bent down, grabbed her skirt back off of the man's chest and pulled the mask from her bag.

A small witch fled into the night.

CHAPTER TWO

Halloween II
Friday 31 October, moon entering the last quarter

Luke, Angel, Helen

Blppp! Luke's text to Lottie got sent from the phone in his pocket just as he reached the lane on the far side of the gate.

This was where her car had left him. All he needed to do was follow his own trail until he reached the place where he'd hidden the bags. That shouldn't be hard. Along the grass, keeping the hedge to his right. Ignoring the wet grass and the whirring shapes that might be bats. Why hadn't he brought a torch? Because it was in his bag, of course.

The dark was closing in as if someone was twisting a dimmer switch. He got to the edge of the wood and couldn't see anything. He remembered how the supermarket carrier had pushed a bow-wave through the leaves. He'd worried that it was leaving a massive trail. Now he hoped it had.

Luke knelt down and started patting the leaves, feeling for the swept track as he waited for his eyes to adjust.

His ears were sharp enough. They heard too much. Not just his own panting breath and the squashy rustle of the leaf cushion but other unidentified sounds; sudden calls and sharp, quick scuffles – like claws. Birds or maybe squirrels would be okay but not badgers, stoats or foxes. And he definitely didn't need any ghouls or monsters. Not flesh-eating hairy spiders either. Or giants. He heard an owl. It was only an owl. The sort of thing you could get in a picture book. It wasn't a disembodied spirit and if it was hunting something, it wasn't hunting him.

Luke's groping hands felt tree roots. He wished he'd never thought that they could be bones. Then his bare hand pressed down on something that was seriously prickly. Baby porcupines? Then he remembered the spiny balls he'd seen earlier. Of course they weren't explosive and he'd only been playing when he used an invisibility philtre to hide his bags.

"Revelatio!" That wasn't right. "Speculandum!"

Oh come on –

He'd been crawling as he searched. Now he sat back on his knees to get his bearings.

Plop. There was something random falling from the trees. Why wasn't there even a moon?

He listened again. From beyond the wood he could hear water birds settling for the night and beyond them a rumble that must be traffic. End of the week. People going home. Normal people. With plans and families.

The damp was soaking through his jeans, his hands felt stained with leaf mould, the sweet wet smell of rot and fungi was going up his nose and into his brain.

He heard sirens.

Lottie and Anna and Liam and Vicky would be at the airport by now. He was going to have to leave the bags until tomorrow when it was light and get back to *Lowestoft Lass*. He didn't want his dad to worry.

Luke stood up, brushing his hands on his fleece. Took a couple of steps and did a header straight onto his cache. The sleeping bag and the buoyancy aid and the backpack and the supermarket carrier were still lashed together by the scarf and the thermals. He couldn't get the knots undone but he wasn't bothered. They could spread them out on the wheelhouse table and sort everything together.

Best to hurry. He should have written a note. As straight down the hill as he could and then left at the creek. Arms full of bags: foot careful. An unexpected glow suggested there might be some building that he hadn't noticed earlier. The light was so dim it was almost brown.

Lowestoft Lass was dark when he reached her but so were the other liveaboards. Not a glimmer anywhere except from a set of three carved orange pumpkin heads grinning from the black Dutch barge.

Where was his dad? He ought to be home by now. He wouldn't have gone straight out looking for him, would he?

Luke found the switch for the wheelhouse light and began to sort though the mess of crushed biscuit, broken eggs and leaking milk. Get it all clean and put away before Bill came back. He'd need to hurry.

Luke had time to mop up every drip of spilt milk; time to eat the most broken of the biscuits and pick out every last slimy piece of eggshell. He had time to find a metal spike to push into the centre of those over-tightened knots and time to wriggle it backwards and forwards until they finally worked loose.

He had time to get properly frightened.

WHERE WAS HIS DAD?

✦ ✦ ✦

Angel had enough sense left to pull off her mask when she was almost home. She kicked it under a parked car and tried to calm her breathing like they'd showed her in those sessions. Then she walked up the path between the faded smiles and the weathered cheeks of her mum's collection of garden gnomes.

She let herself in quietly trying to remember what she'd said that she'd been doing.

"You're late," said her mother.

"You didn't answer your phone," said her dad.

Then they looked at each other and tried again.

"So, how did it go?"

Did what go? Angel stood and shuffled in the hallway feeling desperate.

"I used to love dancing when I was your age. Of course it was quite different then. Irish traditional was what we used to do – though they say it's coming back. I expect you and your friends do that modern style in leotards. Makes me think of cats, black cats usually. I hope you'll let us see."

Her mum had a line in cheery patter that really got on Angel's nerves. Next minute she'd start on about whether Angel had had any tea and what she'd like if not.

Her dad had been watching some programme on the History Channel. If he'd been working he wouldn't have heard her at all. He paused the programme and asked again about her day. He always asked about her day. He didn't seem to notice that she never answered any more.

She used to. Used to pour it all out: every mistake, every hope, every rejection, every thrill and every hurt.

Not now she was in Year Eight.

"It was okay."

"Come and sit down then. We can change the channel." He was trying his best. "Find something you'd enjoy as well. Watch it together. Let Mum fetch you a bit of tea?"

She stayed in the hallway. "I'm going to bed. I'll take my pills myself. I might read a book or something."

Her mum came hurrying towards her. "Are you sure you're all right?"

"I only want to go to bed. Can't you ever leave me alone!"

Her mum hurt and retreating. "I could bring you up a nice warm drink? Hot water bottle?"

Angel ran for the stairs.

"Don't forget to put your uniform in the laundry basket," her mum called after her. She was narky now. "I'll want to take your blazer to the cleaners while you're on half-term."

Angel made it to her room and slammed the door. She leaned against it wishing, like she wished every night, that they'd let her have a lock.

Of course she wasn't going to read. Reading was really hard, even with all them special cards and overlays. She didn't understand how everyone else could do it so easily. Downstairs was completely stuffed with books and her dad went to work in a Records Office where he did nothing all day except read and sort out papers and scan things into files. Her mum had been an assistant librarian before she'd had to give up work to care for Angel. She didn't see how them two top-grade readers had produced her.

They probably didn't see it either. Something had gone badly wrong.

In bed at last she curled herself tight, clutched the grubby doll she'd had all her life and allowed her body to tremble. She was freezing cold and at the same time hot. Whether she shut her eyes or opened them she couldn't stop looking at that man lying on the pebbles with the boat on top of him. Crushing him. She wondered what he'd looked like when they got him out.

If they had.

She should have stayed.

That blue light. Hurt her. She could have had one of her turns.

She'd probably get put in prison if they found out she was there. Angel had been in trouble before. She'd been in trouble most of her life. But this was trouble in a different league. She'd never go down the skate-park again. Never go near them boats.

She was home now. And if she didn't blab there wouldn't anybody find out. The man hadn't opened his eyes and the lads weren't going to tell.

The paramedics would look after him. They'd have blankets and they'd give him oxygen or something. Then they'd call the boatyard or the firemen to come and lift the yellow boat. They had all the gear. And the hospital wasn't far. Not if they hurried. He'd be there quicker than she'd got home.

But if she couldn't ask, she'd never know for certain that he was okay.

There was a banging on the front door. The bell rang.

Too loud. Too long.

Angel lay rigid. Straining every nerve. She should have told her mum and dad.

She heard the TV go off and the front door open. Then she heard giggling and shouts.

"Trick or treat, missus! Trick or treat!"

✦ ✦ ✦

This wasn't the Land of Legends. This was Worst Dreams Come True.

His dad had forgotten he was coming. Forgotten that their holiday had started today.

Luke had made the tea and it had gone cold. He had unpacked his clothes and put them away in the locker; had laid out his sleeping bag and folded a blanket over it.

He hadn't brought his Nintendo. It was part of the special deal for this week. Lottie thought he played fantasy games too much and Anna said she wished she'd never given it to him. Which was so unfair when she was always on her iPhone or her laptop.

Lowestoft Lass didn't have TV. She didn't have mains electricity though she would one day. There was a 12V system that worked off a battery but you had to run the engine to keep the battery topped up and Bill only did that once a week. He said he was going to fit a solar panel but he hadn't done it yet. His first priority was to make her leak-proof for the winter. Fitted boat covers were expensive so he'd bought tarpaulins. He said he'd need Luke to help him put them on. The tarpaulins were folded ready on the foredeck together with a coil of long, thin rope. It was one of the jobs they had planned to do.

But Bill wasn't here.

He'd finished work, must have done, and he hadn't come

home. Maybe he'd stopped somewhere for a pie and a pint. He didn't drink much these days but there were shanty-nights at the Red Lion pub and Bill liked to join in with his concertina. Luke didn't think shanty-nights happened on Fridays but he didn't really know.

There was lots he didn't know about his dad. Like would he have his phone switched on if he'd gone to play his concertina?

If Luke wanted to try and phone his dad he'd have to go back up the hill and through that wood again to get reception. And now it was completely dark outside – except for those horrible grinning pumpkins.

How had he ever thought that Halloween was fun?

Luke decided that he'd just as soon wait. His dad would have to be back when the Red Lion closed. He'd got the wrong day. That was all.

✦　✦　✦

In the deep metal hold of *Drie Vrouwen*, Hendrike was manic. She hadn't taken any of the dried mushroom but she was still getting visions. It didn't seem that she could control them any more.

Helen tried not to show that she was frightened. The only way to deal with her mum in this mood was to keep very calm and do everything she said. Do it as soon as she said it but without getting shaky or rushing, That just wound her mum up more.

They kept chickens in the forepeak on board *Drie Vrouwen*. Hendrike had packed their coop with straw and ferried them across the Noordzee. Most of the hens were there to lay eggs but every two weeks, Hendrike chose and killed one and then she plucked it and took its insides out and they ate it. When they'd eaten the meat she boiled everything else into stock for soup together with the potatoes and the dried peas and the strings of onions and the root vegetables from the sacks that were almost empty.

They had been here since Lughnasadh and now it was Samhain. They had made their own bread, caught and eaten little fish, harvested samphire from the marsh, nuts and berries from the hedgerows. Three months and there was only one chicken and the cockerel left. The wheat for their feed wouldn't last much longer.

Soon they would complete their task and then, on the top of the highest tide, they could leave this muddy creek and return home. Helen dreamed of home as a neat little house in a row of other, identical, neat little houses but she knew that was only a dream.

Even the cheapest canals in Amsterdam would be better than this. Her mum would be given her job back and then she and Elsevier could be as weird as they liked because Helen would be going to school and to the rowing club and out with her friends and there would be cycle tracks and shops – and hygiene.

Hendrike's hair was white. It had used to be the colour of dirty sand. Then she started dying it to make it pale gold like Helen's but something had gone wrong and there wasn't any colour left at all. During the day she wore it in two plaits coiled either side of her head. Tonight Hendrike had combed her hair so it spread like a cape over her shoulders and down her back. She told Helen to go to the forepeak and bring Leo, the cockerel, to the cabin.

Surely her mum wasn't going to do it here? Normally she

managed it seated out on deck, quick and neat, the bird held firmly between her knees. A twist and a pull. It wasn't cruel – if you could accept that killing was a part of living. Both Elsevier and her mum kept telling Helen that.

Helen had asked to become vegetarian. This had not been allowed.

Tonight she felt depressed and sick. She didn't want to fetch the cockerel.

"Wouldn't it be better tomorrow?" was all she managed to say.

"Tonight is Samhain, All Hallows Eve. Tonight the veil is thin between the worlds. Tonight we can learn from the dead. This is the first night of the waning moon, the beginning of the end."

Helen thought of poplar trees planted in straight lines, of gardens filled with bright flowers that had no medicinal or hallucinogenic properties, of living in any place where you could get away from your mother and you didn't have to pretend all the time and hide what you were doing from the neighbours.

"There's someone on the boat next door," she said. "It's probably the man."

"The man," said her mother. "We must get rid of the man."

She had lifted the carpet from the cabin sole and chalked a circle on the wooden boards. Now she was trickling wheat and pumpkin seeds around the circumference, counting them.

"Seventy five pompiert: ninety three woote. Where is Leo? I will wait no longer."

Helen recognised the numbers. Her mother was back in the seventeenth century. There was no danger to the cockerel there. She did as she was told.

✦　✦　✦

It was two in the morning. It was still Halloween. The graves had opened and the ghosts would roam. Bill couldn't have gone to shanty-night because his concertina was here in its box on *Lowestoft Lass.*

Luke's skin was crawling with cold and he couldn't breathe quite right. He'd gone to bed and tried to sleep and this new thought had come into his head like ice-damp.

What if something bad had happened to his dad?

The more he thought the more frightened he became. His dad couldn't have forgotten what day the holiday was meant to begin because Lottie had rung him that morning before school to tell him she was going shopping and to check if there was anything in particular he needed Luke to bring with him "this evening". Those were her exact words.

His dad was more likely to nod than to speak, even on the phone, but he was totally reliable. Luke knew he was. He was gutted with himself that he'd thought any different. If his dad wasn't here it was because something had stopped him. Maybe he'd been jumped by a zombie or river troll.

He had to stop thinking that way. River trolls and zombies Did Not Exist.

But muggers did. Maybe Bill had been jumped by a mugger on his way home from the yard.

Should Luke ring the police? His dad had been put in prison when he shouldn't have been. They didn't much like the police, his family.

The fear in Luke's head was worse than his fear of the dark.

He'd gone to bed properly in his pyjamas. Clean teeth even. He'd wanted to show his dad that it was all okay. That he hadn't been worried; that he could quite well look after himself alone on *Lowestoft Lass* for a few hours. Any twelve-year-old could.

Now he reached onto the floor for whatever clothes were there and pulled them on quick. He used the backlight from his phone to find socks. Should have thought of it when he was in the wood earlier.

Luke climbed up into the wheelhouse. He wasn't happy with himself and he didn't know what to do next. He looked through the windows to the black boat next door. The lights inside the pumpkin heads were guttering. Hours ago he'd thought he'd heard music. A hand drumming on stretched skin and a hollow-sounding pipe. He hadn't any headphones with him. He couldn't block it out.

A patch of cloud gleamed grey as rippled armour. There should have been some moon but the night was overcast. None of the other boats was more than a low shape humped against the dark. He didn't know any of these people. He couldn't wake them up to ask about his dad.

Luke zipped up his fleece. He patted his pocket to make sure his phone was there, then hurried across the gangplank and up the track to the gate.

He rang his dad. He rang Anna. He rang Lottie. Even texted Liam:
Hi Bro!
None of them answered.

He still didn't think he ought to ring the police. Who else did he have in his phone that he could call at two in the morning for help about his dad? It was half-term. They were most of them away. Donny and Skye and *Strong Winds* were at sea. Xanthe and Maggi too. Last proper sail before the winter, they'd said. Taken a good forecast and gone north.

He could ring Wendy and Gerald, his ex-carers, but they had their baby to look after. Anyway what could they do? Luke wasn't sure what Wendy and Gerald deep down thought about his dad. All those monthly visits to the prison and the dogs and that room with the tables and never knowing what to say. Liam being sick on the way back. Every time.

Someone was shouting.

"No! No!" over and over. It wasn't his dad but it was someone in trouble.

Luke ran to the rescue. Along the top hedge, then downhill among the trees. Kept hitting things and tripping.

The shouting strung out into howling. Luke stopped. If he was going to search for his dad, he couldn't risk getting eaten by a werewolf. His heart was beating faster than the skin drum.

Then, in the quiet, he heard a door close. That was such a normal noise.

Luke carried on, feeling his way. Slow and careful now, listening all the time and holding out his arms so he didn't collide with tree trunks and low branches.

Could this dark get darker? Yes, when it was a wall.

Luke's hands felt leaves and rough stone. He moved sideways to his left and then sideways to his right. Only a couple of steps each way. He worked out that the leaves were ivy. Did bats live in ivy? Or spiders?

His right hand flapped into empty air. Then he was round a corner and fumbling along a second wall. Brown light came struggling from a dirty window. And if you peered right close and rubbed a bit you could see there was something inside that was possibly a lamp. And a human shape bent over, pawing its way around some tiny room filled with the backs of books.

A human shape that was covered with fur.

✦   ✦   ✦

It was three in the morning. It was still Halloween until sunrise.

Hendrike and Helen were coming back across the reed beds. They had made their own path using random pieces of debris to mark the way and stolen planks to bridge the drainage ditches. Whenever they had crossed a ditch, they pulled the plank behind them so they could not be followed. It was a clever system and they'd had months to make it perfect.

Tonight they wore dark cloaks with hoods to muffle their shapes and hide their pale hair from the clouded moon. Under the cloaks they carried files and small torches and the sacks which they had used to remove the plaster. They had been sinking the evidence among the reeds as they walked. Their trophy was loose, the escape route ready. As soon as Elsevier arrived they could act.

Helen had been glad to get out from the cabin, even when she could hear the old madman shouting in the woods. Her mother's crazy rituals made the whole boat feel bad. Helen didn't believe in ghosts or witches. Or angels or demons either. Nothing except life here and now. She was a rationalist and Halloween – or Samhain as her mother liked to call it – was simply another date in the calendar. It meant nothing.

Her mother was stupid because she'd messed with her mind.

She was harmless though. She was acting up, she didn't have any power. Even their mission wasn't hurting anyone. It was just a stunt to please Elsevier.

And they would so soon be gone.

Helen looked across to the fishing boat where the man lived. There was a light shining from the wheelhouse. That was okay then. It had been off earlier. Now it was on. There was no reason for her to worry.

CHAPTER THREE

All Saints

Saturday 1 November, first of the waning moon

Luke, Helen

He forced himself to stay flat. This noise! Was it a banshee, a strangling or had the aliens landed? Luke's hand groped for his Nintendo. He always kept it under his pillow when it wasn't in his pocket.

There was no Nintendo. He remembered. Anna had taken it.

The noise was coming from somewhere really close. Malfunctioning smoke alarm? Donkey trying to sing opera?

"Urki-urki-oooooo, urki-urki-oooooo."

Not donkey...cockerel. A full-on, high-decibel, non-stop cock's crow. Not your cosy cock o'doodle-doo. More strained, more painful. And so close. It must coming from the boat next door, that spooky black barge with the pumpkin heads.

"Urki-urki-ooooooooo!"

A cockerel on a boat? This whole place was weird and he wished he'd gone to Italy.

Last night – early morning – whenever – he'd run away from the hut in the woods: from the werewolf prowling through his books. He'd pitched himself across the gangplank, slammed the wheelhouse door and locked it from the inside.

What if his dad came home and couldn't get in?

But his dad wasn't coming and the werewolf might. That

door was staying locked. And he was going to leave a light on. He didn't care if he was wasting the battery: them dark spirits would be afraid of light.

Skid into the cabin. Kick his trainers off. Dive into the sleeping bag and pull a blanket over the opening.

Luke wriggled down far as he could then lay rigid in the stuffy darkness. Fell asleep as if he'd been unplugged.

Not any more. No more sleep with that cockerel leading off.

Was that footsteps, running? Luke sat up to try and listen better. He looked around the cabin. His dad still wasn't here.

Think on a bit…a cock's crow was good. A cock's crow meant that it was morning. It meant Halloween was properly over. All the bad things from last night had gone back underground.

Luke remembered the light in the wheelhouse and the locked door. He rushed up the cabin steps to open it. His dad would be sitting outside, cold and a bit reproachful, in his donkey jacket and his woolly hat.

Except he wasn't.

Luke found his trainers, switched off the light and checked that his phone was still in the pocket of his fleece. The others could have called him back by now but he wouldn't know until he got reception. He wasn't going scampering up that hill any more. He was going to walk along the river wall to the Phoenix Yard and wait there till he found someone who could tell him what time his dad had finished work last night. And if he'd said where he was going.

Sometimes people's dads didn't come home because they'd gone off with someone else. Luke wouldn't be calling Lottie to tell her that. There was going to be a row anyway once she discovered that Bill hadn't been with him for the night and Luke hated rows. He switched his phone off. It was going to stay that way until he knew exactly what had happened to his dad. Then he'd decide who he should call and what he was going to say to them.

He wasn't scared as he walked along the muddy path that led past the sluice and round the top of the creek. He wasn't on a Quest either. He was a practical person setting out to get some information, keeping it simple – like his dad would.

The crowing faded into silence as he walked along the river wall. The tide was high and shiny but the gulls and ducks weren't busy yet. They were mostly floating in their ripple circles, waiting for the ebb.

The emergency halogen lamps in the Phoenix Yard had all been turned off. Anyone could see the yellow and black hazard tape and read the message: Do Not Enter. Luke could see the mobile crane with a yellow boat in its slings. He could see the yard manager sitting on a pile of sleepers and drinking tea as if he'd been sitting there all night.

The manager saw him. "Y're Bill's boy?"

"Where's my dad?"

It came out like a sort of croak.

"Police been trying to get your step-mum but they said you was all away. Then someone mentioned Bill was expecting one of his lads for the week. So I thought I'd stay around, in case you showed up. And check whether anyone was planning on collecting this." He pointed to some small damp garment beside him.

"WHERE'S...MY...DAD?"

Luke didn't mean to shout.

"Hospital. Boat came down on him. Ribs and legs. Don't worry, he ain't dead."

Luke's mouth had dried up.

"You're not with anyone, then?"

Luke shook his head.

The manager stood up. Picked up the bit of clothing. "You'll want to go to the hospital. See him for yourself. Would you come with me in the van?"

Luke nodded. Of course he would. It was only that he couldn't speak.

The manager seemed to understand. He held out his mug for Luke to take a sip of the warm sweet tea.

"I'll fetch the keys. Someone broke the winder last night but they weren't thieving. You're sure there's no-one I can call?"

Luke shook his head again. He still didn't know what he would say to Lottie.

His dad was coming out of the operating theatre. It had been an emergency procedure to lift the crushed ribs off his lungs and they'd set his legs at the same time. There had been two surgeons and it had taken several hours but they said it had gone okay. Luke couldn't see him yet because he had to be taken to intensive care until they were sure he'd come round safely.

"Then he'll need complete rest and sleep. No upset or disturbance."

The ward sister looked stern. Luke had managed to talk a bit in the van but now his mouth had glued itself shut again.

"I reckon we don't mind waiting," said the yard manager,

whose name, Luke now knew, was Derek. "It'll set Bill's mind at rest to see his boy."

"Are you Luke?" said the sister. "He was asking for a Luke before they took him down."

Luke felt his eyes fill up. This long night. His dad had wanted him.

"Perhaps you'll tell him that Luke's here and he's okay," said Derek. "We'll get ourselves some breakfast and be waiting."

"I ought to call Rev. Wendy," Luke managed.

"Vicar? He ain't that bad."

"She's a sort of carer. She'll know what I should say to Lottie. I've got my phone with me but I switched it off when I left Dad's boat and they'll find missed calls from before that. Lottie's my step-mum. If she knows I phoned Rev. Wendy she'll take it better."

"We'll call her from the café. Get some tea and sausages inside us and come back here to wait for your dad." He looked over to the ward sister who looked up from her desk and nodded.

Later, when they were sitting in a side ward, Derek pulled a grubby garment from a plastic bag and showed it to Luke. It was the thing he'd had with him when he'd been waiting in the yard and it was a navy blue blazer.

"Found it after they'd taken him away. Didn't notice it at first. Thought it was a bit of old rag. Must have been underneath him."

"It's a school blazer. It's from Fitzgerald School. I go there and so does my sister."

"Went there myself forty years ago. This un's got a name in it." He showed Luke the neatly sewn tape.

"'Angela Vandervelde.' She's even in my class. Except she

usually isn't cos she gets sent out. She's called Ants. I think she's Special Needs."

"She'll have worse than Special Needs from me if she's got anything to do with that boat coming down."

The double doors opened and two porters pushed a bed into the room. A nurse walked beside the bed wheeling a tall stand with a monitor and a load of drips going into the arm of a body in a gown. The head was tipped back and the eyes were shut.

Luke felt as if his heart stopped. A sensation of breathlessness and a complete terror that he couldn't explain. There was a sort of cage on top of the body and sheets over that.

"Dad?"

Bill's eyes opened and he saw Luke.

"A'rright?" he breathed.

"Yeah, yeah, I'm all right Dad. You?"

"A'rright." His eyes shut and he opened them again with an obvious effort. "A'rright now."

Rev. Wendy spent a long time talking to the ward sister. Then she made the first phone call to Lottie. She explained about the accident and the operations Bill had had. She told Lottie that he was likely to stay in hospital for several weeks at least. There didn't seem much point in abandoning their holiday unless Bill's condition worsened. At the moment he only needed to lie still and be cared for with the minimum of stimulation. He found it hard to speak and got distressed at the thought of them coming home because of him.

"He knows how Liam feels about that football match," agreed Luke. "And Lottie with her new album. They only got there in the middle of last night. I mean of course they'd want to come home but that'd make him feel bad."

Rev. Wendy sighed. Then she squared her thin shoulders and did her best to smile.

"We'll collect your luggage from the boat and you can come back to the vicarage with me."

"No!" said Luke. That sounded rude. "I mean no-thank-you-very-much-for-asking but I need to be with Dad. This was our holiday. I can sleep on *Lowestoft Lass*. I did last night."

Why had he said that – with the werewolf and the pumpkin heads and that Force Eight cockerel next door?

"There's other people living in the boats," he said. "Like next door and that. And I'd only be there in the evenings and at night cos I'm booked on a kayak course every morning and I'd be visiting Dad after. If I slept back at Bawdsey, it'd be much further."

Wendy and Gerald were okay and baby Ellen was sweet but he definitely didn't want to spend the rest of his half-term in Erewhon Parva vicarage. Been there, done that. Not ever again.

He was surprised Rev. Wendy didn't say no straight away. She should have done. She said in that case it was a problem and she was going to have to ring Lottie again to talk about it. Couldn't he think of a school friend he could go to?

Luke had met some good mates since he'd been at Fitzgerald. They went round each others' houses, played on each others' X-boxes and PS3s, sometimes went biking.

"I ain't never allowed to be on my own. And *Lowestoft Lass*'s exactly like a house. She's my dad's house."

"These children and their boats! I can't understand it at

all. There's Grace Everson close by…she's a sensible woman. I wonder what she'd say?"

Rev. Wendy was talking to herself but she still hadn't blown him out. This was amazing. Luke put on his most pleading face. He really wanted to stay – even though he didn't. Last night in the wood had been like he was under a bad spell. Maybe he needed to give it a rerun. Exorcise all them spooks.

There was a faint noise from the shrouded figure that was Bill – as if he was trying to agree? Rev. Wendy noticed it too. Did she look…relieved?

"You know we'd said we'd always Be There for Luke – or for any of the children." She was talking directly to his dad, even though his eyes were shut. "And of course we meant it. And we will…Be There. But Gerald and I haven't had a holiday for years! And Ellen. Such an unexpected blessing at our age. So tiring… with six parishes. The diocese have offered a few days' retreat by the sea in Whitby. After the All Saint's vigil and a combination Year's Mind service. Not easy to please all the congregations. Brought forward from the Sunday by special permission. Incorporating additional prayer into the morning services. Graveyard intercessions. Packed and ready to leave. Though not too late to withdraw, of course."

"Oh yes! I mean no." Luke hadn't a clue what she was on about but he reckoned he got the gist. "You didn't ought to withdraw, Rev. Wendy. Ellen's got to be looking forward to Whitby."

He'd never been to Whitby. Never heard of it. It could be orc-infested Mordor for all he knew.

"Thank you Luke," Rev Wendy beamed. She'd have seen straight through him in the old days. "But even for Ellen's sake

I couldn't leave you to sleep on your own on that…boat."

"Donny does," Luke began. His friend Donny lived full-time on a Chinese junk but he had his mum there with him and often his uncle too.

A small moan. Bill was part of this conversation, but only just.

Rev Wendy carried on. "You'll remember Mrs Everson?"

The old lady in the green beret who Donny reckoned was a leprechaun and who always turned up exactly when she was needed?

"Her daughter, Miss Grace Everson, lives very close to Fynn Creek – on Merlesham Hill. It's a working farm but I believe she also has involvement with the moorings. Possibly she might be willing to take responsibility? I think we could ask. As it is an emergency and only for a few days. She might even offer a bed."

Luke knew who she meant. Big lady with a rowing dinghy. She'd shouted at him once. He didn't want to sleep on her farm though. He wanted to stay on *Lowestoft Lass*.

"What d'yer think, Dad?"

Bill nodded. He definitely did and Rev. Wendy saw it too but it was obvious that he was drifting off to sleep again and Luke knew, without the nurses telling him, that it was time for them to leave.

✦ ✦ ✦

Saturday was Helen's only good day of the week. It was the day she was allowed to attend the River Wall Rowing Club. She could also have gone to the club on Sundays and Wednesday evenings but Hendrike thought that Helen might attract attention if she attended too often or did too well..

"Elsevier believes in excellence," Helen sometimes dared to

say. "Elsevier wishes us to show that we haven't all gone soft. Elsevier tells me to train and to succeed."

She hated Elsevier but she'd say anything to get away from the barge. She ran for an hour every morning before Hendrike was awake. Leo the cockerel got her out of bed and she made sure she was back before her mother noticed she'd been gone.

It was amazing that Hendrike could sleep through Leo's crowing. Helen couldn't. No matter how late she'd been made to work, or how angrily she'd cried herself to sleep when her mother had spent the evening drumming or chanting or taking the powders that sent her...somewhere else, Helen's eyelids flew apart at his first note and she was off the barge almost before he'd taken breath for the second.

Leo was shut in a coop in *Drie Vrouwen*'s forepeak with the hatch cover closed but somehow he still knew when it was dawn. Helen had learned to trust him. She was footsure as she ran up the steep hill through the towering black trees with the sound of his crowing behind her. She knew that when she reached the lane and turned east towards the river there would be paleness. Then, as she ran past the church and the farm and sped out into the maze of tracks that led towards the main river, there would be greys and mauves and pinks. Or violets, oranges and every shade of red. A kaleidoscopic light-show every morning, just for her.

East was sunrise. East was home. East was where they'd point the barge.

Helen filled her lungs with the fresh damp air and imagined the morning when they would be motoring along some shimmering pathway on their return journey across the sea. She hardly noticed which of the tracks she chose. They all took her to the river wall where she ran until she reached the broken section.

In Holland this would have been repaired but not here in England. The wall had obviously been down for years. The river had come though and several hectares of grazing land were salty and unusable. The English were lazy. They didn't appreciate what they had. It was even possible that Elsevier was right – though only on this single point.

Soon she'd be measuring her strides along a line of willow trees or poplars, saying hi to kids outside their houses and catching her breath to smile at cyclists. She'd be back with her friends and her rowing team. So much lost fitness to regain before next racing season…

But for now she had only Saturdays on this muddy English river. Helen treasured every rhythmic moment that she bent and stretched with the weight of her long oars.

The River Wall Club was near the Phoenix Yard. Helen saw the Do Not Enter signs and people pausing to ask one another what had happened.

She didn't stop. Her mother had checked the yard some time ago when they were looking to steal a dinghy trailer. She'd discovered that their security was good and that their neighbour, the man on the scruffy wooden fishing boat, worked there.

Hendrike didn't like men. She'd tried getting friendly with this one in case she could witch him into helping them. He wasn't rude but he obviously wasn't interested. He only wanted to work on his boat – every evening and most weekends as well. Her mother had decided he was there too often. She made a poppet with a woollen hat and a workman's jacket and began sticking pins in it so he'd fall ill and stay out of their way.

Then last night…

Helen needed to get away. Needed to be in her boat and sculling. Needed to escape her own thoughts.

There were so many people talking and staring, that it was hard to manoeuvre the fragile racing shells out from the boat house and down the slipway. The coach asked one of the other girls to help her.

"And you?" Helen said, after they had carried her boat to the water's edge and she was trudging back for her oars. "Do you need a lift?"

"I'm good thanks. Gonna wait a bit. See who else shows up."

"Why are there all these people today?"

The other girl shrugged. She was chewing gum. Shifted it from one side of her mouth to the other.

"Some accident in the yard last night. A guy got hurt. Maybe killed. I dunno."

She didn't sound bothered.

"This man, do you know his name?"

"Nah."

Helen didn't ask any more questions. If the English didn't care what had happened to their neighbours, why should she?

She didn't want to remember…when Leo had pecked a pattern of wheat and pumpkin seeds that had seemed to spell success…the drumming and the fumes … "Sabbat! Sabbat!"

When her mother had crushed the poppet under the runestone Elsevier had given her. Smashed it down on the fragile effigy. Again and again.

It was all stupid. You could buy runestones on the Internet. The man had slept okay on board his boat. Must have. He'd switched his wheelhouse light on. And turned it off this morning.

Helen fitted her sculls into the oarlocks and lifted her boat gratefully onto the river.

+ + +

"Would you like the dog with you?"

"A dog? With me? On dad's boat?"

"Some people like dogs. Other people don't."

"I do! I would. Never had a proper dog. Had a tamagotchi once. Out of the church jumble. Liam dropped it in the bath."

"This one's a terrier. Patterdale cross. Your friends found him. Nice little chap now that he's decided to calm down. Barks though. Not always a bad thing."

That was about the longest bit of conversation Miss Grace Everson had done so far. She was the lady he'd reckoned she'd be. Untidy hair and a red face. She seemed to have forgotten the day he'd thrown a pebble and hit her dinghy while she'd been sitting outside the pub drinking beer. She'd listened to Rev. Wendy, looked at Luke and nodded. He could sleep at the farm. Or she'd keep an eye on him down on the boat. Feed him if he wanted. She was sorry to hear about the accident, she said. Not odd at all, the lad wanting to stay near his father. There were two women on the boat next door. Both Dutch and kept themselves to themselves but the girl spoke English reasonably well.

"I used to be frit of dogs," Luke added. "But not any more. Except Lottie's booked me into a kayak course at the swimming pool from Monday and I couldn't take him to the hospital."

"No. You couldn't."

"But would he sleep with me at night? I could bring him back in the mornings and collect him at tea."

"You could do that."

"That's very kind of you, Miss Everson. And you'll introduce him to the neighbours. A mother and daughter? Providential!" Rev. Wendy looked anxiously at her watch. "I'm sorry I have to leave now. I'm offering a Year's Mind vigil to follow the All Saints service. Candlelit for the six parishes. Not all the church wardens are convinced…Are you sure you don't want to come with me, Luke? I'll be late but Gerald can find something extra for supper. And there'll be Ellen. And the bird …"

"Hawkins! What's happening to him?"

Rev. Wendy reddened slightly. "We couldn't have gone on holiday without…He and Ellen are quite inseparable. Providentially the hostel was brought to understand our position. Then we found a travelling cage for a very reasonable donation and Gerald's packed his favourite toys. As well as food. He's so discriminating."

Luke wished that Anna and Liam were hearing this – or Donny and Skye. Miss Grace didn't get it because she didn't know. This was Hawkins, the rescued canary, going off to some diocesan retreat with all the bits of pirate tackle they'd made him plus his personal larder. A pecky eater!

"Tell him to be sure and send us a postcard then. I'll be okay on *Lowestoft Lass* – 'specially if the dog'll come? "

Miss Grace nodded without speaking and Rev. Wendy hurried away, promising Luke that his father would be remembered in

Erewhon Parva parish prayers every day and twice on Sundays until he was completely recovered.

"Cows're bellyaching," said Miss Grace, after a brief, awkward silence. "Know anything about cows?"

Luke shook his head.

"Cows need milking," she said. "And if you don't know that, they don't mind telling you. Got any boots?"

"On Dad's boat I have."

"Better bring them next time. Cows make cowpats. Want to fetch the dog along with us? Keep him on his lead though. He'll be getting accustomed to you."

She got a lot done in a short time, Miss Grace. Her dozen cattle, assorted age and genders, brought into their respective pens for the night. Hayed and watered and two of them milked. The cattle shed was a nice building, like a house with separate rooms all next to each other.

"Do cows always sleep like this?"

Luke thought only horses had stables.

"It's how I like to keep them. Stops any bullying."

"Maybe I should help while I'm here."

"Your dad does two nights a week on the days I'm over with my mother. I set it against the mooring fees."

"Oh."

Was the moorings hers then? He'd better stay on her right side while his dad was away.

"I'll do what I can. But I'm not my dad."

She put a broom into his hand and showed him where the straw needed to be swept away.

"Old Peter'll step up. He likes the work. Doesn't know what day it is and can't remember names but the cows don't worry."

"Old Peter?"

"Lives in the wood, gamekeeper's hut. His boat's on the creek. In it most of the time."

Brown light through an unexpected window. Spiders in the ivy and...something inside

"Old Peter...is he, like, hairy?"

"He could probably do with a trip to the barber."

"Hairy all over?"

She laughed. It was more like a snort.

"Can't say I've looked that close. He uses the shower block at the moorings, same as everyone else. I check his hands are clean for the cows. Make him take his coat off too. They don't like the fur."

"But it IS a coat? It's not...I mean...real fur?"

She frowned now. "Of course it's real. You want to smell it! He hasn't popped into Ipswich and bought himself a fashion state-ment. It's how he keeps warm."

She stomped across to her Land Rover. Motioned him and the dog to follow.

"You don't want to worry about Peter," she said, once she'd wrestled the vehicle into gear. "You might hear him shouting out at night. He's lonely and he's confused but he'd be worse if they took him in. He's got his cat to look after. Dog stays there sometimes. He can tell a good story – as long as you don't want names with it."

How could you get on without names? Even online you needed to know who you were playing – screen names anyway. The black dog was perched on his lap His long nose was stretched towards the windscreen, his whole body trembling with eagerness. Luke put his arms round him, to help him stay steady.

"Is the dog still called Ben Gunn?"

"Mostly he's plain Ben."

She had a key to the gate so they bumped all the way down the track in her vehicle. She parked near the moorings and showed him how to access the toilet block and where there was a payphone. Gave him her number and said he was welcome at the farm whenever he liked.

"You can think you'll be all right by yourself. But sometimes you're not. You won't know till you try. It won't trouble me if you change your mind."

Then she rang the bell by the gangway to the Dutch barge and introduced him to the people who lived there. Hendrike and Helen. He didn't get a surname. The mother was short and dumpy. She wore a sort of smock and stretchy trousers and had white hair in two buns. Her English was quite hard to understand. She told Miss Grace that she'd keep a watch on him.

There was something in the way she said this that made Luke hurry to explain that she'd wouldn't never see him, what with the kayaking and the hospital visits and helping with the cows. He really wouldn't be there hardly at all. Impossible that he'd cause her any trouble

The girl wore jeans and trainers and had fair hair scraped into a high ponytail. She didn't speak or smile but when Miss Grace explained about Luke's dad having an accident she looked as if she was about to faint.

"This 'Year's Mind' Rev. Wendy was on about, what is it?" he called after Miss Grace when she'd already said goodnight.

"Something they do in churches. Ought to be tomorrow. Souls not Saints. Remembering the dead. People bring a candle. It's for anyone who's died in the previous twelve months. Doesn't have to be."

"Oh. Thanks."

She went then and left Luke on his own with the dog. He wondered whether he could get a candle and light it for his mother. She'd died so long ago he hardly ever thought of her.

Except that he had thought of her. Today. In the hospital. When his dad had come in covered under that sheet with his eyes shut. It was like he'd seen it all before. He supposed they must have brought him and Liam in to say goodbye and she must have been lying like that, her body propped up and her last life gone.

The old fishing boat creaked as she lifted with the tide. Luke had found a candle and put it on a saucer and lit it for his mum. He wasn't using any electricity so the small warm glow was ringed around with darkness. Ben was curled on the bunk. He looked as if he was asleep already. Both his eyes were shut and he had one long front paw crooked behind his ear.

Luke stared into the heart of the flame. He did his best to focus on his mother but if he was honest, there wasn't much that he could bring to mind. Liam had once said he hadn't any memories at all. Not even what she looked like. Maybe they ought to ask their dad for a photo.

He picked up the candle and walked round the edge of the cabin with it. Like he and his mum were visiting together. He even introduced her to Miss Grace though they didn't seem to find much to talk about.

Lowestoft Lass's cabin wasn't panelled or even painted. His dad had been stripping everything away so he could check the real state of the timbers. There weren't any books or pictures or anything that was personal. There were rust stains where the damp had seeped through iron fastenings and a few damp marks where the water was leaking from the deck. Maybe it was just the shape that made her feel so homely.

Luke gave up. He couldn't reach his mother here. It'd been silly trying.

Ben's black head was up and watching. That was good because Luke was going to have to visit the toilet block before he went to sleep and if he had any nerve he'd go up the track and send the others a goodnight text. They'd definitely have sent him one.

Ben's short fur rippled over his bone and muscle. He had a deep chest and his legs set far apart like he was a fighter. He totally didn't mind when Luke put his arms around and hugged him.

"He's a beggar for warmth," Miss Grace had said. "He'll be down your sleeping bag if you let him."

That'd be okay.

"C'mon boy," Luke said, putting the candle back onto the table and clipping the extendible lead to Ben's collar. "Race you to the top of the slope. Liam'll be sick when he hears that I've got you staying."

The night air was damp but not cold and the moon was high above the reed beds. It wasn't especially bright and was a bit less than half full.

Luke forgot that he and Ben were meant to be racing. He stood there on the aft deck of the fishing boat gazing upwards. Someone had been holding him once. Someone had showed him a moon like this and had giggled.

"Look at the moon, Lukey. She's trying to suck her tummy in. That'll be a while before I can get a shape like that again."

Someone had been happy, making a small contented joke. Someone whose soft hair and warm cheek had been next to his. Someone who wanted him to see what she was seeing and share the happiness she felt.

She must have been telling him she was pregnant, he realised now.

There were maybe three or four specks of light escaping from the other boats. That meant there were other creekies sleeping here. The low windows in the Dutch barge next door were glowing and they hadn't shut their curtains. Luke couldn't resist quickly glancing in.

There were candles all around the cabin, hundreds of them; small ones mainly, creamy white, their bright flames dancing even though there wasn't any breeze. They covered every surface. The girl was there. Sitting in the corner looking fed up.

The mother was right in the middle of all the lights: waving her arms and twirling round. She'd undone her hair and her eyes were shut like she was in some kind of trance. She was wearing a sort of robe and with that hair and all those candles...

well, it was a good thing the daughter was keeping awake.

Lowestoft Lass shifted slightly and Luke realised that he didn't ought to be spying. If that mother and daughter were remembering those many dead people, they must have been in a disaster somewhere.

Luke hoped he'd got it wrong and that they just liked candles.

CHAPTER FOUR

All Souls
Sunday 2 November, second of the waning moon

Luke

Ben kicked Luke with his hard claws as he burst out from his share of the sleeping bag. He flung himself at the cabin side and barked frantically. He was white teeth and red gums and front legs braced and back legs ready to spring.

"Hey boy, it's okay. I know how you feel. It's a cockerel, that's all."

Ben wasn't hearing him. He was wild. If Luke touched him, would he bite?

"Good boy, calm down...just a cockerel...like they have on farms."

Ben lunged towards the ship's side, his ears flat to his head, upper lip pulled back in a crinkly snarl. He was Cerberus, he was the Grim, he was Black Dog Shuck.

He was also, Luke noticed with relief, clever enough to avoid bumping his nose each time he lunged. All the same he'd be waking the whole creek if he carried on like this. Other people would complain. There'd already been steps running from next door.

Luke chucked his clothes on and found Ben's lead. He was quite nervous about attaching it except he remembered something Xanthe had said about Ben scaring himself with his own fury. Or was it Donny said it? And was it Ben or was it baby Vicky when she used to have those tantrums? And did it matter which it was? Talking all the time, mainly to himself, and feeling his hands cold and sweaty and trying not to let them shake, he crept up close to the barking dog and clipped the lead to the collar.

"C'mon fella. Let's go see the size of him."

Ben swung round when he felt the click of the lead and Luke's fingers brushing his fur. But it was okay, he didn't bite.

When Luke stepped towards the companionway Ben charged for it. He scrabbled his way up the ladder and was heading across the gangplank to the shore almost faster than Luke could keep up.

"You're a pussy cat!" Luke accused him as they made it to the wicket gate at the top of the hill, both of them panting. "You were more scared of the bird than I was."

The cockerel knew nothing of the trouble he'd caused. His crowing sounded small and distant from up here. Mechanical even. The girl from the barge came springing past in her clean white trainers.

"Sorry," Luke called after her but she didn't speak or look round.

He took Ben home to the farm then watched Miss Grace do the morning milking. He scrubbed buckets and pushed barrows. Learned how she liked her tea.

The girl passed him again on his way back. This time she slowed to a walk. She looked like she was ready to be friendly.

"How is your father?"

Her English was clear but quite careful. She didn't seem at all out of breath.

"Dunno. Haven't seen him yet."

"What has happened to him?"

"A boat came down in the yard. Crushed him."

"That's dreadful. Why?"

"Why what?"

"Why did the boat come down on him? When was he there?"

"Dunno. It's where he works. The yard manager thought there could have been kids messing about. There was someone called 999 and there was a school blazer. Belongs to Ants Vandervelde. You don't go to our school so you don't know her. She's trouble."

"When was this...accident?"

"Friday. Evening sometime. He wasn't back here when I arrived but I could have took a while."

Or his dad could already have been lying there, trapped, waiting for help. Wondering whether his son would think to come looking for him. Luke felt ill when he remembered how he'd been mucking about playing Land of Legends in the wood. So much for making his dad feel proud of him. He should have gone straight down the track and onto *Lowestoft Lass*. Then he should have started for the yard.

"It must probably have been dark when it happened, else you'd have thought someone would have seen him."

The girl turned slightly and stopped in front of him so he had to stop as well.

"That's not enough," she said. "We must know!"

What did it matter to her?

"Police'll find out," he suggested. "They gotta investigate for the insurance, Derek said, as well as to see if there's prosecutions.

They'll check when the call was made and then they'll go interview Ants. 'Spect they'll talk to Dad too – when he's well enough."

"Listen," she said. "Will you discover the time of the fall please? It's important for me."

He wanted to ask why but she ran on again.

"Goodbye!" he called. "Nice meeting you."

She didn't answer or glance round. The Dutch woman was standing at the *Drie Vrouwen* gangplank with her big arms on her broad hips. Her face looked red. He saw the girl sent below. Heard the mother shouting.

Luke hid in the shower block. He hadn't got his washing kit but if that was him getting yelled at, he'd rather other people hadn't heard. Unless they were already his friends and he didn't know whether he and this girl were friends or not. One minute she was all concerned about his dad and the next she didn't even say goodbye.

Maybe she wasn't allowed to talk to boys. There were people who were funny about that. It was religions or something.

Anna would know. But Anna wasn't here.

If he did jobs on deck until it was time to go to the hospital then he'd be doing helpful stuff for his dad – practical stuff – and if the girl's mother came up he could say good morning. Maybe then he'd get a feeling if it was him that was the problem or if it was something between her and her daughter. And if the girl came up he wouldn't say anything at all unless she spoke first.

He didn't like that mother. He just didn't.

So, what jobs could he do? Luke walked around. He checked the warps. Dodged down behind *Lass*'s high sides pretending she was a fortress and the gaps beneath were arrow slits. Crept down along one side and up the other knowing he was invisible. Wished Liam was here to set an ambush.

No Liam this week. No dodging games. Those high sides were to stop fishermen being swep'over in rough seas. His dad had said.

Luke found a brush and began to sweep the decks, same as he had Miss Grace's barn. There were a few dead leaves blown down from the wood. Some of them had heaped up against something that had a few sacks over it.

He moved just one.

And then another.

It was a kayak. It had been red and white once – more brown-ish-grey now – with the Scout Association symbol and a set of paddles. Luke forgot about the sweeping. He sat and stared. Tried not to dream.

Miss Grace came with him to the hospital that first afternoon. She said the nurses might be funny about unaccompanied children till they got used to him. It turned out also that she'd brought a notebook and pen. She thought Bill might want to tell Luke about how things worked on *Lowestoft Lass* and, if he couldn't talk easily, he might rather write them down.

It was a good idea but, as it happened, Bill couldn't write. He was white and shaky with the pain but he'd refused to have any morphine as he said it made his head go funny. He'd have it later, after they were gone.

Even whispering seemed to make him get shiny with sweat but that was what he did. He whispered and Miss Grace wrote:

all the instructions for turning on the gas cylinders and checking the bilge pumps and running the engine to charge up the battery – answers to questions that would never have occurred to Rev. Wendy to ask. Miss Grace read aloud as she went so Bill never had to whisper anything more than once.

He kept stopping to tell Luke to tell Lottie not to worry. This was extra words and Luke could see how every word hurt. He wanted to help him think of something else.

"I checked the warps, Dad, and they were okay and I swept a bit and I found a kayak…?"

Bill nearly smiled.

"F'you. Scouts were selling 'em."

For him! His own boat! All the older ones had boats – racing boats, dinghies, *Strong Winds* – even Anna had *Hirondelle* somewhere. He didn't think anyone had noticed how much he wanted a boat of his own.

"I'll share it with Liam then?"

"No engine," Bill mouthed.

Luke grinned. His younger brother was obsessed with engines. He and their dad seemed to get on so easily like that. Liam was always looking at the instruments and opening the engine room doors and asking what things did.

"Now I know why Lottie booked me on that course. I thought she was just trying to keep me outer your way when you were working. Didn't know it was a plot!"

He'd been really hacked off at his step-mother for signing him up for a beginner kayak course at the swimming pool, an hour every morning Monday to Friday, right through the week. And making him bring that buoyancy aid and waterproofs.

So maybe she and his dad did talk to each other sometimes.

"Thanks Dad! And I'll text Lottie thanks as well."

A kayak! He could come in and out Fynn Creek whatever the tide was doing. He could maybe pull the kayak over the flood wall and go right into them reed beds. He could go up the main river, past all the boats and the yards and under that bridge where boats with masts had to stop. Or he could go down the river towards the sea. He could explore!

"Not on yer own." His dad was panting for breath. "Not without I'm there. Or someone to keep an eye."

Miss Grace was staying quiet but Luke could see she was agreeing.

"Trust me, Dad. You don't have to worry."

By the time his dad was well again Luke would have done the course. He was really looking forward to it now.

"So, did you ask your father?"

She caught him near the shower block as if she'd been lying in wait.

"Eh?"

"At what time exactly the boat fell down on him."

Her pony-tail swung impatiently; her voice was urgent. He didn't get why she was bothered. He wanted to ask why her mother was so angry but he couldn't find the words.

"No. I didn't. I forgot. And my dad's not well. He probably wasn't exactly looking at his watch."

One of the doctors had come into his dad's room when he and Miss Grace were still at the hospital. He looked important and there were three or four other people following him. They had stethoscopes and scannable name badges and a couple of them carried clipboards to write down everything the main man said.

Luke thought they'd have to leave the room but Miss Grace merged into the background. Maybe she'd learned that skill from her leprechaun mother. Luke merged too.

The doctor kept asking Bill if the feeling had come back into his legs yet. He was asking questions about bladders and bowels, which Luke wished he wasn't hearing and Bill didn't answer. One of the nurses looked at the notes and answered for him.

The doctor didn't let on whether the answers were right or wrong. Both Bill's legs were in plaster so what was he meant to be feeling? The bit that looked bad to Luke was when the doctor stood at the end of his dad's bed and asked him if he could wriggle his toes.

Bill couldn't. Even though you could see he was trying really hard.

"Early days," said the doctor. "Your body's still in shock. There was no obvious indication of spinal damage. It's just something we're keeping an eye on. If there's no change over the next forty-eight hours I'll ask a neurologist to take a look. For now you're best left as you are. Get all the sleep you can. Those ribs must hurt. Pain relief? Diamorphine?"

He was asking the nurse.

She checked Bill's notes again.

"Not today. The patient refused medication as he needed to stay awake for his visitors."

"Look here," said the doctor to Bill. "You've had a serious accident. You could have died under that boat from the shock alone. I'll go so far as to say that you were incredibly lucky that you hung on alive until the paramedics reached you. You must give your body its best chance to stabilise. And that means sleep. You can't sleep if you're in pain so that's why I'm prescribing routine doses of morphine. You're not going to become an addict. You're simply going to sleep better and longer. I'm sure your family will understand how much it matters."

So the doctor had noticed they hadn't left. He was saying this for them to listen.

"Can I still visit?" Luke asked. "There's only me and I won't mind if he's asleep."

The doctor looked at Miss Grace.

"The rest of Mr Whiting's family are away," she said. "I'm a friend. He doesn't want them called back unless it's an emergency. Is it an emergency?"

"No. If the movement's not back in the next two days I'll be asking for some further tests. That's all. And you can come," he was talking to Luke, "During visiting hours, if your dad promises not to wake up. And if you promise that you won't wake him. Bring a book or a game to keep yourself quiet. Got one of those electronic things? Bring that!"

"My dad could have died," Luke told the girl.

She went white again.

"I'm sorry," she said. "Please. Discover for me the time and I will explain."

If her mother was truly dangerous she'd have to turn her in. Especially now this boy was here. Hendrike didn't like him. What if she made a poppet of him and began another harming spell?

Worked herself up communing with the dead and smashed his effigy with her runestone?

She shouldn't allow herself to think like this. Magic didn't exist. Not in the seventeenth century and not now either. Hendrike hadn't gone anywhere near the man on Friday night. Or the boatyard. She'd been acting up in the cabin and then they'd crossed the reed beds to continue filing away the fastenings on the trophy. Helen had been with her all the time.

"I'm not allowed to talk to you," she told Luke. "It's best you don't see my mother too much either."

"Because I'm a boy?"

"Maybe. We are secret people. But please believe I do not wish harm to anyone. All I want is to finish our task and go home. I am not truly living here."

CHAPTER FIVE

The Red Lion

Monday 3 November, third of the waning moon

Luke, Angel

Ants Vandervelde was on the kayaking course. He didn't recognise her straight away because he wasn't expecting to see her and also she had a swimming hat over that crazy mane of hair.

The first thing they had to do when they got to the pool was jump in and prove that they could swim fifty metres with clothes on. Anyone who couldn't would have been chucked off the course. But everybody could so they were told to get changed into their swimming things and come and sit on their towels while the instructor introduced some basic concepts.

Luke noticed her then because she couldn't keep still. She was standing up at random moments and twitching her body and looking round in all the wrong directions. Just as she did at school.

Then everyone had to say their name and their motivation for coming on the course. She had to be asked twice because, as usual, she hadn't been paying attention.

"I'm Angela Vandervelde and I'm here because my mum always signs me up for something when it's holidays because I annoy her in the house and she keeps hoping I'll find something I like and make friends. I never do though."

The instructor said something about kayaking being a team

sport for individuals and a big part of the course would be learning how to assist each other in situations like a capsize or if a paddler became over-tired.

"If conditions are suitable we may get you all out on the river by the end of the week and then you'll see how important it is to use supportive techniques such as rafting and rescue."

"I ain't going near that river."

"No-one's going to make you do anything you're not comfortable with. Next please."

"I'm Luke Whiting and my dad's bought me a kayak and I'm here because I want to learn to use it properly."

There was a lot more he could have said – along the lines of his dad not being able to help him with his kayak because a boat had fallen on him and he'd nearly died and no-one had been able to explain what had happened but that SOMEONE had left her NAMED school blazer behind and the police were going to be asking her questions and it wasn't surprising that that person didn't have any friends because she always caused trouble wherever she went.

But Luke had learned early at primary school never to say anything more than he had to. Not in public.

He planned to stalk Ants and catch her when she was on her own. Then he'd ask her about the blazer and how it had got to be underneath his dad when there was a boat on top of him and no-one around to see he was okay. And how come that someone had made a call but that no-one had waited to tell the paramedics what had happened? Or get in touch with the owner of the boat or the other people at the yard? He was going ask her how she was going to feel if his dad couldn't ever walk again.

And then he was probably going to tell her how he felt about it. And how Liam was going to feel about it. And Vicky and Anna. And even Lottie. He was going to make her sorry. Sorry for everything.

He smiled back politely when the instructor smiled at him and hoped, privately, that there wouldn't be too much more talking before they were allowed to get the kayaks out.

Ants couldn't wait that long. She got up while the instructor was still talking and went across to the row of kayaks that had been put out ready and started messing about with the sets of paddles. The instructor asked her to come back and sit down but she didn't, so he got the whole group to start choosing paddles while he tried to regain Ants's attention by using her as his model to show everyone else how long the paddles should be and the difference between right- and left-handed pairs.

She started waving to people and jiggling up and down. Hawkins the canary could have shown more self-control Luke thought, disgustedly.

The instructor ignored her while he explained to everyone about getting into their kayaks on land to check that the seats and footrests were positioned correctly. Then he got his revenge by telling Ants she could be the first to get in when the kayaks were lifted into the water. He didn't tell her how she should do this. He must have guessed she'd be too quick.

As soon as she began scrambling in, excited and careless, the boat shot away from under her, tipping her headfirst into the pool.

Everyone laughed.

The kayak had filled with water but the instructor didn't say anything about emptying it out. So when Ants tried getting in again, it sank completely and everyone laughed some more.

"Who wants to learn how to get in their kayak properly?" asked the instructor, smiling at Luke.

It was tricky, even when you were used to dinghies. All the same every member of the group (except Ants) managed it first time with the instructor kneeling beside them, explaining step by step and helping them keep the kayaks steady. Then he talked them through the correct procedure for getting out again.

Ants had pulled her waterlogged kayak away from the rest of the class and was struggling to get it up onto the side of the pool so she could empty it. She wasn't having much success.

"Heavy?" asked the instructor, once he'd got the rest of the group sitting safely on the edge holding their kayaks and watching.

Ants nodded without answering. She was a small girl for her age and looked smaller in her pink swimming cap and plain black primary school costume.

The kayak was as stubborn and as slippery as a dead seal. She had hold of the bow end with both hands and was staggering around as she tried to drag it out. She gave an extra heave when she realised everyone was staring. The kayak rose a few inches then lurched round and sank again, almost pulling her in with it.

"Anyone want to show her?"

Nobody did. They knew they didn't know how because they hadn't been taught. They weren't going to make fools of themselves trying.

"Anyone want to try and help her?"

Nobody moved.

Luke felt bad for a moment. Then he remembered that she'd

probably left his dad lying injured and alone in the dark.

"You can hurt yourself lifting a waterlogged kayak without help," the instructor told Ants, as if that wasn't obvious. She'd got hold of the cockpit rim and was struggling to tip instead of pull. "But, like most things, there's a knack to it." He manoeuvred her out of the way and made the emptying look easy, though he still didn't explain how she should do it. "Let's try again and see who can remember the technique of getting into the boat and not into the water. Then we'll learn some basic strokes."

This time Ants folded herself quickly and neatly into her damp kayak and waited for at least a minute before she started fidgeting.

The instructor was in his own kayak and was facing the class, explaining optimum grip positions and correct posture while Ants had one paddle blade down in the water stroking gently to and fro, experimenting.

Her boat started to slip sideways towards the sculling draw. She slid the paddle further forward still rotating it rhythmically in a sort of arc. The kayak began turning in response. She reversed the blade: the kayak changed direction.

She was in her own space at the far side of the class, completely absorbed and concentrating, her body weight shifting with the different angles and her kayak answering every request. Her confidence increased: her sculling grew more dynamic, the water churned, a wave splashed against the side of the gyrating boat.

It was like one of those whirling Russian dances, Luke thought, where the music gets faster and faster and you hold your breath for the dancer as their legs begin to blur and their centre of gravity sinks down until you know that one false move must cause disaster. He watched her, mesmerised.

The instructor blew his whistle, piercingly. You could see Ants jolt with shock. She dug her paddle far too deep and plunged face forward into the pool with her kayak flipping on top of her.

"Cue for another rescue demonstration," quipped the instructor and most people tittered.

He surged forward as Ants broke surface. He dragged her kayak across the front of his and rocked it to and fro to empty it of water. He didn't say anything until he'd finished and her boat was floating alongside his own. Then he put the paddles across both decks and told her to hook her legs over them keeping an equal amount of weight on each boat.

"I'm not as keen as you are on unscheduled dips."

He held the kayaks together as she wriggled up onto the front deck and then back into her own boat.

"Can you understand now why we work as a team in this sport?" he said, smirking.

She didn't answer and she didn't seem to want to try any more. She didn't bother to take her paddle when he held it out. Simply let her kayak drift back towards the side of the pool then used one hand and her weight to guide it the last few feet to the edge. She leaned her arm onto the concrete and hid her face on the crook of her elbow. She'd lost her cap and the back of her head looked small and unfamiliar with her ginger mane soaked through. Her skinny shoulders stuck out like dislocated chicken wings.

When Luke glanced over a while later she'd pulled her kayak out of the water and left.

He'd told Miss Grace that he'd take himself to the hospital. She'd agreed without comment and asked if he had any money and if he knew the bus times from opposite the Red Lion pub. She also invited him to tea.

"It's one of the days I feed Peter so I make a proper meal. It won't be any trouble to cook an extra helping. You can take the dog back afterwards."

He walked the long way using the road. There must be a path along the edge of the wood or through the reed beds and across the field but he wasn't sure and he couldn't afford to miss the bus if he wanted to arrive at the beginning of visiting time.

Even the long way made him early. Luke stopped at the main road junction and looked across at the pub sign. It was a sort of emblem bolted onto the wall, underneath an overhanging gable and next to a peculiar old window. He crossed the road and got as close underneath as he could.

It was red all right, crimson as spilled blood. It looked more like a Chinese dragon that a lion. Its mane was painted purple, so deep you'd think it was black. Wasn't like any lion's mane that Luke had ever seen. It was more like a king's wig, the sort they wore in history.

Thick dark curls clustered round the lion's eyes. Though you couldn't hardly see its eyes from on the ground. You saw flaring nostrils and a gaping mouth; a pointed tongue and sharp incisor teeth. Then you noticed claws clutching at a purple shield and more waves of wooden hair that looked as if they'd been arranged by some top celebrity stylist.

The lion's heavy torso bulged from the pub wall. It was like it was coming for him. Wanted to attack him, ride him down. It would have pulled the whole pub with it, if it could.

Luke saw it was a war sprite. He hoped the fastenings were firm.

Below the jaws and chest it sort of tapered, like the top half of a seahorse. There was something missing from this monster. It was like a captive genie struggling to escape.

The more Luke stared, the more he felt the carving's hidden power. He could have battled it on his Nintendo and that would have been well exciting but standing on the pavement on his own, he felt unsettled and defenceless. There were heavy guns in the smoke behind the lion, a flash of steel and a crack of flame. People screamed and died. It would crush him if he didn't get away.

Luke held his breath as he stepped sideways out of the path of the monster. Then, as soon as he could, he turned back across the road and hid in the brick bus shelter beside the flat stone bridge.

If Liam had been here they'd have dared each other to scramble up onto those solid parapets. Run across and drop a twig or a stone into the hurrying stream. Luke sat still and waited for the bus. He felt sick. It was like he'd had some sort of vision and he'd got to clear it right away before he saw his dad.

Bill might know about the lion from going to those shanty-nights. But Luke would be selfish if he started asking stuff like that. The doctor had said that his dad needed sleep. He had to give his mind a rest so his body could heal faster.

Bill wasn't properly awake: but he wasn't restful either. He might have seen that it was Luke but he didn't say hello. It was like he was talking in his sleep. His eyes were open but the things he was saying must have happened in a dream

Luke had never heard his dad like this. He said he'd met an angel. Bill's angel was like a warm glow when everything else was cold. He'd felt himself drifting helpless into banks of fog.

Thick, wet, smothering fog. There wasn't nothing he could do. He was lost and couldn't move. Then his angel came and pulled him home.

Bill smiled at the hospital ceiling. Then his face changed and went grim and he stared at Luke and started telling him urgently about the demons. There were dark shapes walking in the hour before dawn, Bill said. Dangerous spirits seeking revenge. Blood gelt for deaths that happened long ago.

Luke couldn't look away. He stared and he nodded and he tried to look as if he understood. His dad was talking in a whisper as if he couldn't breathe for fear.

Then Bill clicked back into himself again. His voice changed to normal-but-quiet and he told Luke about the generator he was hoping to install on *Lowestoft Lass*. He'd said it all before but that didn't matter. Then he made Luke promise not to let Lottie worry and reminded him, for about the twentieth time, to tell Derek that he wouldn't be able to get into work for a week or two.

"But first you got to thank my little angel. You got to thank her and keep safe."

It was like some really confusing challenge where Luke didn't have any of the key controls.

"Yeah, okay Dad. That's exactly what I'll do. I'll thank your angel and I'll tell Lottie you're okay and I'll talk to Derek and I'll have a go at tracking down those demons. I'm going to have tea with Miss Grace at the farm when I get back from here. It's great having the dog at night but he doesn't like next door's cockerel."

Bill's eyes had shut and his breathing went slow and steady. Maybe Luke could talk him to sleep.

"I checked the main water tank like you said yesterday and

I know where the hose is now so I'll top it up when I need to. My kayaking course was good by the way. We learned getting in and out and water safety and forward paddling and backward paddling and stopping. I'm going again tomorrow. One of the girls from school was there but she fell in twice. The second time she went right under and her swimming cap came off. It was well funny."

Bill's eyes flashed open. You could see the white all round them.

"Drowning," said Bill in a strange hoarse voice that wasn't his at all, "Drowning is a terrible death. Fishermen drown and sailors too. Some are washed up along the shore: others drift with the tide, lower and lower until finally they sink. Then the scavengers come. I see them edging closer with their pincers and their busy teeth. There was blood on the foam."

Luke wished desperately for Lottie or Anna to be there.

"You don't have to talk like that, Dad. We ain't at sea. We're at the hospital in Ipswich and you're going to be okay. You had an accident and the doctor says you've gotta rest."

Bill stopped almost as quickly as he'd started. Looked like he'd gone to sleep again.

"Is my dad all right?" Luke asked a nurse.

"Doing fine," she said. She checked Bill's blood pressure and looked at the notes on the chart. "Running on a bit, is he? It'll be the morphine. They mostly sleep but everyone's different. Some of them get a bit high: others try and tell you that they're seeing pictures."

"Morphine…that's okay then."

The nurse looked at him. "You're a bit young. Haven't you got an adult with you?"

"I'm okay. I was only asking."

He was okay. His dad was seeing pictures. It was because he was on morphine.

Bill let his head fall sideways on the pillow. It seemed like the only bit he could move. His mouth was open and his eyes were shut. Luke hoped that meant the pictures had switched off.

He sat beside his dad's bed on the plastic hospital chair. Didn't dare move in case he woke him. There was a TV in the corner but he wouldn't risk turning it on. Instead he began to doodle in the notebook that was meant for writing instructions. Angels and lions mostly. Then waves along a shore and a warship with rows of cannon. Puffs of smoke and cracks of flame. Kept adding to the waves. Drew bulging clouds, bigger and darker as his pencil wore down. Began imagining a sea monster attacking through the storm.

Tore the whole page out and threw it away.

There was a fur coat hanging inside the farmhouse door. Great shaggy thing, not fluffy or sleek like something you'd want to stroke. Inside it looked like old raw skin and it smelled Bad. Luke got away from it as quickly as he could and made for the other side of the big table. Ben was jumping up and wagging his tail and squirming. Luke squatted down to make a fuss of him in return. He sneaked a look at his fellow-guest as he did so. He still felt a bit shaky and he wasn't too sure about eating with werewolves.

Old Peter was a small man with very long grey hair, right over his shoulders, and a long beard. He looked as if he might have tried to brush them before sitting down to tea. His hands were gnarled like tree roots but they were clean and his nails were cut neat and short. Somehow Luke had thought he would have nails like scaly yellow claws.

"You can wash your hands in the cloakroom," Miss Grace ordered him. "Get all that hospital dirt off. I don't have germs in my kitchen or near my cows."

The werewolf's jersey had once been navy blue, like a seaman's, but it had been darned with so many different wools that Luke couldn't confidently have guessed which patch had come first. His eyes were also blue, though faded.

Miss Grace introduced Luke as "Bill Whiting's boy from the fishing boat."

Luke said 'Hi' and did his best to smile. Old Peter stared without speaking, as if the connection was too hard for him. One of his eyes was watering all the time but the old man didn't seem to notice. There was no expression on his face. Not even puzzled.

Ben sat next to the werewolf's chair. Peter rubbed the dog's wrinkled forehead and nodded very slowly. Then he looked at the food on his plate as if he wasn't certain what it was. Miss Grace put a knife and fork in his hands and suddenly he smiled.

"You're a goot girl, Maroosia."

His voice was unexpectedly clear. Then he began eating as if he might forget what to do if he stopped.

Tea was sausage and mashed potato and red cabbage and apples and big slices of sponge cake. Mugs of tea of course. More of everything when they wanted it.

"Father doing all right?" Miss Grace asked Luke.

"A'rright, thanks."

Old Peter got up from the table and wandered round, searching. He found it in his coat. One pocket had a book: the other contained a bag full of those spiny balls that had been dropping from the trees on Luke's first night in the wood.

"For you, Maroosia."

"Chestnuts," she said, thanking him and tipping them into a bowl. "Beggars to open if you don't know how."

Luke didn't mention that he'd thought they were attack missiles in a forest war. He watched as she stripped out the plump brown nuts that were shaped like tiny treasure bags. Then he tried to do it himself and was soon sucking his fingertips. Those spines were well sharp. He hadn't been that far off when he'd thought porcupines.

"Vanya?" asked old Peter.

"No. Sorry," he said, removing his finger from his mouth. "I'm Bill Whiting's Luke and I'm living on my dad's boat. Just for this week."

Miss Grace cooked the chestnuts on a metal sheet in her Aga and they were soon struggling to eat the creamy kernels without burning. You had to toss them between your hands. Peter wasn't nearly quick enough so Luke passed some peeled nuts across to him.

"Ah, Vanya," sighed the old man. "It's goot that you're here. Soon you will be asking for a story."

"We're all one or the other," said Miss Grace. "Vanyas or Maroosias. He doesn't do names any more. Still likes to spin a yarn if he finds someone to listen."

The werewolf slept quiet in the woods that night but Ben growled in the graveyard hour. Luke woke and shushed him and hooked his fingers into the dog's collar while stroking him urgently with his other hand and whispering reassurance. The dog was fully alert and trembling as if he was caught in an electric current.

Luke didn't have enough free hands to check his watch, but there was no hint of light in the sky beyond the cabin roof and no sound from the cockerel next door. *Lowestoft Lass* shifted as if she too was wakeful. Was this demons?

He heard footsteps crossing to *Drie Vrouwen*. Human footsteps. Confident. Striding.

"Settle down, fellow." Luke sighed with relief. "Next door's needed a visit to the toilet block."

CHAPTER SIX

Doorways
Tuesday 4 November, fourth of the waning moon

Luke, Helen

Luke hadn't thought Ants would turn up to the kayak course again but she did. Her mother came too. She looked like Ants, except more tired and pale, and her hair was mouse brown not red henna. She talked to the instructor for a while then went to sit in the spectator area.

Ants didn't speak to anyone. Once she'd changed into her swimsuit she stood with her towel clutched round her flat chest looking down at her own white feet as if she didn't trust herself to move. She still wasn't listening. When the instructor had told everyone to go to the store for their kayaks and paddles, Ants stayed stationary.

"Hello, Angela. We're all going to fetch our equipment now. I can give you all the help you need." The instructor was using that specially slow and careful voice that people use to idiots.

Luke felt a flash of anger towards this stupid girl.

"Oh, by the way, *An*-gela," he said, plonking his kayak and paddles down beside where she was still standing as if she was in a trance. "Did you get your blazer back okay? The one with your name in that you left at the boatyard. On the night my dad had his accident and nearly died?"

He said it quite loudly. Most people were busy lining up beside the pool but some of them heard.

She didn't react for a moment. Then she chucked her towel down and was pressed against him, her cold skinny body pushing at his bare skin, her fingernails digging into his upper arms.

"Is that man your dad? Is he okay? I've been wanting to see him every moment. I can't think of nothing else. I don't care about the trouble."

Luke pushed her away and she tripped backwards over someone's kayak. Hit her backside and elbows hard against the concrete. Then she was up at him and fighting. Crying while she did so. Hysterical sobs. Head-butting and kicking. Her eyes were squeezed shut and she was wild.

Luke was first shocked that he'd pushed her over and then he was slow knowing what to do. Hadn't ever fought a girl before though he'd seen Ants in action at school. People used to set her going when there wasn't much else to do. Took bets how long she'd last before some teacher put her into isolation or sent her home.

She bit his chest. That hurt. Luke forgot she was a girl and started fighting back as if she was Liam. They kicked and pushed among the litter of kayaks and paddles and people getting out of the way.

He'd shove her in the pool if he could. That'd cool her off. She was a pincher too.

"Angela! Stop it!"

The mother shouted out. Then the instructor blew his whistle right up against them both. Luke was too angry to stop but Ants's mum got in there and started pulling her daughter away. So then he had to let go.

"That's it." The instructor was possibly the angriest of all.

"You're both off this course. Get yourselves dressed and don't come back. I'll inform the management and you're banned from the pool as well."

Ants's mother might have been trying to apologise but the instructor wasn't going to listen.

"You've already told me about your daughter's Special Needs. I'd say what she specially needs is old-fashioned discipline. Thank you very much."

Luke was shocked and shaky. He couldn't see where he'd put his towel. The instructor picked up a paddle and looked ready to chase him through the exit.

"And if your parents come and see me, I'll say exactly the same to them. Disgraceful behaviour. Now does anyone else think they've joined the karate club or shall we carry on kayaking?"

He didn't know whether to be quick or slow in the showers but when he came out they were waiting for him.

"I saw you push my daughter," said Mrs Vandervelde. "That wasn't very nice was it?"

Huh?

"And did you see her attacking me? I've got tooth marks on my chest. I hope I ain't getting rabies."

The bites were well painful. Livid red semi-circles. He'd looked at them in the changing room mirror. You could almost see the puncture holes.

"She's a little blood-sucker. I hope you keep her window locked at night."

"Now, now, no need for that. I think a nice apology would make all of us feel better and then we can go home."

"Mum," said Angel, "You've got it all wrong."

"I was watching, Angela. I know what I saw."

"You don't know nothing, Mum."

It was funny how she seemed to be able to shrink, to stop being all hair and teeth, get even smaller and paler and go really quiet.

Her mum turned round and stared at her. "What is it, Angela? What don't I know? Is there something that you haven't told us?"

"I'd say there's quite a lot you haven't told her, isn't there, An-gela?"

Luke heard his own voice, nasty and sneery and bitter. That was how he felt.

Ants looked at the floor and nodded. But then she stared up at Luke again, stepped forward so fast – and pulled herself back out of touching distance. As if she knew there'd be a re-run.

"All I was askin' you was if he's okay? I never meant for it to happen. You gotta believe that."

"No, he ain't okay. He nearly died out there when you left him to it and now he might not never walk again. I don't give tuppence what you meant."

Ants sort of collapsed with shock, arms over her head and moaning. Mrs Vandervelde looked desperate. She pulled out a mobile and pressed speed-dial.

"Mike," she said. "I need to you come home. Yes, I know you're at work. I think Angela's in real trouble. Yes, I know you came home when I asked you last week. And the week before. You'll just have to explain to them. Again."

Then she knelt down and put her arms round her daughter, trying to persuade her to stand up and lean against her and start walking. Then they could all go home and Angela could tell them whatever it was when she was feeling better. And her father would be there and they wouldn't be cross. She promised they'd do their best to help her sort it out – as they always did.

"And what about your mother?" she asked Luke. "Is this something she should know? Do I need to ring her too?"

Luke felt a little bit sorry for this wispy woman. He didn't say anything about his mum. Just shook his head.

The Vanderveldes lived on the far side of town, near Fitzgerald School. It took a long time to get there and they didn't speak on the way. Ants soon shook off her mother's arm and walked with a big gap between them, head down and shoulders hunched.

Luke followed at a careful distance. He wanted to know what she was going to say. He wasn't going to let her get out of anything. Then her parents could deal with her.

A small house in a cul-de-sac with a sunrise on its gate. A double line of ornaments along the path and a weathervane like a square-rigged ship.

Luke sat on an upright chair closest to the door in the Vanderveldes' front room. He accepted a cup of sugary tea and fixed Ants with a stare.

"It were Halloween. I didn't stay late at school and I didn't go round a friend's. That was all lies. I ain't got no friends, you know that. I went to the skate-park and I hung out. There were lads there. I don't know any names. They let me do stunts for a bit and then they got bored. So they took some little bikes into the boatyard and we were going under the boats real fast. But there was somebody there and I went under first and the one behind me didn't make it and he hit the legs and the bloke was running towards the boat and it come down on him."

She stopped.

That wasn't nearly enough for Luke.

"Yeah? Then what? Who called the ambulance? Who tried to get the boat off? Who went to find help? Who looked after my dad? Who stuck around to explain what had happened? Who CARED for him?"

She was sitting on the sofa and she'd gone sort of rigid.

"C'mon," he said. "I need to know."

"You'll have to be patient for a moment." Mr and Mrs Vandervelde were sitting on either side of their daughter. The mother was holding her again. "She's having a seizure. It's stress-related. It'll soon wear off. Please tell us, how is your father?"

"His legs are broken and they had to operate to lift two of his ribs off his lungs. An' at the moment he can't move his toes so they don't know whether he's damaged his back and whether he won't never walk again. The doctor said he could have died."

"That's…terrible," breathed Mrs Vandervelde. "I'm so sorry."

"But we can't say it was directly Angela's fault," said her father. "Of course she shouldn't have been there and I'm very, very dis-appointed. But it does sound as if it was one of the others who had the collision that brought the boat down. Not Angela."

"That doesn't exactly help my dad."

Mr Vandervelde's shoulders sagged. "No," he agreed. "Though the question will have to be asked why he was running towards a toppling boat. If indeed there are any witness statements other than our daughter's."

"Haven't heard of any. Derek from the yard said nobody was with Dad when the ambulance got there. They couldn't even trace who made the call. Apparently someone broke the office window and used the yard phone to ring 999. Derek wants them for criminal damage, he says."

"And there'll be a big insurance claim." Mr Vandervelde was watching his own hands, which had started twisting round and round each other, like two small struggling creatures. "Are we quite certain Angela was there, Nelly? This couldn't be another of her stories, could it? She's already said she lied about her movements. She's only twelve."

Ants shifted on the sofa and looked for her mum. Mrs Vandervelde was holding her close. Now she started stroking her cheek.

"There, there, darling. Better now."

"Yeah, I'm only twelve an' all. An' my brother Liam he's ten and Vicky, that's the youngest, she's three."

"Three children and the father possibly incapacitated," Mr Vandervelde informed his writhing hands. "Third party liability."

"And your mother?" Mrs Vandervelde asked Luke again.

"Is dead. Mine and Liam's. Vicky's mum is Lottie. I reckon she'll want to be in touch as soon as she gets back. Or Anna will. Anna's a prefect at our school. She knows your daughter."

Mrs Vandervelde was hanging onto Ants and blinking back what looked like tears. Mr Vandervelde's hands were diving round each other like trapped rabbits. His mouth was hanging open as he stared at Luke.

Luke stood up and edged towards the door. He badly needed to get away from them. "Derek's got the blazer, b.t.w. The one *An*-gela left behind with her name sewn on."

"Noooo," he heard Mr Vandervelde actually groan.

"YES!"

He let himself out and hurried down the gravel path between the gnomes. The whole front garden seethed with ornaments. There were hump-backed weasels and snuffling hedgehogs: birds poised to fly and cats to pounce.

Except they didn't seethe. They were stone and pottery so they all held still. It made him think of the courtyard at Cair Paravel and the frozen victims of the White Witch of Narnia.

He wondered if his dad had meant Ants and her friends when he was babbling on about demons? Nah! Ants and her friends weren't that smart. They were trolls if they were anything.

He checked the time on his phone as he headed for the bus stop. There was a text from Lottie: Coming home asap Thursday. Flights full but paying extra for first class. With you PM. Worried. Hospital not saying much and Bill nothing. You must tell us truth if needed any sooner xxxx

He'd tell anyone the truth, obviously. He discovered that he wasn't quite so certain that he knew what it was

Bill was dozing when Luke got there. It seemed like a healthier doze – more like proper sleep? There were still drips going in and some sort of drain coming out. (Luke sat the other side of the bed from that.)

Why did he feel that his dad was getting better? Was it only because that's what he hoped or was it because Bill wasn't ranting on about angels and demons? It could be something to do with the colour of his face. Because Luke had been thinking of pale stone creatures in the Narnian moonlight, it was easy to jump forward to that bit of the story where the magical lion had blown on the statues and the first tinges of colour had come licking in like flame round the edges of white paper. His dad's face looked that bit more pinkish.

"How's my dad getting on?" he asked a nurse.

She didn't answer but a few moments later a more senior-looking one came into the room. He had a feeling that she was one of the ones he'd seen before. Could have been the sister even?

"How's my dad getting on?" he asked again.

"He's making progress. The sensation's certainly back in his legs and he managed a little movement when the surgeon examined him this morning. That's one big area of worry ruled out. The ability to move has brought an increase in pain which is why we've rigged up an epidural. It's a mix of steroids and anaesthetic and it's made him much more comfortable, as you can see. He's sleeping off a sedative now. He still needs rest so we'll keep him out of the main ward as long as possible. You can tell your family that they're not doing any harm by staying away. Your mum's been ringing a lot, worrying about flying back."

"Step-mum, not mum."

"Step-mum then." The nurse looked at Luke as if she was wondering whether she needed to re-assess his family situation.

He didn't like that look.

"She's nice, my step-mum, I like her. And she's very sensible. It's just she's got the others to think of as well, my brother and sisters. It's their holiday and they'd been looking forward to it ages. She's doing a recording and my brother's got tickets for the San Siro."

"It must be difficult, I see that. There's someone looking after you isn't there? An adult, I mean?"

"I'm with neighbours," Luke replied. It was obviously the right answer.

"Then you can help us reassure your step-mum that rest is the best thing for your dad right now and he'll be glad to see them later in the week. Or whenever it is."

The nurse had been talking in a normal voice, not whispering. That was because of the sedation. She didn't expect Bill to wake up so she didn't have to bother being quiet. It was a bit like sitting with Sleeping Beauty or Snow White, Luke thought when she left them alone again. He and his dad didn't usually touch but after a while Luke discovered that he wanted to hold Bill's hand. Mainly to be sure that he wasn't either a statue or an enchanted princess.

It was a hard-working hand, rough skin and a bit paint-stained with dark hairs on the back of it. Not stone. Not Snow White. Bill's hand was warm and alive and Luke carried on holding it. He didn't bother with drawing or anything. His dad's hand felt so comfortable, so…familiar. He must have held it quite a lot, he supposed, when he and Liam had been kids.

"That's what my angel did," said Bill unexpectedly. His voice was okay.

Luke dropped his dad's hand as if it was a witch's comb. Not that friggin' angel again.

"Sorry, Dad. Thought you were asleep."

"Mmm, probably was. Think they gave me something. Been sitting here long have you?"

"A while. Probably have to go soon. Lottie'n'them coming back late on Thursday."

Bill didn't look either pleased or un-pleased.

"Y'lose track of time here. What's today then?"

"Tuesday. Afternoon."

"Liam'll have been to his big match, will he? Wouldn't want him to miss that."

"That's tomorrow night. You can't blame them for wanting to come back. They're worried about you."

"I've got you, haven't I? Though it's not exactly the week we'd planned."

"Long as you're okay, Dad."

Bill was quiet for a bit. Then he started to talk as if he was repeating his thoughts out loud. "Shouldn't have run at that boat. Saw she were coming down. Trying to be some sort of have-a-go hero was I?"

"I wasn't there, Dad. I dunno what happened."

"Not entirely clear meself. There were some kids on bikes. Going under the boats. Dangerous it was. Could've hurt 'emselves."

That would have been Ants and her gang.

"They didn't though, did they? You were the one who got hurt."

Something of Luke's anger must have come through in his voice.

Bill frowned. Stared at that ceiling again. Eyes a bit narrow; worry-lines getting deeper. "There was a littl'un – proper little zinger. He weren't the one that brought the boat down though. That were the one behind. Then they shoved 'im off his bike and the boat was still coming down. I thought it'd get him."

"You sure he was a boy?"

Bill frowned again. "It was getting dark. I was finishing-up. Maybe I only thought he were a boy. Bent right down on that little bike. Going like merry hell. Lotsa hair. Could've been a girl…"

He sounded uncertain. Luke didn't feel so sure either. Then the nurse was back in telling him that visiting time finished twenty minutes ago.

"See you tomorrow, Dad. That's our last day. You save your strength up. Liam'll be full of it!"

"Keeping busy in the evenings?"

He'd gone to the farm to collect Ben. Miss Grace was doing her cows so he'd offered to help. He'd been promoted to spreading clean straw then, afterwards, she offered a cup of tea and some cake in her kitchen. Luke had never drunk so much tea in his life as he'd drunk this week. He supposed he'd get to like it in the end.

"I've been going to sleep mainly. And drawing. I suppose I could have asked Dad for some jobs."

"I like to read a bit before I go to sleep. Just a chapter or two. Find it sends me off."

"I've got books on my Nintendo as well as games. But I didn't bring it. Books keep me awake if they're any good."

"Old Peter's got books. Piles of 'em. And more soaking on *Ra*'."

Once adults started going on about books…you'd think they were the only ones who'd ever read anything.

"What's *Ra*?"

"His boat – whatever's left of her. Drop him in some pie on your way home, would you? Dog knows the way."

She had a big pork pie on the table and was cutting it into quarters. Put one on her own plate then wrapped one on its own and two together.

"That's for you and t'dog. He's a beggar for pie."

Oh, okay. There was a lot of Lottie's shopping still to eat but he wasn't sure it had included pie.

"Guy Fawkes tomorrow. Creekies light a bonfire and let off fireworks. Dog doesn't care for them. He'll need to stay here. There'll be a bed for you if you change your mind. You won't be any trouble."

The hut was so covered with ivy that it looked like a bush. All the cracks between the roof tiles had been stuffed with moss. There was a pile of logs and a brick- built chimney. The chimney was smoking therefore the werewolf was at home.

Luke's heart sank.

Ben was straining at his lead so hard that he could hardly breathe. It was surprising how heavy he was for a not-very-big dog. He was on his hind legs, scrabbling at the door. Then he burst in, panting with excitement. The werewolf looked bewildered before that sudden change like sunlight came across his face.

"Bayan!"

It was a funny way of saying Ben but the old man's accent was odd anyway. Miss Grace had said he was from Russia.

The extendible lead was jerked out of Luke's hand. It rattled across the threshold and past the old man's legs. He looked confused again.

"Hi, it's Luke. Bill Whiting's son. From the fishing boat. Miss Grace wanted me to drop you in some pie."

"Vanya?"

"Luke."

"Come intside. You must have tea."

"No. No thanks. I've had tea. Lots of tea."

The werewolf didn't seem to understand. He was beckoning Luke into his hut. Luke shoved the wrapped pie at him and looked round urgently for Ben.

The hut was tiny and very warm. You couldn't hardly see the stone walls because they were all covered with books. It was clever really. Someone had sawn cross sections of logs and laid them on their side with planks on top. That made the book-shelves and the books were heaped on them as tight as they could go. There must have been hundreds of books crammed into the hut – they were like its insulation.

There was a black metal stove with an odd sort of kettle. It had a tap and the werewolf was filling a mug. Two mugs. A small table with the lamp and a single chair. The bed was more planks on top of logs with a heap of plain grey blankets and a mattress that looked like it had come off a boat. Ben was already on there, looking quite at home, next to a large brown cat.

"Genia," said the old man handing Luke a cup of tea. It didn't have milk and the old man didn't offer any.

"Thanks," he said, trying a cautious sip. It wasn't like any tea he had ever tasted but it didn't feel poisonous. The cat was watching him with round, unblinking eyes. It had a broad face, almost like an owl.

"Won't you sit, Vanya?"

Luke sat on the bed next to Ben and away from the cat who fluffed out her mottled fur and growled deep in the back of her throat.

"My Genia will haf no liberties," said the old man, moving the single chair closer to Luke.

"No," said Luke, wondering why he hadn't simply handed

over the pie and left. Because of Ben, of course.

"Have you been here for long?" he asked, trying to break the silence.

"I came on my boat but she is old and wet. Now I am in this house with my books."

There was another silence. Luke stroked Ben. The werewolf drank his tea. The cat sat still and stared.

"I can't read my books any more."

Surely he should be in a Home or something? He was older than old: he was Ancient.

"But I help Maroosia with her cows and I tell stories to my Genia. And stories to Bayan when he comes. Would you like a story, Vanya?"

Old Peter's eyes looked bright. He pulled his chair closer. "I can tell you about the woman who has crossed the sea. I can tell you about the good wheat that she threw into the water and how the harbour was choked and the people starved. The name of the town has gone from my head."

He stopped for a moment and Luke tried to stand up. The tea was scalding hot; he'd be here all night if he stayed until he'd finished it.

Old Peter leaned towards him, breathing fast. "She means harm and the girl is her apprentice. I hear them from *Ra'* when they walk at night. A dark sorcerer has arrived to make them three. Now they will have power. I can tell you stories you haf never heard."

His long hair straggled beside his face, his pale eye dribbled. Luke could see inside the werewolf's mouth. He didn't have fangs; he had stumps.

The old man's face was sort of glittering with excitement. He touched Luke's arm with his bony hand.

Luke leapt up from the bed and grabbed Ben's lead. Genia sprang away and sat underneath the metal stove, glaring and yowling.

"Sorry. It's time I went. I'll be expected."

Peter was panic-stricken by this lie. "You haf family? I am so sorry. You must run with both your legs. Your mother she will be out of her mind."

He was pulling Luke towards the door, pushing him out into the wood. Luke tried to explain that he'd got it wrong and there wasn't anyone. Then he said he'd come another day but the old man couldn't understand. He was weeping with distress. Luke had never seen anyone so upset.

"Run, Vanya, run. My story is a bad mushroom and your mother will be counting her lost chickens."

He hurried back into his hut and Luke could hear him: "Oh, oh, oh".

He knew he should have stayed and listened to the old man's spooky tale. How hard would that have been?

The Dutch girl was hanging around near the shower block. Same as yesterday. At least he had something to tell her.

"I talked to my dad. His accident happened when he was finishing work. Sort of five-ish on Friday. He said it were getting dark. Is that what you wanted to know?"

"Certainly not later? Not, for instance, at nine or ten pm?"

"Deffo. He was in hospital by then. He had to have scans and stuff. And, now I think of it…"

He'd heard the sirens himself when he'd been up there at the top of the slope. That must have been the ambulance going for his dad. It had taken him this long to make the connection. Slow or what!

The girl looked as if she'd made a connection too. She flung her head and her arms back and let out a huge sigh of relief. Her face went rosy and it was the first time he'd seen her smile.

"What did you think?" he asked her.

"I thought…" Then she stopped. Clearly she wasn't going to tell him. "I thought it was something different. I'm glad that I was wrong."

Her mother didn't have the power to harm people. It was okay to go along with her and Elsevier. They'd take the prize and leave. It was only a thing. No-one would get hurt or even mind very much.

At last she could go home.

CHAPTER SEVEN

Bonfire Night I
Wednesday 5 November, fifth of the waning moon

Helen, Luke

Helen was out of her berth and into the forepeak almost before Leo's first crow. She pushed an empty wheat sack over the cockerel's head and tied string round the open end. Then she took the direct route up through the forehatch and ran, holding him (not too tightly) in her arms. There was no need to pause and shut the hatch as there were no birds left. Her mother had killed the last of the hens to make a feast for Elsevier.

Both adults were asleep, she hoped. They had all been out after midnight and into the early hours, showing their Kapitein what they'd achieved. The escape channel had been inspected; the sluice gate mechanisms greased and tested; a trailer had been requisitioned (stolen) and parked near the pub for so long that it must by now have become invisible. There was a (stolen) punt moored under the bridge.

They had ropes, a mattress and the tarpaulins. All stolen. Reparations, Elsevier called them. Helen didn't know for what, exactly.

Hendrike made her own particular nightcaps and slept soundly but, after yesterday's dawn welcome, Elsevier had said that if she were ever disturbed again by Leo's outrageous noise, she would throttle him herself. Helen believed that Elsevier was capable of this but not that she'd know how to kill neatly, almost painlessly, as Hendrike did. Leo was the only creature Helen cared about and she wasn't going to let this happen to him.

She'd run past Merlesham Hill Farm often enough in the early mornings. She'd heard the cows and seen white doves along the red roof tiles. The farm felt like a good place and it was Leo's only chance. If the farmer didn't want him then the end would presumably be efficient.

It was her one act of resistance.

Until yesterday, when the boy from the fishing boat had confirmed that his father's accident was just that – an accident – nothing connected with her mother's crushing of the poppet, Helen had been ready to sabotage the entire operation.

Elsevier had been unbearable, strutting around the cabin with her trousers tucked into the tops of her boots, striking the poses that Helen knew she'd copied from museum paintings of the Golden Age. Her arrival had to be kept secret but Elsevier was always in need of an audience. Helen and her mother hardly counted yet still she'd alternately postured, harangued and sulked. What had driven Helen close to treachery was the fact that she'd brought Hendrike a 'present' of magic mushrooms from her supplier in Amsterdam.

"She can't take them. Her visions are out of control as it is. What are you trying to do to her?"

Helen often wondered what would happen if she told someone about the drugs. Would it separate her mother from Elsevier?

The two women had met when Hendrike was still an assistant curator at the Rijksmuseum. Elsevier had entered their lives with a swirl of her cloak and a flourish of her broad-brimmed hat. Had begun inviting Hendrike to Amsterdam's brown cafes where they sat late at night in a haze of smoke and conspiracy.

Then her mother had sold their small flat and bought *Drie Vrouwen*. She began experimenting with various seeds and moulds and fungi which she'd discovered in her seventeenth-century research. She experienced hallucinations and called them visions. Took up drumming and chanting. Said she was a wicca, a woman of power, a new age seer.

She lost her job.

Elsevier stole Hendrike's research and used her visions to impress new followers. She was building a cult. Wreken de Dame – Avenge the Lady. The two of them had twisted some stupid folk-tale about a woman who was accused of blocking a harbour and used it to legitimise stealing back an old ship's figurehead. Wreken de Dame was supposed to be about making the Netherlands great again. Really it was just to make a bigger stage for Elsevier and give her an excuse for getting rid of anyone she didn't like.

Helen couldn't believe that anyone could take Elsevier seriously but apparently they did. She was interviewed in newspapers and local radio, then invited to join discussions on late night TV. It seemed the more outspoken Elsevier became – including rude and insulting – the more people flocked to Wreken de Dame. It was charisma, apparently.

The Kapitein suspected that Helen might not be loyal. She had rattled her cabin door late that night and found it locked. Had growled a throaty message for Helen's ears alone.

"It is possible that my relationship with your mother may have run its course. If this mission is successful, there may be a parting of the ways."

Helen would do anything for that.

"First the mission must succeed. That is essential. Do you understand?"

She'd do anything – except let Elsevier get her grasping hands round Leo's feathery ruff.

The farm was his best chance. And then she'd be back on board *Drie Vrouwen*, ready and willing to conspire. And if Elsevier and her mother didn't split when they got home to Holland... Helen didn't know what she'd do.

Luke and Ben were walking up to the farm as Helen was coming away. Miss Grace hadn't been keen to take the cockerel.

"There's a reason I don't have one already. My hens lay better if they're not being bothered all the time."

But when Helen, without looking up, had asked her in that case whether she wouldn't mind killing the bird speedily, Miss Grace had relented. She appeared to accept Helen's explanation that they were planning to go home soon and her mother didn't want the cockerel on the Noordzee crossing as it was likely to be rougher in November than it had been when they'd arrived. Also she didn't ask any awkward questions about what had happened to the hens.

"Is he pinioned?" she asked instead.

"I'm sorry," said Helen, "What is pinioned?"

"Have you cut his main wing-feathers? Can he fly?"

Helen shook her head. None of the poultry could fly. Her mother had seen to that.

"No matter. We'll put him in a coop for now and I'll take a look later. I've known them grow back if the bird's still young.

The dog, the old man, the boy and now a cockerel. Should I be opening a refuge?"

Fortunately she didn't seem to want an answer.

"Remind your mother to tell me when she's ready to vacate the mooring."

"Hi," said Luke. "Have you been running?"

The girl's cheeks were blotchy red.

"No."

She couldn't face going back to *Drie Vrouwen*. She'd thought she could. But she couldn't.

"I will go and look for ceps."

"Ceps?"

"*Boletus* edulis, fungus you can eat. They will pay for them in the town or at the pub. Or my mother makes soup."

"They might be toadstools."

"Not if you understand correctly. We also pick berries, nuts and seaweed. Either we eat them or we sell them to the pub. You English are too lazy to look."

He ignored the insult. He'd nothing else to do this morning now he couldn't go kayaking. Thanks to Ants.

"Okay. You show me. We'll take Ben. This is Ben, by the way, the dog. He doesn't like your cockerel."

Helen looked at the terrier. Didn't smile. Didn't speak.

"He's probably only scared – real softy is our Ben."

"Ben is your dog?"

"I wish. Belongs to Miss Grace. She's letting him keep me company – you know, cos of Dad. My friend Xanthe rescued him – Ben, not Dad – but then she couldn't manage to look after him full-time. That's why he's on the farm. If I find any mushrooms maybe I could give them to Miss Grace. She's been good to me."

"I think she is good also."

Luke didn't notice that Helen had come mushroom-hunting with no basket. He took his fleece off and offered it as a carrier when they found a colony of oyster mushrooms on the trunk of a dying beech tree.

"It's okay. Lottie's coming home tomorrow. She won't mind doing some washing."

"Lottie?"

"My step-mum. And my step-sister and my brother and my half-sister, Vicky."

"You have so much family."

That made him feel bad again about last night. When the old man had hurried him away, believing that he had a mother waiting for him.

"Maybe I ought to give some to Peter as well. He lives in a hut near here."

"The mad man?"

"He's just old. And a bit forgetful."

She shrugged. "You'd better not. You have to be careful with mushrooms. Some can make you sick. That's not good for old people."

"Wow, look at those! They are totally Super Mario."

Almost a complete circle of red mushrooms with white warty bits. They had to be the most classic toadstools Luke had ever seen. Was it Alice in Wonderland where you ate bits and grew bigger? The girl was on her knees, pulling them out from their roots.

"What are you doing? – I'm really sorry, I've forgotten your name – You can't pick those. They have to be poisonous."

"My name is Helen. Helen who wants to go home and yes, you are right, these fungi are poisonous. They are *Amanita mus-caria*. I pick them and then I crush them and I bury them under leaves so no-one else is fooled."

Only part of that was true. She was removing the fly agaric from her mother's sight. Normal people would be scared off by the vivid colour and the spots and the remains of the white veil round the base. Hendrike went looking for them wherever there were birch trees. She had read too much.

"So, what are you doing?"

Luke had spotted a big white mushroom, perfectly round – twice as big as a tennis ball. He ran up to it, ready to chip it neatly into goal, exactly as Liam would have done, but instead he stopped and picked it up and threw it for Ben and then he and the dog raced together to retrieve it. It was well fun.

"Stop it! That's food. People can eat that!"

Oh. It had looked…extra-terrestrial.

"I'm sorry."

"You are very ignorant. Now follow me and I will show you chicken-of-the-woods."

Luke shortened Ben's lead and made him walk to heel and neither of them said anything at all when they discovered that chicken-of-the-woods was a golden fungus that grew on the trunks of sweet chestnut trees.

"I wish," said Helen, "that people would remember it is good to eat natural food and then they don't have to kill so many animals."

Luke nodded seriously and held out his fleece. Anna had tried to make him eat tofu once. It was like chewing bathroom sponge or expanded polystyrene. This looked a bit similar except for its smell. He knew he ought to want to be a veggie but…

They picked a whole pile of delicate-looking purple fungi and then Ben was pushing leaves about with his nose and Luke noticed a scattering of mushrooms which looked like over-cooked buns. Helen was delighted.

"These we give to the farmer as our gift," she said. "These are ceps."

They put the ceps for Miss Grace on the kitchen table and Luke said goodbye to Ben.

"Thanks for letting me come," he said to Helen as they walked down the track. "Are you going to be around for the bonfire?"

"Maybe. Maybe not if we have to pay. I don't know why it is?"

"It's because it's the fifth of November. Guy Fawkes tried to blow up the King and the Houses of Parliament. He had barrels of gunpowder and he hid in the cellars all night. But he got found."

"Why?"

"Someone grassed him up – told on him."

"No. Why did he wish to blow up the King?"

"To do with religion, I think. Most things were in them days."

"Which religion was this Guy Fawkes?"

"Not sure." Luke felt embarrassed. He liked history. He ought to know. "Maybe Catholic. Or Protestant?"

"We are Protestants," said Helen, firmly. "The French and Spanish, they were Catholics. The French plotted against us with you English."

"Oh. Er…sorry."

"Sorry is not always enough," said Helen and ran away from him, back to *Drie Vrouwen*.

It was going to be lonely without Ben. Maybe he'd accept Miss Grace's invitation and stay the night up at the farm.

He met Peter and said Hi but Peter didn't answer. Luke tried walking along beside him chatting. Peter didn't recognise him so Luke gave up when they reached the moorings. He said goodbye and watched the old man as he plodded through the double row of boats that were standing out of the water for the winter.

He did look like an old and mangy wolf. Luke's first impression hadn't been so far wrong. He could track Peter. Discover his day-time lair. That's what he'd do if Liam was here.

The old man went back into the wood and shambled along a section of path that they hadn't yet explored. It was muddy and there were boards crossing three or four small streams that must be draining back into the creek. There was a length of rope tied to a tree. It led out into a band of reeds. A plank jetty also led into the reeds. It was narrow and a bit uneven but it seemed you could hold the rope and follow it along. That's what Peter did. Then he disappeared.

Luke waited for a while, then went back the way he'd come. He would watch out for Peter's return then explore the jetty when the old wolf was at the farm or in his hut.

Ants Vandervelde and her parents were standing beside *Lowestoft Lass*. There was no way he could avoid them. Mr Vandervelde was writing something. He stopped when he saw Luke.

"Hullo. Good morning. Glad to see you."

"Er, hi."

"We were going to leave a message."

He wished they had. He wished he'd stayed in the wood or gone down Peter's jetty. Anywhere.

Ants and her mother were hanging back, leaving the father to do the talking. He kept pushing his glasses back on his nose. Ants was fidgeting and looking from side to side at all the boats. She was holding her mother's hand. Or her mother was holding her, which seemed more likely.

"This is your father's boat?" Mr Vandervelde stopped pushing at his glasses and pulled his wispy beard instead.

"Yeah."

"Is there somewhere we can talk? We've been to the Phoenix Yard. We have told them the whole story. And to the police. We've been to the pool and explained the provocation. You can return to the course or we will offer your parents a refund for the fees they paid. We are here because Angela is desperate for news of your father. As we all are," he added.

"NO." Luke nearly shouted.

Ants began to cry. Her mother tried to put her arms right round her but Ants pushed her away. Her mother still hung onto the hand while Ants stood and sobbed. It was so embarrassing. That girl, Helen, and her mother would hear her. They'd assume these were his friends.

"Stop doing that. Okay, come on board – if that's what it takes. I don't know what my dad would think."

He did know what his dad would think. His dad was helpful and kind. That was his dad's big mistake.

"It was you lying on the ground wasn't it?" he asked Ants,

when they were all in the wheelhouse with the door closed. "You went under the boat first but you didn't knock it down. Then the others pushed you off the bike and legged it. My dad thought you were going to get crushed so that's why he ran towards the boat. So he nearly died and it was ALL YOUR FAULT."

She nodded without speaking. Her gold-brown eyes were huge, her small face white and her dyed red hair even more startling than usual.

"Angela has made a full statement to the police and also to the boatyard manager. She has admitted trespassing but not with intent to cause damage or endanger property – or life, of course. She claims she does not know the names of any of the boys who were with her and she refuses to attempt identification. We don't yet know what further proceedings the yard or their insurance company intend to take against us." Mr Vandervelde looked down at his hands which seemed ready to begin their uncontrollable twisting. He put them out of sight behind his back. "All that truly concerns Angela is your father's condition. She wants to see him but we've told her that it couldn't be allowed."

"When he were on the ground and I thought that he were dying I promised him that he were going to be okay."

She was leaning towards Luke, sort of quivering. He wondered whether she was going to attack him again. Her mum must've thought the same cos she was still hanging on

"Gold star promise, I told him. He was so cold and his breathing was going funny and I tried to keep him warm and stop him from like slipping away. I tried my best."

Luke looked hard at her wide face with its short straight distinctive nose and that mane of hair. He remembered what his dad had felt and what the doctor had said.

He'd got it so wrong.

"You did! It was you who was Dad's angel!"

"Hardly, in the circumstances …"

Angel ignored her father. She needed to tell Luke exactly how it had been. "I ain't good at focussing. I ain't good at sitting still. There's something wrong with me but I don't know what it is. They try putting me on programmes but I'm always getting chucked off. But this time I did it. I sat with your dad and I stayed stone-still and I sort of poured my promise into him. Then the ambulance came…and I ran away."

Luke stared at her almost as hard as she was staring at him.

"I want to tell him that I was sorry. It was the light, see? I know I should have said something to my mum and dad but I didn't. I want to know if my promise worked. I totally need your dad to be okay – for me and him."

She stood without moving.

"I think," said Mrs Vandervelde, after a while, "that we should all have a nice cup of tea."

"Hate tea," said Angel, jerking back to her normal self.

"And I've drunk so much that I might be turning brown," said Luke. "But I'm sure my dad would want me to offer you something and anyway I haven't had breakfast yet. Ants…I mean Angela, can come to the hospital with me later when it's visiting. The nurses can be a bit funny about kids but I know Dad would like to see her. He's been asking."

He made them tea and ate beans on toast himself. Offered some to Ants but her mother said she shouldn't because they were orange so she just had the toast.

Then he showed them round *Lowestoft Lass*. The tide was up and she was floating. Everyone seemed more cheerful and when Ants spotted the kayak and went nearly dippy with excitement, Luke managed to persuade her parents that it would be okay to launch it in the shallow water and have a quick paddle round. Conditions were ideal. The tide was slack and there was very little wind.

It was a good thing Lottie had made him bring the buoyancy aid and waterproofs. There was a sort of skirt thing folded inside the kayak which he managed to fit on and, without exactly saying anything untrue, he allowed Ants's parents to think that he was doing this all the time. You could see that they were fussers.

"The weather forecast's not good later in the week," said Mr Vandervelde. "People who want fireworks need to have them now. Better not to wait for the weekend."

"I'm probably not staying much longer. The rest of my family's coming home tomorrow and then I suppose we'll go to our house at Bawdsey. Unless my brother Liam or any of the others want a night on board."

"I would," said Angel.

Luke shut his ears to that. There were limits.

He had first turn in the kayak. It was well fun. He went up to the sluice and felt the water pouring though from the stream the other side. There was a sort of lagoon bit that he hadn't noticed before, half-hidden behind the flood wall. The water was shallow and there was a load of rocks, as if maybe the wall had crumbled. Luke didn't go in because he was worried about damaging his kayak but he looked across and saw an old boat lying at a crazy angle in the reeds.

He paddled back to *Lowestoft Lass* as casually as if he did it every day.

Ants's parents said she wasn't allowed to take the kayak away from the fishing boat. "You're not experienced as Luke," they said and he had to pretend that he wasn't listening.

Ants was staring at the kayak. She was hopping from one leg to the other and flapping her arms by her sides. What if she did something stupid and fell in again?

"You gotta concentrate, remember," he told her, shoving the paddle at her

He should have saved his breath. She stepped so tidily into the kayak that the flimsy vessel stayed completely motionless. Then she pushed her paddle down into the water and made the kayak move away fast from the decking, first sideways and then into a long, curving, reverse sweep.

She did exactly as her parents had said and stayed close to *Lowestoft Lass* all the time. Watching her was like watching someone in the middle of a private dance, or skating complicated figures on an empty ice-rink. She didn't look up and no-one interrupted.

The kayak was gyrating, powering forwards, swooshing backwards, twirling in and out of the cat's-cradle of mooring lines between *Lowestoft Lass* and *Drie Vrouwen* as if they were markers in a slalom race. Ants was bent towards the paddle as if she and it and the water were a single unbroken connection. It was...beautiful.

When she'd finished and was sitting up again, there was an outburst of applause. Some of the creekies who'd been gathering old wood and rubbish for the bonfire had stopped what they were doing to watch.

Ants was obviously startled but she managed not to panic. She made a few quick strokes which brought the kayak alongside the decking and allowed Luke to take hold of it while she got out.

"Thanks," was all she said.

"That was awesome."

"Does she do stunts?" someone shouted from the bank.

Ants's parents had no idea what to say – to her or to each other.

The ebb tide was sucking the water away from the moorings which meant that it was almost lunch time and they needed to make plans for going to the hospital. Luke said that Ants could come on the bus with him but her parents said that they'd take her home first so that she could get changed into something more suitable. Then they'd drive her in later when Luke had had time on his own with his dad and had double-checked whether it was going to be appropriate for her to see him.

"Of course we want Angela to make a proper apology but we'd hate to risk upsetting your father in any way."

"It's only two people at a time visiting."

"Don't worry about us. We'll sit outside."

"We could give you a lift home afterwards, if it would help. We don't mind waiting."

"I'll be okay. There won't be any special hurry. I'm not doing anything this evening."

He wished he'd thought of calling one of his mates from school. Fireworks were only really good when you had someone to chase about with. He supposed it was Liam he was missing.

"Everyone's invited to the party," one of the creekies stopped by to say. "We heard about your dad's accident but you can bring your friends."

Ants looked at him with such a flash of hope. But then down at her feet as if remembering all that had happened.

"Do we have to pay?" Luke asked.

"Nothing for kids. You do need an adult to be responsible and they bring a fiver and some food or drink. Or a firework if you prefer."

Mrs Vandervelde was shaking her head already but her husband looked at Ants, then at Luke.

"Did you want to attend?" he asked. "If your father had been here with you, would you have gone?"

"Dunno. Might've done."

This would have been half way through their week and instead it was almost the end. He'd made loads of mistakes and he hadn't turned practical either. Now that he'd seen Ants he knew he wasn't even going to be anything special at kayaking.

"Go on my little Luke, say yes. You have to say Yes if you want adventures."

It was like a voice that had always been somewhere in his head, encouraging him on, not pulling him back.

"You can come if you like. And…Angela can come. I've got loads of food left. Sausages mainly."

"I really can't…" This was Ants's mother.

"I know you can't," said her husband. "But should I? And take Angela with me? Would you mind?"

"What about the burning? Would they be burning a guy?"

"We'd have to ask."

Mr Vandervelde could see Luke looking confused.

"Angela's mother is a Catholic. She was brought up in Ireland when there was still a lot of fighting about religion. And killing. She knows it's not the same any more but she can't quite get over it."

Luke had never thought about that: people minding about a real Guy Fawkes. Like believing that there were properly witches when it was Halloween?

"So which side was Guy Fawkes? Someone asked me earlier and I wasn't sure."

"He was a Catholic of course. Seventeenth-century and probably a bit simple. He was the fall guy and he had a cruel end. Tortured then executed by disembowelling."

"Mike, please!"

"Sorry dear."

"The girl on the boat next door says she's a Protestant. Is that what most people are? Am I one?"

Mr Vandervelde looked at the black barge.

"*Drie Vrouwen*, three women. Are there?"

"What?"

"Three women on that boat?"

"Just Helen and her mum. And a cockerel. I haven't been on board. They're not English and I don't think they like us very much. I don't know why."

"Only a historian would understand that. I assume they're Dutch."

"Are you a historian?"

"Yes."

"Is A...Angela?"

She stopped staring at the water and looked at him instead. It was a miserable, furious, dare-you look. "You know I ain't. We're at the same school. I can't even read properly."

CHAPTER EIGHT

Bonfire Night II
Wednesday 5 November, fifth of the waning moon

Elsevier, Helen, Angel, Peter, Luke

As soon as it was dark she closed the sluice. The cow and the girl had worked for weeks to clear the stream of submerged branches and trailing fence wire but she wasn't certain how deep the carving would float and they would need plenty of water to hurry their prize to the barge. High water in the creek would be close to midnight, too early for her purpose.

Elsevier loathed these English tides. In Holland they had controlled their inland waters and enclosed them into meers. The English didn't have the organisation or the skills. They didn't seem to care. Look at the way they let their seawalls crumble until they breached. Then it was an emergency and people rescued from their homes and pictures in the news. That's not how she would run a country.

If it were not for the rise and fall of this night's tides their mission would be so simple. The best time to take their prize was the dark time before dawn when lesser people had gone to sleep and even the road was quiet. But by then it would be ebbing. There would be only centimetres of water in the creek unless she had it stored in advance.

The fastenings were loose – she had checked that they had been correctly filed through. She would superintend the removal herself. That was an action too crucial, too symbolic to be entrusted to underlings. Then the girl would need time to transport the trophy from the bridge to the sluice. She disliked the girl but assumed she'd manage this efficiently. It was in her interest.

Remove the electricity and bring the darkness forward. Let the cow cause havoc. They had to get the trophy onto the barge before first light. The girl had done them a favour running off with that appalling cockerel – but she wouldn't mention that to the mother. More power to her if they were fighting.

She slipped carefully down the creek side of the flood wall and checked that there was no water coming through. No gurgle from the metal grille. Just the occasional popping of methane bubbles in the smelly mud and the rustle of a hunting rat. She could hear the distant sounds from the party at the moorings and see the glow from the modest fire. So that was their idea of enjoyment.

✦   ✦   ✦

Helen and her mother joined the bonfire party as they'd been ordered. They'd helped themselves to the five pounds entrance fee from the honesty box near the showers and Hendrike was carrying a cauldron of steaming chicken and mushroom soup. It smelled delicious. She'd told Helen that it wasn't for her.

"Why? Have you made it with something bad?"

"No. But it has stock from the hen and since you are now so squeamish, the Kapitein and I have decided that you are permitted no more meat products until you apologise for your behaviour in taking the cockerel. You have to learn obedience to your elders."

Helen didn't care about the soup. She wanted to be a vegetarian anyway but she was tired and hungry and she'd been up most of last night being obedient to her elders and she knew she'd be up most of tonight as well. Her mother hadn't asked her why she'd taken Leo. Didn't seem interested in understanding anything about her. She'd loved him because there was nothing else left.

"Please, moedertje, can't we give up and go home? Now, before we commit more crimes? Elsevier doesn't care about us, you know. She doesn't truly grieve for the sorrows of the past. Wreken de Dame is all about her."

Hendrike slapped her. She was glad to feel her heavy hand stinging her daughter's skin.

"You are never to speak like that. We women will succeed where men have failed. We will bring home this symbol of the Golden Age. We will drive out the foreigners and once again we will become a strong proud nation."

Helen couldn't cry. She felt as if the last traces of feeling had been slapped out of her. She looked forward to hurting someone else in return.

The boy was there, standing close to the bonfire and drinking lemonade from a plastic cup.

He'd been away all afternoon. Visiting his loser father in the hospital, she supposed. It had made it delightfully easy to siphon the last drops of diesel from the fishing boat's tanks into their own. They'd already taken the tarpaulins, the long ropes and a petrol can.

He looked childishly pleased to see her. Wanted her to meet his friends: the irritating little redhead who'd been showing off in the kayak and her father, who he introduced as a historian.

"He can tell you about Protestants and Catholics if you want to know, though it's actually not very nice. And it's okay for you to be here if you're a Protestant because if we were burning anyone – which we're not – it'd be a Catholic. Which is why Ants's mother isn't here. This is Ants. Her real name's Angela but it doesn't suit her and she says she doesn't mind. My dad thinks that she's an angel but that's particular to him. We've been to the hospital. He seems a lot better."

Helen-at-Home might have asked the girl what name she liked to be called. New Helen didn't bother and the only reason that she stood still and forced her lips to smile was because she and her mother were under orders to be as visible and as cheerful as possible throughout the evening. The creekies were a friendly lot when they came out from their boats. They were keen to make everyone welcome even though the women from *Drie Vrouwen* had been avoiding them since August.

This time tomorrow they would be gone. Goodbye muddy creek.

Helen confidently expected that they could avoid answering any awkward questions by pretending that their language skills weren't too good. Except it turned out that red-head's father spoke Dutch.

All the months they'd been here Helen hadn't met a single English person who spoke Dutch. Now here, on their last evening was this man who spoke her own language. Spoke it in the formal, slightly old-fashioned way that her mother's friends used to speak in the days when her mother's friends were other academics and curators. Not self-styled charismatic leaders – or weirdoes.

It almost broke through her self-control.

He was a small, enthusiastic, wildish-looking man. Said his name was Michael, asked her to call him Mike. He had untidy white hair though he probably wasn't very old; glasses perched on the end of his nose, a wispy beard and an irritating habit of rubbing his hands together when he got excited about what he was saying. He followed her around eagerly though she tried to get rid of him onto her mother. He seemed to have some obsession with getting her to tell him about the Dutch education system and the way history was taught in schools. She wanted to say that all she cared about was getting back into the Dutch education system. She didn't mind what she got taught.

He was terribly excited when he learned her surname.

"And you a de Witt! And I, would you believe, am a Vandervelde! The surname run together in the English way and not in any sense a direct descendent of those admirable artists. But when I look at the sketches VV the Elder produced tossing about in some little galjoot between the great ships and their cannon, I do feel proud of the association, however slight. Did you know that they moved to England after Sole Bay? Watched the later battles from the other side. And are you connected with the lamented brothers de Witt?"

"De Witt's a common name in Holland. I've never thought about it."

That was such a lie. Her mother would hardly let her think of anything else. Hendrike said that they were descended from the great Johan de Witt, who had led the United Provinces into their Golden Age and had then been shockingly murdered. Her mother said that the direct connection was a secret, which she had established though her research. Helen was not allowed to tell anyone in case it might tempt her to brag. As if people her age would have been the smallest bit bothered. Why should they care about some failed politician three hundred years ago?

Hendrike had different rules for herself. She shared her Big Secret with anyone she wanted to impress. Helen assumed that was the main reason Elsevier had taken her up. That and her mother's belief in her powers and her knowledge of all those maritime prints and drawings she'd been employed to catalogue. If Hendrike hadn't obsessed over the detail of all the warships in the Van der Velde pictures then Elsevier would never have hatched up this hateful stunt.

She kept her smile fixed. "So sorry," she said.

Mike looked disappointed. "History and religion. No interest to the young of today. I forget what a boring old fart I've become. Last week I got so desperate I repeated my entire lecture series to my wife's collection of garden gnomes. They didn't ask many questions but at least they kept smiling and stayed where they were until the end. So tell me, my dear, what do you enjoy? Those electronic games, perhaps?"

She talked about her rowing club for a while and then her mother came up with a helping of the chicken and mushroom soup. Helen assumed that her mother would have laced it with her knock-out nightcap. She wanted to tell Mike not to have any but she knew that she mustn't. She couldn't bear to watch him drink it so she said she was off to see whether the fireworks would soon be ready.

It was a dark night with no moon and a feeling of damp in the air. Elsevier had been passage-planning as she hid in the cabin all day. Mainly to make sure they were back in good time for her press conference. She had told them that the barometer was falling and the forecast bad, but – as long as everyone obeyed orders and the heist was successful – they would make the crossing whatever the weather.

"The blood of seafarers flows scarlet in my veins," she'd declared.

Helen didn't see that Elsevier's blood colour was going to make much difference to the weather but she didn't say anything because she wanted to get home to Holland more than anything else. Her mother looked adoring. How stupid was she! She didn't know she was going to get dumped.

The creekies were trying to sing. They couldn't get the right notes.

"We need Bill's concertina," someone shouted.

"Where's his boy? He was here with the old man."

"Saw him in the gents. Not looking so good."

"Must have sampled some of your home brew!"

There was a lot of laughter about very little and the bonfire was beginning to die down. Soon they would have finished their fireworks and then what would they do? Would they go back to their boats or would they stand around still drinking beer? She had been ordered to tip it away wherever she could.

"But if they have no more beer then they'll go to the pub."

"The Kapitein will be commanding from inside the bar and you will wait in the dark for her. I will bring them flocking at the time decreed."

The tide was beginning to trickle in over the mud. Helen had not been able to discover precisely what Elsevier and her mother had planned.

"We learn from the actions of the past," Hendrike stated. "And from the daring of our forbears."

The past. People trying to blow each other up for being the wrong religion. That's what these stupid English were celebrating wasn't it? Helen's head ached and her face burned and she wanted to cry. She couldn't stand the cheerful people offering her chocolate and baked apples any longer. She slipped away and went to sit in the quiet space between the fishing boat and *Drie Vrouwen*.

"Oh, hi, are you wishing you were on the water?"

It was the irritating girl.

"I can't wait until I have another chance. I was in a kayak this afternoon and it felt totally special. I've never felt like that before. If I wasn't in so much trouble I'd be begging my parents for a kayak. I'd even go back to the lessons. Except I don't suppose they'd have me. But anyway I'm in trouble so I've got to keep quiet."

"Trouble?"

"With the police and the boatyard and the insurance company and my parents of course. But at least I've made it up with the man."

"What man?"

"Mr Whiting, Luke's father. My new friend Luke. I'm with him here this evening. We were invited. I never get asked to anything. But he seems to have gone off somewhere. I haven't seen him for a while. There was an old man came in a fur coat and ate sausages but then Luke said he had a stomach ache. My dad's not very well either. He's gone really strange. As if he's seeing things."

Helen felt a flash of anger. Her mother just couldn't resist, could she? She hadn't used nightcap, she'd sprinkled fly agaric powder into the soup with all those beautiful fresh mushrooms that Helen had picked that morning. Okay, they needed to make sure that the next-door neighbours were out of action but she didn't have to poison them.

Hendrike came up behind her at this moment. She was carrying her empty cauldron and breathing heavily.

"What are you doing here?" she demanded. Close up Helen could see that her face was flushed as if she'd been standing too close to the bonfire.

"I'm sorry mother. We were talking. Some people aren't feeling very well." She felt it was safer to speak in English.

"That will be the fault of the boy and his sausages."

The red-head had caught the contempt in Hendrike's voice. She was squaring up to her. "Luke's my friend. Don't talk like that."

"So," Helen intervened, "we were discussing water and how calm it makes people feel."

She noticed that the dinghy, which belonged to the fishing boat, had been moved over to *Drie Vrouwen*. She didn't know why.

"You are in the wrong place, daughter. I think you have forgotten the time. Soon there will be fireworks. I will take care of this child. She may like to move a small vessel for me."

"Oh yes please," said the red-head with a ridiculous skip.

"There." Hendrike was beaming. With her white hair in those twin buns and her portly figure and the large white apron she'd chosen to wear this evening, she looked like every dear old housewife from every child's picture book that featured houses made from gingerbread and trays of rosy apples and poisoned fairings. "I've got a proper helper now. You'll paddle very carefully won't you, my dear?"

The girl was jiggling on the spot, her mouth slightly open and her wide eyes bright. She was an idiot thought Helen. The sort of idiot who'd carry your drugs bag through customs if you asked her nicely.

I don't like the person I'm becoming.

"Goodbye daughter." Her mother's lips continued smiling but Helen recognised the tone. She had no choice. She left.

✦　✦　✦

It was quiet on board *Ra'*. Quiet and sad and comfortingly familiar. Peter knew every cleat and handhold on this boat and all the different sounds she could make when her hull moved against the water. He knew that *Ra'* was dying. She lay where she'd been thrown when the hurricane came raging over southern England, uprooting trees, breaching walls and tearing boats from moorings. Peter had tried to put things right but the damage was too great and he was already old.

When had he been born? Too long ago. Before *Ra'* herself had been built by that Englishman, escaping with his Russian woman.

Peter had been an observant, interested child. He'd followed them around, listening to their strange accents and odd behaviours. When they had built their yacht and left, he promised himself that, one day, he too would sail to England.

And here he was. Together with *Ra'* – the scraps that were left of them both.

The English thought that he was Russian. Even the kind Maroosia who let his yacht remain where the storm had thrown her and who gave him food and work and his small hut and the cat to keep him company. Even Maroosia assumed that all the Northlands, all the countries along the southern shore of the Baltic Sea were somehow…Russian!

Peter knew that Maroosia had much to think about. She had a mother to consider as well as the farm and the moorings. He never ceased to be grateful for her kindness so he never tried to explain the size of her mistake. To confuse Russians with the neighbours they invaded!

Peter had suffered too much fighting. He wanted to end here on his boat or in his hut among his books. There was no Vanya.

The tide filled the space inside the wrecked yacht until she wallowed for a moment deep below her waterline. Then it retreated and she lay back with a wooden sigh.

Peter had made a mistake. He couldn't remember what it was: the facts had gone; only the feeling remained. The worry of his mistake had pushed him from his hut and sent him to *Ra'* for comfort. He sat wedged in the angled cockpit, his old bones huddled inside his wolfish fur.

He slept and woke. The day had passed and the light was fading. Peter looked across the small, deserted lagoon towards the flood wall and the sluice. His eyes were still good at a distance. He watched the cloaked stranger who was waiting there and he wondered.

He couldn't find the right words to wonder with so he left *Ra'* and felt his way back across the planks. Then he walked round the wall to the sluice.

The stranger had gone. Peter watched the water backing up along the stream, spilling over into the reed beds and slowly raising the inland water level all the way to the bridge near the pub where he used to go in the days when he had a little money in his pocket.

He'd forgotten what the pub was called but he began to remember the heavy taste of English beer and the good fellowship of shanty singers. Scraps of tunes came dancing into his head. The days in the north when they'd held hands and sung, refusing to be sent home by tanks and bullets. Long ago and far away.

When Peter had forgotten why he was standing at the sluice, he set off to find the man on the fishing boat. A man whose name he couldn't recall but who owned a concertina and would sometimes make music with him if they met in the evening when the day's work was done.

✦   ✦   ✦

Luke hurried to fetch Peter fat sausages in a roll. Said yes to onions and slathered them with mustard and tomato sauce. He really couldn't see that it mattered whether the old man had paid five pounds or not. He'd miss his own sausages and fill up on the soup if anyone made a fuss. He told Mr Vandervelde that he should talk to Peter: that Peter had lived in Russia and that he had a hut full of books. This seemed to go quite well though

Peter kept glancing round as if he was looking for someone who wasn't there.

Ants had run off. Maybe she thought Peter was a werewolf – or maybe she couldn't stand still any longer. He'd never known such a fidget. And it was like she was obsessed with the kayak. Kept telling him that it was the best thing that had ever happened to her and that it was going to change her life.

When he asked why, she said it was the water. It slowed her up, she said; she could feel it like she couldn't feel air. It slowed her mind and gave her time to think.

Whatever.

Luke was beginning to wonder whether he was feeling quite okay.

Hendrike was carrying two pepper pots in the pockets of the large white linen apron she'd put on for the evening. Most people were offered a shake of pepper with her delicious soup: only the near neighbours of *Drie Vrouwen* were allocated the alternative – a personal cocktail of dried and powdered fungi that could produce a range of disabling reactions.

Some people assumed, with embarrassment, that they'd had too much to drink: others, that something they'd eaten had not been properly cooked. Suspicion had fallen on Luke's sausages. Hendrike told people that she'd noticed they'd been lying open in his wheelhouse since Friday.

"In Holland, where I come from, we would keep them in a fridge."

So that's where you should have put them for him, thought Helen, hating her mother even more.

"Poor lad, he's learning his lesson the hard way," said some-one who was kinder and not sick. "Who's for a trip to the Lion when we've finished with the fireworks? Beer didn't last long."

"I don't think I'm going to be able to drive us home," Ants's father gasped at her. His face was sweaty and he smelled of vomit. Helen could only pray that Hendrike had had enough sense left to be sparing in her doses.

"I want you to take my phone and ring your mother and say we'll be staying here for the night. Can you do that Angela? She's not to worry and we'll be home in the morning. Young Luke and I are going to pool our sorrows." That was a bad choice of word: his stomach heaved as he spoke.

✦   ✦   ✦

The man who sang shanties wasn't there. There was a boy who kept apologising and saying that he didn't have a mother and he did like stories. There was another man who talked as if he was giving a history lecture. There was food which was hot and very good indeed. The witch-woman was offering soup. Peter knew better than to accept that.

Then the man and the boy had disappeared and the fire-works began. He hated fireworks: they stirred distant memories of gunfire. Bursts of killing in city squares, from the windows of houses and around street corners. Rockets which brought death with a whistle or mortar bombs which delivered it with a distant flash.

Peter hoped his new friends had taken shelter. He hurried back into the trees; you were always safer in a forest. The gunfire soon finished and he saw other people beginning to make their way along the path that led along the edge of the wood and beside the reed beds. Back towards the main road and the pub. He wondered whether they were refugees.

CHAPTER NINE

Bonfire Night III
Wednesday 5 November, fifth of the waning moon

Peter, Luke, Helen, Elsevier

The front gable of the pub was illuminated and the letters of its name cast soft shadows on the creamy plaster. Light leaked from behind the thick curtains of the downstairs bar; cars hurried past with their headlights blurring in the damp air. Some vehicles turned in to park; doors opened and shut; sounds spilled briefly onto the empty pavement.

Peter could only see the lion. It gleamed from the darkness, blood-red and menacing. He began to feel the motion of an unknown vessel, to hear the thud of cannon balls and to smell the acrid stink of gunpowder. The monstrous figurehead was bearing down on him. He must take cover.

A gust of laughter blew out from the saloon bar. There was someone making a speech, telling jokes, playing to an audience. Perhaps a recruiting officer whipping up enthusiasm for war? Peter trembled. He was an outcast, a sick man, haunted by old violence and treacheries, not fit to tell a story to a child. The boy had been right to run from him.

He couldn't go near that door or risk being seen from the window. If he stepped out into the road again he would put himself within range of the warship.

There were firework displays in the nearby towns:

shellbursts, rockets and small arms fire. Peter was trapped. He huddled backwards into a shadowed nook between the bow-window and the pub wall. He hunched down and pulled his fur coat round him. His blood was slow and fear felt very cold.

The last buses passed but didn't stop. Cars became occasional. The distant fireworks subsided into drifting smoke. The speech-making from inside the pub had subsided into rhetorical questions and cheerful agreement. Peter began to wonder whether it was safe to move.

A fire engine came screaming by. It paused opposite the pub and turned left down the narrow lane towards the Fynn Creek moorings. Now people were running out from the open door, shouting to each other. Most crowded into cars. They too headed down the narrow lane.

Then all the lights went out.

Peter must take this chance. He must start back now to *Ra'* or to his hut.

There was a dark shape immediately beside him. A flaring match beneath a broad brimmed hat. Another, smaller shape hurried across the road, pulling something.

Peter pressed himself against the wall. They had no idea he was here. A low trailer with wheels pushed up beneath the lion. A gun carriage?

Ropes thrown up and round. A muttered command. Both figures pulling. The lion toppling down and onto the limber.

It was captive.

Peter struggled for words. The war beast trussed and bound.

The two figures ran with the gun carriage as neatly as if

they'd been trained. Peter followed. He'd lost the ability to think for himself.

There was a single lamp-post still burning on the bridge. A moment of high risk. Peter pressed himself into a prickly hedge and watched without understanding as the two figures paused to wrap a tarpaulin tightly round their prize. They tipped one end of the trailer up against the orange-tinted sky. The bundle slid from sight.

One figure ran on. The other…vanished.

Peter stood a while. He thought he might have had a dream. He wasn't sure if the dream had been the sound of cannon or the dark shapes hauling down the war beast from the wall and dumping it. Maroosia was angry when cars were burned and abandoned beside her fields or sacks of rubbish left in gateways. He had found old cookers or fridges in the wood.

There were brambles in the hedge and blackthorn twigs. They clutched his fur like greedy fingers. By the time he had set himself free there were candles behind the windows of the pub and beams of torchlight questing in the car park. He should go back to his hut. Genia would not have been offered any supper. Genia was quite capable of getting supper for herself but she would not be pleased about this.

✦   ✦   ✦

Luke and Mr Vandervelde were holding the high bulwarks of *Lowestoft Lass*. They were staring at the flames and wondering what to do.

It was hard to think clearly when every step made you want

to topple over. Luke felt that his head and his body had got disconnected somehow. *Lowestoft Lass*'s friendly grey deck would every so often seem to tip sideways from under his feet and the griping stomach pains were so sudden and so…productive.

Fire. How could this be?

"You should stay in your cabin," said the Dutch woman next door. "You're no use here. I haf called the fire-fighters and you may prevent them from their work."

"I'll watch out," said Angel, nervously. She couldn't have done anything to cause this, could she? It was sort of the direction where she'd paddled that dinghy.

"I am telling my daughter to stay in the cabin. She will not be seen. I will not haf her in this danger."

The fire was at the far end of the line of moored craft. One rogue firework, not properly ignited? A rocket perhaps, caught by rigging as it fell?

The beginnings of a breeze were blowing in the wrong direction.

"Buckets," thought Luke. They were using buckets already.

"Does your…have a hose?" asked Mr Vandervelde, weakly. He was agitated and sweaty as well as sick.

"The fire is not coming here," said their next door neighbour. "I make certain of it. You go away to your beds."

She was gazing at the flames as if she was mesmerised. Angel could hear her muttering under her breath. Then she began to swing her arms forwards and upwards, almost as if she was conjuring.

Miss Grace had driven down from the farm in her Land Rover. She had never liked fireworks. They upset all the animals. And for what? So people could watch good money going up in smoke and run around in the dark like barbarians. Where was everyone who should be here? All gone drinking at the Lion.

She attached a long hose to the nearest of the standpipes. Luke followed dizzily as she stamped along the decking, unrolling the hose behind her. Mr Vandervelde stayed near the tap, holding on to it.

Their jet of water was a disaster.

"There's petrol there!"

Petrol floats. The flames from the first dinghy were washed swiftly onto the next small vessel, a tiny wooden cruiser with a gas bottle in its aft locker. The bottle exploded.

Hendrike swelled with joy. Her research was exploding into life before her eyes. Fireships were the guided missiles of the seventeenth century. Manoeuvre them into position and let them to wreak havoc. The colour, the sound, the searing destructive power. She began to hyperventilate.

"Are you okay?" Angel asked her.

"Heilige vlammen! Kracht van der Leeuw!" She grasped the last rags of her sanity. "I go to the cabin. To calm my daughter."

Now they needed to make a firebreak – a gap between the blazing small boats and the rest of the vessels. Miss Grace was untying warps, cutting them if necessary. Luke, Angel, Mr Vandervelde couldn't get the un-burned boats away. The flood tide was still running, pushing them against the pontoon. Luke's fingers were thumbs, his balance was precarious. Mr Vandervelde was retching uncontrollably.

Angel was bewildered: Miss Grace exasperated.

"We need to tow them off. I wish I had *Margery* here"

"There's my dad's fishing dinghy."

Luke tried to run back to *Lowestoft Lass*. He couldn't keep a straight line and the dinghy wasn't there. He thought it had been moored by the kayak.

"Kayak, Ants? I don't think I…"

He knew he'd be hopeless.

"Good idea," Miss Grace agreed. "Then we'll need a long light warp."

Luke and the man she didn't know looked at her as if she was speaking in a foreign tongue but the red-headed girl was onto it. She untied the kayak and was ready as soon as Miss Grace had found the long thin line that had been lying on the cabin top of the barge and had fastened it to the nearest of the moored boats.

"Take it straight across to the other side. Let it pay out as you go. You others get over there and pull hard as you can when she passes it across. You can surely manage that much."

The fire had taken two more of the small boats. You could feel the heat on your face. It was so noisy. Luke hadn't known fire made such a noise. As if all the devils in hell were munching popcorn.

"Don't just stand there! Get on with it!"

The fire engine arrived, followed by fastest of the creekies. There was plenty of help now. Miss Grace was tying boat after boat together as Angel paddled urgently across towing the long line. The newly-arrived saw what was happening and ran round to take over from Luke and Mr Vandervelde as they struggled to pull a flotilla of small boats one after another against the tide and out of the way.

They'd made the firebreak.

"There's petrol at the end." Miss Grace told the firemen.

"Petrol? Thanks for the information. We'll use foam."

Angel wondered whether she should tell someone about the dinghy that she'd moved. She'd looked at every one of the boats they'd pulled to safety but it hadn't been there. She wished she could find the older girl. Her dad had gone completely weird and Luke was being sick again.

✦   ✦   ✦

The banks of Fynn Brook had been reinforced with sandbags and cement to carry the weight of the road. It was a blind drop into the black water beneath the bridge. Helen hit the floating lion as she fell.

This was the last time she'd ever enter this hateful stream with its faint smell of rot and chemicals leached from the fields. Her hands shook as she retrieved the stolen punt and tied the trophy to its stern. The steady flow of the current was already pulling at the boat and the bundle. The water was so much deeper than usual and the night was so dark. No breath of wind, no gleam of light slipped through the overarching trees and high scrub-covered banks.

She'd asked for a head torch but had been refused. Why had she obeyed? It would have been just another theft. No one was going to see her here.

The wrapped prize floated awkwardly. It was much bigger than it had looked when it had been fastened to the pub wall. It kept rushing her from behind and hitting the stern of the punt, then getting across the current of the stream and pushing the punt off course. She had only a single oar. Normally the brook was too narrow for sculls.

She and her mother had worked here night after night to clear fallen branches, oil drums and other debris from the stream. She couldn't believe how many snags remained. Again and again she was climbing out of the punt to free the carving from some half-hidden obstruction. It felt as if the lion had a will of its own and it didn't want to take this voyage.

She was wet already. She might as well wade and tow them both. Never mind how often she'd stub her foot on some underwater rock or embedded rusty can. She looked at her watch. It was almost high water in the creek and she hadn't even reached the reed beds yet.

Peter padded anxiously along the path that ran parallel to the stream. He was struggling to find words to fix his memories. Words which he could use to tell Maroosia what he'd seen. The stranger waiting by the sluice. The water trapped and rising. The two shapes tipping their burden into the stream beside the bridge.

How could he explain the explosions and the warship? His grief for his lost mind overwhelmed him and he howled.

Helen lost her footing in the soft mud and went completely under water. She had reached the next stage where the stream came out from the trees and into the expanse of reeds. There were no more stones and she was out of her depth and that old madman should be safely in his hut.

When she broke surface in the darkness she couldn't see the

punt or the prize at all. The water had risen so fast that the shape of the stream had been lost. The feathery tops of the reeds stuck up around her as if they had been startled. Where was the punt? Was it ahead of her, caught by the current, towing their trophy towards the sluice on its own?

Where was the sluice anyway?

Helen forced herself to think. Madman must be somewhere along the path through the wood. There was no other dry land within earshot. So madman was south and the current was pushing east. Okay, she had a fixing.

Except that meant that the wild orange glow ahead must be coming from the moorings.

Helen trod water as she tried to understand. The sky above the creek should be dark. More dark than usual. The bonfire and fireworks had finished hours ago. Her mother's task was to offer nightcap to any creekies still awake, then trip the main electricity.

Something heavy came bumping past. It was the punt. She reached to grab it then something even heavier collided solidly at an angle with it and they both whirled away with the flood. If that second big hunk of timber had hit her, she would have been unconscious. It was the carved lion and it was gone.

The madman howled again and Helen was tempted to reply. She continued struggling to stay logical. The fact that she was physically out of her depth must mean that she was still in the main channel. However fast the flood had risen over the last seven hours since Elsevier closed the gate it couldn't have raised the entire level more than a metre overall. She could see the tops of the reeds. There would still be shallow places.

She'd crossed this swamp so often, returning with her mother along their secret paths. She remembered how wildly the stream meandered as it approached the flood wall. The punt and the trophy would surely stick round one bend or another. As long as she continued to swim where it was deep, she knew she'd find them. They'd be trapped in some side stream or dead end.

Poor sad old man. She'd never heard his loneliness with such clarity before.

Fireships! That's what her mother had done. She'd copied some vile seventeenth-century battle plan and set a boat on fire. Her mother was out of control. She'd end up killing someone.

✦   ✦   ✦

Luke came out of the toilet block and headed towards *Lowestoft Lass*. He was dizzy and exhausted. He'd reach his bunk and then he could sleep.

The fire wasn't so frightening now it had nowhere to go. The burned end of the decking still glowed red but tide had turned and the charred and melted dinghies would soon settle onto the mud. The main electricity supply had failed and the continuous violent blue flashing from the fire engine seemed to make everywhere darker still.

Ants's dad – who kept asking him to call him Mike – had told his daughter to go down into the cabin and not look out. This was because of her sensitivity to strobe effects and Ants had gone without argument. Helen's mum said that she'd told Helen to stay below because the situation was too dangerous. That seemed like a mistake when Helen would have been so much more use than him or Mike in helping to reduce the danger.

There were two or three fire-fighters keeping watch and talking to Miss Grace. They were trying to put together some report on what had happened. The initial alarm call had come from the owner of *Drie Vrouwen* but they hadn't got much sense out of her since. She'd waved her arms around a lot and said that her daughter must remain for ever in the cabin and they would be leaving on the next tide.

Good, thought Luke.

Then he heard Peter howling.

✦   ✦   ✦

Elsevier sat beside the sluice wrapped in her thick cloak and waiting for the girl. She had underestimated the volume of water that would build up in the hours since she had closed the gates. It had been a wet autumn and the brook, which ran past the pub and under the road bridge and through the reeds, had been collecting run-off water from fields and streams for almost twenty miles before it reached the flood wall. The ditches were already full.

Elsevier was angry. Not with herself, of course, but with the girl who was late and the cow who had caused so much additional chaos that the fire-fighters were still at the moorings. The water on the land side of the wall was no more than half a metre from the top. On the creek side the mud was uncovering fast. She needed that girl to arrive. And soon.

The high, trapped water would help them pull the punt and the trophy over the wall so they slid down the steep slope on the far side. Then she would open the sluice gates and release the flood into the channel that led down the creek. The girl could float the prize to the barge and wait in the dark until the authorities were gone.

Elsevier had mastered the tides. She relished the power and brilliance of her plan.

The grazing land on the far side of this shallow valley would be flooded – Elsevier didn't worry about animals – and the weight of water piling up against the wall must be considerable by now. It was possibly surprising that there was water continuing to flow out from the shallow lagoon on the creek side. At this stage of the ebb that lagoon should be dry. It didn't trouble her. She knew that she was in control.

The current was rushing her the wrong way. Helen had found the punt and the prize caught on an abandoned plank round a shallow bend. She'd climbed back into the punt without difficulty, retrieved her single oar and began navigating as directly as she could towards the mid-point of the wall. It was almost visible – a black line against the dull glow in the sky. She thought she could see the metal railings on either side of the sluice gate. The Kapitein would be waiting there.

Suddenly the water had begun to take her sideways. She was being carried towards a section of the wall that was nearer the trees. This was wrong. However hard she struggled she couldn't make the punt change course. The trophy was riding up hard against its stern as if it were urging them towards catastrophe.

There had been a breach – she could see it now. A part of the flood wall had given way and the water was cascading over and down into the shallow semi-enclosed lagoon where the old man's boat lay on its side among the rushes.

Helen had seen what happened when these walls collapsed. There'd be a mass of broken stone and concrete blocks on the further side. The elderly punt would be smashed to matchwood.

She didn't have time to think what would happen to her if she too went over in the torrent with the heavy trophy tumbling behind. All her fears were focussed on the lion. Would the tarpaulin protect the ancient carving? Even if it survived the fall, the water would dissipate across the wide space of the lagoon. Their prize would be stranded where it fell. Trapped for all to see until the next high water – which was in the middle of the following day.

She knelt in the bows of the punt working the paddle with all her strength. It had a thick shaft and a narrow blade. Completely inefficient design. The wood was rough: her palms burned. Her back and shoulders ached. The punt refused to respond.

The water seethed white as it poured through the breach. Helen didn't grasp what that meant. With a final desperate pull – and an unexpected side eddy – she swung the bows of the punt leftwards and rammed into a section of the wall that had remained intact.

She jumped out and heaved at the short front rope trying to heave the punt further along the wall towards the sluice and relative safety. She didn't expect this to work. She expected that at any moment the cord would be jerked from her hands as the prize plunged down into the lagoon dragging the punt behind it.

The wrapped lion swung sideways. And it stuck.

Only the top layers of the wall had been washed away. The rest was still there – for now. The flood water was pouring over a shallow sill. That was why it was churning white. The figurehead lay wedged across the gap as if it was a boom to make a dam.

More water began to pile up. This couldn't last. Soon the lion would be lifted over or the lower sections of the wall would give way.

She pulled frantically on the rope. The punt was anchored by the weight of the trophy. Another heave and the fastening pulled away from the rotten wood.

She tried pushing from the side but the boat was stuck fast. If she couldn't move the punt, she had no chance at all of shifting the prize.

There was only one possible course of action. She must run to Elsevier and get her to open the gates. That would reduce the pressure, lower the water levels, give her a chance to pull the prize away from the gap and move it along the wall to the sluice. Perhaps the Kapitein would help?

✦ ✦ ✦

Luke headed straight for the plank pathway that led out into the reeds. That was surely where the old man would be. Maybe he was ill: maybe he was trapped and afraid. Confused by the sight of the fire.

Luke used the backlight of his phone to pick out the cheap blue plastic rope that was knotted round the tree. He gripped it firmly in his right hand. The makeshift jetty lurched randomly from side to side as if someone was pressing the rotate button on a controller.

It wasn't the jetty, it was him. He'd never been ill like this before. He had to stop quite often, stand completely still and hold tight. Concentrate on feeling the planks beneath his feet. Gravity was a miracle.

The reeds rustled all around him, whispering their comments in their own alien language. Luke didn't call out. He told himself that was because he didn't want to risk startling the old man. His mouth had gone dry and it tasted disgusting.

The boat at last. The hull of a yacht. She must once have been painted white like Maggi and Xanthe's beautiful *Snow Goose* but now she was a dim and pale skeleton. No moon to light her and her name faded away beyond the first two letters – *Ra'*.

As soon as he touched the deck he knew that the wood was rotten. Surely Peter shouldn't come here?

"Hi," Luke whispered very softly, almost as softly as the reeds. "It's … Vanya. Hi, Peter, are you okay?"

He found the empty cockpit and shone his light into the deserted cabin. Miss Grace had been right. There were more books here. Soggy books and mildewed charts.

Now Luke could hear voices blowing across from the far side of the lagoon. He needed to get back across that jetty, urgent. That sweaty, shivery feeling. The hot flush and the pain.

✦ ✦ ✦

The old man had already reached the Kapitein. What instinct for trouble had sent him nosing round towards the sluice? He must have crossed that section of wall only moments before it crumbled. Now he was standing there, facing Elsevier, pointing to the water and then to the gates, unable to find words. Helen knew what he was trying to say. She said it for him.

"You must open the sluice, Kapitein. There's breach further down and the prize is caught fast across it. Until the pressure is reduced there's nothing I can do to shift it."

"You're late."

"I am."

"Why should I do as you ask. A girl who can't keep to time or to a plan."

"Because if you don't, the prize is lost. Morning will come and it will be grounded in plain sight."

"And this old fool?"

"Is old and will forget. No-one listens to him."

Elsevier flounced and she stamped and she swore but she did it. She cranked open the metal grille and watched the water stream through into the empty creek.

This immediately began diverting the current away from the breach and back into its regular course. The punt and the prize were no longer pressed so hard against the wall. Elsevier would do no more but the old man came with Helen and helped her to manhandle them along towards the sluice. He seemed to have an instinctive understating of floating objects and their ways.

He also appeared to be congratulating her for having cleared the item that had been dumped beside the bridge.

"Maroosia will be pleased," was all she understood – and that made no sense either.

Wordlessly he assisted her to heave the punt and the prize over the wall and down into the creek. The escaping water was carving its way along a runnel between the mud banks. Helen climbed down into the punt and knew she had the depth she needed for the final leg of her journey to *Drie Vrouwen*.

A certainty flashed into her mind. The old man had seen too much. He was inessential now. She shouldn't leave him alone with Elsevier.

CHAPTER TEN

Troublesome Reach
Thursday 6 November, dark of the moon

Helen, Angel, Luke, Mike

"People who mess with their heads are so…un-Dutch."

"What about people who mess with other people's heads then?" Helen didn't see why she should be polite any longer. It wasn't she who'd brought the hallucinogens from Amsterdam and she'd done her best to prevent her mother accessing the English alternatives.

"They were a present. She's worked hard for me."

"Bring her flowers or a box of choccies then."

"I told her they were for later."

"And I told you that she's got no control any more. It's a pity that you're such a great speaker that you only ever listen to yourself."

She saw the older woman's dark eyes narrow, her cheeks flush red. She raised her hand. Helen wasn't having that.

"And if you think of hitting me – or if you touch me just once in any way at all – I'm out of this boat and I'm telling the authorities."

"No more little house on the polder and rowing races on the Bosbaan for you in that case."

"Prison for you, I hope."

"For me? But they loved me in the pub and, apart from that,

I was never here. Who saw me? Except one crazy old man – who you chose to cherish. Make no mistake, oh child of the pure white trainers and the principles to match, the moment you leave this boat or make that call, I'll be gone and you'll be the person with the spaced-out mother and the stolen property. Rather a lot of stolen property, isn't there? I imagine most of these muddy peasants will find something on board that they've lost. As well as the large and valuable seventeenth-century artefact."

How Helen hated her. Would the boy back her up if the old man couldn't? But he'd seen nothing, really. She'd got to stick it. Not too much longer.

"Perhaps we'd better think how we're going to ship your precious trophy home for you. Now that you've put my mother out of action I don't see how we're going to get ourselves away from this creek, let alone across the Noordzee."

Hendrike had been raving by the time they returned. The thrill of the flames, the mind-bending present from her Kapitein. Once she'd helped them heave the lion on board, she'd been locked in her cabin and told to keep her visions to herself.

Elsevier was pacing backwards and forwards in *Drie Vrouwen's* main saloon. She executed one of her dramatic swirling turns and stopped still, flinging out an arm towards Helen.

"Your point being?"

"That this boat is too long to manage the tight bends of the creek easily, even at the top of the tide. We can't trust the marker buoys to be exact. There was too much bad weather in October. At least two of them dragged. They need repositioning but no-one will do it until next spring, if then. It might be the same with the buoys at the river mouth so we'll need plenty of water there as well. It's difficult. If we want a good depth of water at the river mouth we must get out of here as early as we can – unless you want to wait another tide."

"It's imperative we leave this country as soon as we can. Or before."

"The way we got the barge into this creek, if you remember, was having me rowing ahead in the inflatable dinghy, checking the depth on each turn. You were steering and mother was on the foredeck watching me and directing you. You can't see the pilot when you are at the helm. The barge is too long. You're too far back."

"And your solution?"

"Is obvious. We need a third person. Or we could wait until my mother's better – if she is."

The older woman brushed this idea aside.

"Too risky. The fire investigator will be back and I assume even the English police will make some sort of search for the carving. The weather's getting worse and the tides will be falling away after tomorrow's high. We've got a long trip and I've scheduled the press conference and the photoshoot for Martinmas. Perfect timing to catch the popular mood."

"Martinmas? They'll be arresting you next Tuesday then."

"Not at all. Next Tuesday 11th – which, as you rightly say, is Martinmas – I'll be on prime-time TV across Europe asserting our national right to a lost item of our national heritage. Your mother's research was good. I'll claim back the carving for the United Provinces and our Golden Age. It'll become an international incident – like the Elgin marbles which the English stole from the Greeks. Or the treasures they lifted from the Pyramids."

"Lots of controversy means lots more publicity for you. You don't care about the rights and wrongs at all."

"I'll be in government by the next election." Elsevier doffed her hat and bowed. Then she raised it high, in response to the cheers of her rapturous populace. She scowled as Helen failed to oblige. "Back to the immediate problem. Who do you have in mind to join us? Can they be bribed?"

"Shouldn't think so."

"Good. We resort to tactics of the English press gang. Who is your lucky volunteer?"

+ + +

Angel didn't know how she should feel when the fair-haired Dutch girl tapped politely on the door of *Lowestoft Lass*'s wheel-house. She guessed the girl was at least a couple of years older than her and she looked like the sort of person who was really together. Probably good at everything. She'd seemed friendly last night but then Angel had lost sight of her in all the confusion and the fire. And now she'd probably found that the dinghy had been burned.

"Hi," she said. "I'm really sorry about your mum's dinghy. Do you think that it was anything we did wrong – I did wrong, I mean – that fire happening just exactly where I'd moved it? Have you talked to those insurance people? I hid when they came round. I didn't know what I should say. It looks horrible at the end of the pontoon. I didn't want to go anywhere near it."

She hadn't woken her dad or Luke. Hadn't phoned her mum either. She still had her dad's phone but the reception down here was bad and she hadn't gone up the hill to use it because she knew her mum would know that there was something wrong as soon as she heard her voice. And then she'd start worrying and they'd probably have a row and her mum would get on her bike and come peddling round to help, even though her dad had the car and would be fine to get both of them home later – now that he'd stopped sweating and being sick and saying weird things.

"Hi," said Helen, stepping inside. "Yes, that was quite a night! And it is about the dinghy that I must talk to you. How are you feeling this morning?"

Her hair was swept up into her pony-tail with none of those stray, wispy bits that would have happened if Angel had ever tried a style like that. She wore a white polo neck and a sporty-looking dark blue windcheater with some sort of club logo.

Angel hadn't eaten anything at all last night. It had all been too exciting. And then scary when it was the fire. So she'd tried to cook herself some breakfast and she seemed to have left cutlery and dirty pans everywhere. She'd burned the toast as well – though that was nothing. You could smell burned plastic boats in the air outside. It was a bitter, chemical smell not at all nice like a garden bonfire.

Bonfires! Her mum had had the right idea for once. Angel didn't think she'd ever want to go to any more Guy Fawkes parties. This had been her first and would be her last.

"Hi," she said again, trying to clear a space at the small wooden table so the other girl could sit down. "Um, would you like…?"

She wasn't sure what she should offer and she couldn't remember if she should know the other girl's name. The girl made herself a space at the table with what seemed like two effortless movements. She shifted a pile of plates and mugs over to the sink, set them to rinse in fresh water and sat down, smiling at Angel but looking serious too.

"No, I'm very well, thank you. My name is Helen by the way. You must forgive my English. I'm not sure what name you like to be called?"

Angel sat down with a bump, not noticing that she'd put her elbow in a cereal bowl that was still half full. No-one ever asked her that.

"Well, my parents call me Angela and that is my proper name. And the teachers do of course and those sort of people. But the other children in school, they call me Ants and I hate it – though I have to pretend that I don't. It's happened at every school I've been to and I can't remember how many schools that is. You might not understand as I don't think you're English, though you speak it very well. There's a saying about people who fidget having ants in their pants and I do fidget. I can't seem to help it. It would be all right if Ants was just, like, a nickname but the trouble is then some kids get on to the pants bit and then they say they want to see what's inside my…"

Why did she always say too much? There was no need for her to tell this cool, clean, Dutch girl about the number of times she'd been held down in the playground, kicking and biting, so that some clever-clever group of chanting children could check that she hadn't got insects in her underwear.

"That's not at all nice," said Helen who found the red-head's hurried way of speaking quite hard to follow but understood that she had been bullied at school. Too bad for her.

She smiled at the younger girl. "So what name do you call yourself – in your head, privately?"

No-one had asked her that question. Not even when she'd been taken to the psychologist and they'd made her do all those things such as drawing herself as an animal. She'd been a wild-cat of course. A wildcat making out she were a noble lion.

She didn't like the psychologist or any of those people with the fake-nice voices who asked all those questions and never told you any answers. But this tall girl with her beautiful fair hair and her blue eyes and her careful way of speaking had asked politely, as if she wanted to know.

"Well you're not allowed to laugh. I call myself Angel, see. Because it's Angela without the feminine bit – that's what an 'a' does to words in English – and I don't much like being a girl. I hate pink for starters and I don't never feel like I fit in. That's at home as well as at school, with my mum and dad. So I thought if I'd come from somewhere else it would explain it." She tried to lighten up. Didn't want to sound as if she was pitying herself. "I know I haven't, of course. But if I had come from somewhere where everyone was good – like angels would be good – then if I were living there, I'd likely be good too. Because I can't seem to manage it down here."

Helen took the single word. "Angel – okay, that's a nice name. In Dutch it's 'engel' which is both English and an angel. I can use that because I am hoping that you will be for us an angel. My mother is sick and we want to go home. Today the tide is high at twelve and we can get the barge out of this creek. I have one friend who will steer but we need a pilot to go ahead and find the deep water. And now we don't have a dinghy. Would you go first for us, in your kayak. Or your friend perhaps?"

Would she! Getting back into the kayak was the one thing she'd been thinking about all morning. One of her reasons for burning the toast and forgetting that she'd already got cereal. Not that it was any different than usual. She was always rubbish when she tried to make her own food.

"It's not mine. And he's not well either, though he might be better by now. He and my dad ate something that didn't agree with them. Luke's worried that it might have been his sausages. I don't know because I didn't eat anything. There was so much going on. Did your mother eat sausages?"

"I'm not sure. I would really like to take her home to Holland." Angel jumped up.

"I'll ring my mum. I can run up the hill. Then she could come and help. We've got the car here but she could use her bike. And my dad could as well. Help, I mean. They do make a fuss but, if your mum's that ill, she maybe wouldn't mind. My mum could ring our doctor for you."

This was certainly more than Helen wanted. The prize was lashed on *Drie Vrouwen*'s cabin roof. It had been hosed clean and re-wrapped in the stolen tarpaulins but she couldn't risk unknown adults looking around and asking questions. She had a lot to do if they were getting to sea in the next few hours. She needed this girl but she didn't need any extra mothers. And definitely no doctors – not until they were in Holland.

"Don't worry then. I'm quite busy. I thought you would like to assist in the kayak. It doesn't matter."

"I so do! You don't know how much. I don't have to tell my mum." Luke, she mustn't upset Luke. "...but I really do have to ask

THE LION OF SOLE BAY

my friend. The kayak's his and I messed up so badly last time I was using something that wasn't mine. My dad'll be okay. You could talk to him. You did last night. I expect he went on about history."

Okay, thought Helen. She'd take all three. They could maybe do with extra crew – if only to irritate Elsevier. The Kapitein hated males.

Also she probably needed to stop the boy talking. There'd been no time last night (or early this morning) to discuss what they should say if anyone asked awkward questions. It wasn't only the fire. The boy had come mushroom-picking with her. She might have said something about the fly agaric. Then he'd been very sick. She didn't want him or the girl's father deciding to go and get the source of their illness analysed.

Plus he'd seen her last night when she'd left a furious Elsevier to manage the last section of the journey herself. He'd showed up when Helen had been struggling to get the old madman safely back across the gap in the wall. He said he'd been searching for him and had heard voices.

He was still sick and unsteady on his feet but he'd got the phone number of the farmer, which was a help. He'd rung her and they'd got the old man across the breach and walked him slowly to the end of the track where the farmer had met them with her Land Rover.

"I think he has had a fall. He seems confused," was all that Helen said as explanation.

She didn't want to stay. She couldn't think why the madman wasn't kept safely in some hospital. She had been completely unprepared when he put his bony hand on hers as she was settling him into the farmer's vehicle.

"Thank you. You are the young Maroosia. I think that you have saved me."

He had such a lovely smile. For a moment she wished he was her dear old grandfather. If she'd had one. Which she didn't.

Then she'd hurried away to *Drie Vrouwen* and helped to haul the prize on board while the sky was still dark. She'd watched Elsevier turn the key on her mother and had finally locked herself into her own cabin for a few hours' sleep. She didn't know where the boy had gone after that or what he might have seen.

She'd get all these people on board. Take them out of the way for a while.

"Good," she said to the girl. "We leave as soon as the water's up. In an hour, maybe two. I'll show you how you will test the depth for us. And your father and your friend can come with you on the ship and see that you are safe. A little river trip, what fun! If you speak to your mother, tell her you are all helping your neighbour and you will return later. Goodbye for now. I must make preparations."

✦ ✦ ✦

Luke was jealous of Ants as she paddled away from *Drie Vrouwen* in his kayak. Helen had asked him so sweetly that he couldn't refuse. He and Mr Vandervelde – Mike – were going to help with the warps and the fending-off as she left her mooring but then they would be passengers while Helen watched Ants and shouted back instructions in Dutch to her friend with the big hat who would be steering.

"Her name's Elsevier, but she's perfectly happy for friends like you to call her Elsie," said Helen.

Luke didn't think Els…waddever…was happy about that at all. He saw the way she scowled at Helen while pretending to smile at them with her big white teeth. He'd sometimes wondered what a 'wolfish' smile looked like. Now he thought he knew.

Mike looked as if he wanted to ask Elsie more about her name but Helen was hustling them both into their positions and explaining what they needed them to do to get *Drie Vrouwen* out from her tight spot alongside *Lowestoft Lass.* She was worried about her mother and desperate to begin their voyage home as soon as they could escape the shallow waters of the Deben.

Luke had a bad feeling that all this illness could have been caused by him forgetting to keep Lottie's sausages in the fridge. He and Mike were wobbly but okay this morning, except they were both very tired and he couldn't imagine himself wanting to eat another sausage EVER. Or even accept another helping of that brilliant soup. Made with the mushrooms that he had helped to pick! His single achievement of the holiday – if you didn't count learning to spread straw for cows.

He hoped Helen's mum would soon be up and about. It seemed a long journey for them to be starting with just Helen and Elsie to manage everything on the boat. Helen had said all she needed was help out of the creek; otherwise he'd have volunteered to go with them and be their crew.

His holiday was over. When he got to the hospital everyone else would be there. Reunions two at a time to keep things calm in Bill's ward. Not that he'd have much to tell and Liam wouldn't listen anyway. He'd want to go on about the Inter/Man U match and the amazing San Siro stadium. He'd probably been texting already. Then it would be all of them back home to Bawdsey.

Luke imagined himself down there in the kayak, piloting the barge out of Fynn Creek. He wondered what *Drie Vrouwen*'s broad metal prow would look like if it was going to be the last thing that you saw – shaped like the top of a wrestler's torso, two massive shoulders in a black cloak without a head. Plus the black anchor and its black chain hanging there like a madman's mace ready to finish you off.

Good thing Ants was focussing on her job. She had to paddle from buoy to buoy, keeping exactly to the centre of the narrow channel and letting the kayak glide every few strokes while she probed to the bottom of the creek. *Drie Vrouwen* needed nearly two metres depth. That was almost all the water that there was up here at the top end of the creek, hardly enough such a long boat trying to manoeuvre round the sharp twists of the narrow channel.

Helen was watching the kayak, calling out to Elsie and using her arms to indicate the direction of each new twist. More than once the older woman didn't appear to follow what Helen said. Then *Drie Vrouwen*'s bow ran into the invisible shallows and stuck as her stern struggled to come round after it. Elsie muttered harshly accented swearwords and crashed the powerful engine into reverse. Once she did this so hard that they ran aground backwards on the opposite side and Luke had to struggle not to laugh.

Everywhere – river, riverbanks, sky – was grey, grey-brown or charcoal. Heavy rain was forecast later. Sooner seemed more likely.

Ants's paddle went deep. She tried again, pushing it down so hard that her arm went right in and the kayak threatened to roll. She couldn't touch bottom. They were safely out of the creek and into the main river.

Luke noticed something else as well. Two somethings – something that wasn't there; something that was.

First he noticed that the barge didn't have a dinghy. Helen had said that she would put them ashore once they were out of the creek. But how could she do that if she didn't have a dinghy?

Then he noticed that Helen's friend had a gun. A gun which she was pointing at him.

"Give Miss de Witt your phones then go below," she said to him and Mike. *Drie Vrouwen*'s engine was dawdling in neutral. "You have no idea whether my weapon is real or fake but you cannot ignore my power over the child in that kayak. She is so close to the barge, so unsuspecting. My name is Elsevier and I am your Kapitein. You don't EVER call me Elsie. We need additional crew for our trip and you have been selected. Go down into the cabin and the child will join you."

"I won't let her hurt Engel, truly," said Helen. She looked rather white but she didn't look surprised.

"But I can't," Luke said. "My family expect me to meet them at the hospital."

"You'll be a few days late, that's all. A few days late, I think you'll agree, is preferable to arriving many years too soon – especially as you'd be arriving via the post mortem entrance."

Her rasping English was better than Helen's. There was no possibility that they hadn't understood her correctly.

"Please give me your phones and do as she says," said Helen. "She's dramatic and bad-tempered and she likes to act a scene. It's only for the Noordzee crossing. One day. Two at the most."

Mike sat down where he was. This was his daughter they were threatening. There was no way he was letting her out of his sight.

Okay, thought Luke. That was passive resistance. They'd done Gandhi at school. He sat down as well. Never had a gun pointed at him before. Not for real.

The River Deben looked huge now it had been filled by the tide – and so empty. There were no racing dinghies today. No cyclists or walkers on the river wall. No rescuers. What wouldn't he give to see the three distinctive masts of the junk *Strong Winds*…

Elsevier ran at Mike and pushed him overboard. *Drie Vrouwen's* side decks were narrow and her guard rails low. He was caught completely by surprise.

"We'll keep the boy, coward," she shouted after him.

Helen grabbed Luke and pulled him towards the cabin. He fought her as hard as he knew how. Kept trying to grab onto things but she was faster that he was, tall and strong. She must have noticed last night which pocket he used for his phone as she had it out immediately.

Elsevier looped him with a rope as if he'd been a wild bullock. She dragged him to the companionway and pushed him down for Helen to finish off. Luke kept on fighting though he knew that he had lost.

"I can explain," said Helen. "Later. I have to tie you up for now."

The cabin must previously have been a hold. There were two stout metal poles to reinforce the roof. Helen had him securely fastened with a few efficient movements.

"You're well in practice then," he said, bitterly.

She looked as if she wanted to answer but then there was a shout from on deck.

"To me, girl," Elsevier called down. "The fools are giving themselves up!"

Her dad wasn't a good swimmer and he was wearing all his clothes. Angel had no idea how he could have fallen overboard but she managed to haul him onto the front of the kayak just like the instructor had hauled her. She remembered to smile at him and talk reassuringly as well.

"The woman on that boat has a gun," he said, as soon as he had caught his breath. "She tried to force us below; to press gang us for their North Sea crossing. Paddle for the shore, Angela. Quick as you can. We must fetch help."

"Where's Luke?"

"Still there. Hurry. We have to call the police."

Her paddle stayed motionless across the cockpit rim.

"No way am I leaving Luke. Not like I left his dad. You go ashore if you want."

Should he? His phone was drenched of course but he could swim and then he could run. He could get someone with authority to stop these madwomen before they reached the end of the river. But how could he leave the children?

He couldn't run his hands through his hair or pull his beard whilst balanced on the front of this kayak. How could he think?

"Listen, Angela," he said. "Here's the plan. I want you to paddle towards their boat and I'm going to wave my handkerchief. No I'm not, it's a tissue. I'm going to hold both my hands up and you're going to put me back on board. I solemnly promise that I'll take care of Luke. I'll be climbing up and talking to them, surrendering – whatever it takes – and I'll push the kayak away with my foot. Then you head straight up to Woodbridge and call the police."

"You said she had a gun…"

"My darling, I don't believe she'll use it. And…I can't think what else we can do."

"We both go back to keep Luke safe." The barge was moving away but not fast. It was tough paddling the kayak with someone sitting on the front. Her dad was trying to balance. He'd never been athletic at all.

"Then no-one knows where we are. We'll have to go to Holland with them."

"Dad, I don't want to be shot." The terror of it gripped her. Her whole body felt weak and her hands sweating. Tiny specks of light beginning to dart across her vision, the smell of honey…

"Dad…I've got that feeling…I think I'm going…"

She was about to have a seizure. Out here in the middle of the empty river with her wobbly dad on the front of her kayak.

"Help!" Mike shouted to the lunatics. "Wait for us. We're coming back!"

Then he leaned forward and started scooping water with both hands as he felt his daughter's body slump behind him.

CHAPTER ELEVEN

Deben Bar
Thursday 6 November, dark of the moon

Helen, Luke

The ebb had settled in: the wind was undecided. Sudden gusts, mainly from the north and north-east, blackened the surface of the water: died to nothing then returned, slightly stronger every time.

A three-masted junk, hurrying up the river while there might still be enough water to make a surprise detour into Fynn Creek, had given up sailing and was motoring hard in the opposite direction to *Drie Vrouwen*. Two dark-skinned girls and a boy waved from her cockpit. Elsevier didn't bother to acknowledge them.

Helen was below, sorting out their wet and angry captives, feeling more and more convinced that they were going to be more trouble than they were worth.

"Can't we put them ashore somewhere?" she called up to Elsevier. "I've taken their phones and there are plenty of places that aren't near houses or roads. We'd be long gone before they found anyone to complain to. And what have they got to complain about? The other people in the creek saw them come on board quite willingly. The girl sent a message to her mother. Then she had a seizure in the kayak. That wasn't our fault."

Naturally she was speaking in Dutch. She forgot that Elsevier didn't know that the man would understand them.

"You think no-one will have noticed that the lion of the *Stavoren* has gone?" the older woman replied. "You think the English are so stupid they won't have made the connection between a Dutch possession being taken down and a Dutch barge leaving? If this riff-raff are no use as crew, we'll keep them prisoner in case we need to bargain. Then dispose of them once we're home. I'm not stopping now."

Helen had padlocked Mike to the second metal post with the stolen trailer's chain around his middle. She had allowed him his arms and legs.

"I don't think you'll attack me. Here's a towel for you to use before I tie your hands. I'll find you some dry clothes. They'll be my mother's, unfortunately."

"Is she ill," Luke asked. "Or was that another lie?"

"She's ill," said Helen.

So now Mike was wearing large and unattractive trousers, a peasant blouse and a smock. Hendrike was stout and unstylish: he was small and rather thin. The only thing Helen couldn't find were shoes to fit. Her mother had several pairs of wooden clogs but they were too small. Slip-on sandals were the best she could manage, with thick knitted socks. Mike looked stupid but he was talking sense.

"Does your friend with the gun not realise that your own country will hand you back if you've committed a crime over here? We're all part of the EU. We have agreements."

"She's not my friend. She's my mother's friend. I'm co-operating with her because I want to get home. After that I hope I never see either of them again. And, no, of course she doesn't think like that. She thinks she can get away with anything. They want to rerun the seventeenth century but with women in charge. My mother's simply lost her mind but Elsevier wants to be a dictator. I'll spoil it for her if I can."

"Elsevier! Wreken de Dame! *Stavoren*! Now I understand!"

Helen was ordered on deck at that moment. They had reached the mouth of the river where there were banks of shifting shingle. The Kapitein needed her to keep checking that they were following a dead straight line between the two crucial channel buoys. The north-westerly wind had strengthened and was helping the ebb tide to push them out fast. If they ran onto the shingle they were going to hit it hard.

"What was all that about?" asked Luke. Mike and Helen had mainly spoken Dutch but he'd been watching Mike's body language and he'd heard the tone of voice in which he'd repeated that name. He was sore and grumpy and miserable but he supposed he might as well try to understand what was going on. "What's so special about Elsevier?"

Mike tried to step forward as if he was standing on stage answering a question from the audience. He forgot he was tethered round the middle so he almost fell over. Luke didn't laugh.

"There are two Elseviers. Lots more of course but two that matter to us. This one is the lunatic politician who wants everyone thrown out of the country if their ancestors haven't lived there for at least three hundred years. I can't think why I didn't recognise her at once in her hat and cloak. I suppose I hadn't expected to find her pointing a gun at me in the Deben."

Luke hadn't expected anyone to be pointing a gun at him anywhere – outside of a Play Station or an X-box or his own Nintendo screen.

"The other Elsevier," Mike carried on – this was his specialist subject – "was the captain of a ship that was captured at the Battle of Sole Bay – May 28th 1672 (old style). She was the *Stavoren*, built in Edam, named for a trading town on the Zuider Zee, and sailing with the Amsterdam Admiralty under the overall command of the great Michiel De Ruyter. Take the old road to Ipswich and you can see her figurehead outside the Red Lion pub. Or, you could see it there. I'm guessing that this Elsevier stole it last night as some sort of nationalist publicity stunt. And we're helping her to transport it home."

"The Crimson King…" breathed Luke. He was remembering the teeth and the claws and the fury of that creature struggling to break free. "You think he's on this boat with us?"

Mike wasn't listening. He often didn't when he was working out a theory.

"So, Elsevier shares a name with the *Stavoren*'s captain therefore she thinks she's justified in snatching back what was captured all those years ago. She's not, of course. It was taken fairly and sold on legitimately. But how that girl and her mother are involved I can't think. They're de Witts. They should be on the side of peaceful trade and the rule of law."

"I think Helen's mum's a witch," said Luke. "I heard things in the night when I was sleeping on *Lowestoft Lass*. They had a cockerel and they lit loads of candles. And Ben didn't like her."

Mike was beginning to object that that didn't necessarily prove sorcery but then Angel began to cry. She was tied to the same post as Luke. She couldn't reach her dad and he couldn't reach her. She hadn't understood all that they were talking about, especially the stuff in Dutch, obviously, but she always felt emotional after her seizures and needed reassurance. She'd been limp when they'd carried her down so it had been easy for Helen to wrap the rope round several times. Helen, who she had thought was her friend.

Angel wanted her mum. Her mum who was so annoying and such a fusspot and got everything wrong and never understood – but who would be holding her close and stroking her as she came back to normal.

Mike looked desperate. His hands were twisting and he was pulling at his chain. Luke would have tried patting her or something but he hadn't any hands.

This was a different Ants from the one he was used to seeing spitting and kicking in the school playground. Or the one who'd bitten him at the community pool. He tried to think of something reassuring that he could say though in their current situation there wasn't exactly much that came to mind.

An unfamiliar grinding noise. *Drie Vrouwen*'s engine roared. They felt her slowing to a stop. Elsevier was swearing – though not in English.

"Shut up, Ants," said Luke. "We need to listen."

There were feet running urgently along the deck. The noise surrounded everything inside; a sliding, scraping noise; percussive against the metal hull. Luke recognised the sound of shingle.

They could hear Helen shouting in Dutch from the foredeck. Mike listened and translated.

"The barge has struck a spit. The bows are free; she's caught by the stern. The de Witt girl says there's deeper water immediately ahead."

The sound of the engine changed. Put into reverse? Full throttle. Straining.

The pebbly sound wasn't scraping the hull any more. That didn't need translation.

"Stuck fast," said Luke.

Mike nodded. Angel began to breathe very quickly and wriggle inside her ropes as if she was possessed. She could have been going to get free but the next moment Helen was there, untying them all.

"You have to come and push," she said. "We have to shift the cargo forwards."

"What if we don't?" said Luke.

"Then we're wrecked together. Get on deck and do it."

She didn't wait for their response. She hurried to a side cabin and unlocked the door.

"Mother," she said, controlling her voice into a supplication. "We need your power. Come to the foredeck please. Be our lady."

"Get up there. Quick!" she told the rest of them.

Angel was out of her ropes and scurrying up the steps. Mike and Luke looked at each other, shrugged and followed. Hendrike lumbered behind. Her white hair was loose and she was wearing some sort of robe. She was muttering, ignoring everyone, making gestures without meaning. Luke understood now what sort of 'ill' Helen had meant.

Outside the sea was churning past. He recognised the red-painted buoy which marked the Deben Bar, the shallowest point of the river exit. He turned and looked back over *Drie Vrouwen*'s port quarter. There was Bawdsey Manor – his home – where the rest of his family would arrive in just a few hours' time.

That made his heart thump and his breath get a bit tight

and he thought that it might be him who might start crying next. So he blinked a couple of times and looked ahead.

He'd watched boats of all sorts coming in and out of this river. He knew that the barge was on the correct side of the buoy. She should have been okay. Except she wasn't – and the tide was running out so fast.

He'd heard the older ones talking about the way the shingle had shifted when there'd been gales and high tides in October. Donny'd said he'd only be taking *Strong Winds* in and out of the river on the flood until he was certain that the entrance had stabilised again.

Drie Vrouwen's wooden rudder was wedged. This was the ebb. She'd be stranded soon.

Elsevier was already cutting the ropes that bound a wrapped object to the cabin roof. Luke recognised the tarpaulin. It was his dad's tarpaulin from *Lowestoft Lass*. When would he stop feeling shocked by all of this stealing?

Hendrike went immediately to the foredeck and stood there arms outstretched. The wind was pressing her robe and her hair from behind her as if she was a bellying sail. She was shouting some sort of incantation.

"There is no-one here to rescue you," said Helen to the three of them. "We must all push together."

"Or someone goes overboard and we lighten the ship that way." Elsevier had her gun out again. They still couldn't see whether it was real. Her dark cloak was whipping in the wind, her feet firmly one before the other, her left arm crooked to steady the gun, her right hand curved around the handle, her eyes squinting along the barrel, her finger on the trigger. She swivelled to point at Luke.

"You have the choice," she said.

The afternoon sky was already dark, the tide was foaming past. There was a terrible sense of urgency.

Mike broke first.

Then Angel almost as quick.

They did as Helen ordered. They got behind the bundle that must be the stolen figurehead and began struggling to push it forwards. Luke gave in and joined them, Elsevier was beside him all that time. With that gun. He couldn't look away from her.

Helen ran to the stern, lashed the tiller and put the engine ahead, full throttle, then she hurried forward again to add her slim weight to theirs. Together they pushed the lion as far as it could go towards the bow.

Drie Vrouwen shuddered, plunged, heaved herself free of the invisible obstruction and was moving ahead once again.

Elsevier twirled her pistol round her right forefinger then replaced it in her leather belt. She couldn't have done that if it were loaded with live bullets. Could she?

She strode astern and took the helm. They passed close by the red bar buoy and carried on as far as the Woodbridge Haven. This was a red and white buoy, bright against the racing grey-brown sea.

"I know this one," said Luke to Mike and Ants. "It's called a safewater mark and it's to help you find the entrance to the river. I've been out here before, with my friends. That's our house back there."

"Your house? That, like, mansion?"

"Only the top floor. But it's still mega. My sister inherited it from some great-uncle or something."

"Couldn't you wave for help?"

"No-one's there. They were going straight to the hospital to be with Dad first."

Elsevier turned the barge north-east. Her broad bow butted hard into the waves and Hendrike got wet. She left the foredeck and walked three times anti-clockwise round the captured lion, staggering a little as the barge began to rise and fall with the waves. Then she went below. It seemed she didn't notice anyone else existed.

Drie Vrouwen settled to her new course: Helen made them push the cargo back amidships then she retied the cords as best she could. Her fingers were cold and Elsevier had slashed the ropes in random places. Water was running down the metal side decks. The prisoners were shivering.

"You must hold on where you can," Helen told them. "Then it's best to return below. We have a long voyage ahead. I will organise the watch system."

Luke, Mike and Angel looked at each other.

They wondered what they'd done.

CHAPTER TWELVE

The Whiting Bank
Thursday 6 November, dark of the moon

Luke

Helen didn't bother to tie them up again. Luke could see why. They had shown that they were weak. By helping shift that cargo they had agreed to their captivity. They had drunk to the bottom of the beer mug and taken the King's shilling.

Drie Vrouwen's main cabin was a living space without warmth or comfort. There were old books in plain covers and pictures of warships covered with figures and symbols. Luke, Mike and Angel sat in depressed silence on hard bench seats which were covered in dull brocade and felt as if they had been stuffed with horsehair. All the windows and the portholes were curtained with thick, dark, light-absorbing velvet that swung heavily backwards and forwards. You would never guess that a young girl had spent her summer here.

The barge was bumping and lurching. Luke didn't think that he'd be seasick – what had he left to be sick on? – but he wondered about the others. Ants was no way as tough as she made herself out to be and Mike…Mike had been a lot worse than he had last night.

Helen appeared to have read his mind.

"Here," she said, holding out a blue packet of Stugeron. "You should all take these. We have a long journey and it is not fun if you are ill."

"We won't be so much use to you, you mean," said Luke.

"That also. It is necessary to be practical when you are at sea."

They took the pills.

"I have your phones. I can send one text from each if that would help," said Helen.

He knew that she despised them. He almost hated her more now she was trying to be nice.

"What would you say in the text?" Mike asked. "My phone's ruined anyway."

"To your wife? That you and Angela have been offered a trip up the coast by your friends and you plan to stay another night. Whatever will help her to be calm. This is your choice. It's okay by me if you decide to let her worry."

"I have a job!" he exploded, waving his arms pointlessly. "Yesterday I explained I had a family crisis, continuing from the day before. Today Nelly will have rung and told them that I'm sick. How can I expect her to phone in tomorrow and tell them I've gone boating up the coast?"

Helen shrugged. He was speaking English, not Dutch, but it seemed she'd got the gist. Also that she didn't care much whether she had or hadn't.

Elsevier was at the helm: Hendrike had changed into a long plain dress that looked as if it was made of brown felt. She moved around restlessly, paying no attention to anyone. She didn't speak to Helen, Luke noticed. Didn't even look at her.

She had called out some question to Elsevier and the answer had apparently been yes. Then she'd tied a big apron over her dress and might have begun preparing something in the galley area.

She kept stopping and walking away. Then she'd come back

and carry on again. Her balance wasn't very good. Finally she coiled her long white hair into two buns like ear-muffs. Maybe this blocked something out? It definitely appeared to calm her down and she began to look as if she were cooking seriously. It was almost a whole day since he'd eaten.

"Mum will be out of her head with worry," said Angel to her father. "Do you think she'll ring the police?"

"After the session we had with them yesterday? No."

"She'll definitely bike down to the creek."

"And we'll be gone. Poor, poor Nelly."

"Then she'll have to cycle home again. On her own. Not knowing."

"ALL RIGHT! Send my wife a text, Mejuffrow de Witt. How can you do this to us? You seemed such a nice girl when we met. So sensible. You share a great name – whether you know it or not. You don't deserve it."

"It's called necessity," said Helen. "We've taken a prize. We need to get it home safe."

"Use the ferry service."

Helen didn't bother to answer.

"And you?" she said to Luke.

"You know my dad's in hospital. Send the text to my sister. She's called Anna. Her number's in the phone. She understands about adventures."

Anna was so clever. Anna was his only chance. Anna would surely guess that there was something wrong and then she'd find out how to track the signal from the phone and rescue them.

Helen wasn't stupid either. Mike's mobile was dead after its dunking in the river so she sent both the texts from Luke's, then went on deck and dropped it overboard.

"I have still my phone to make a call tomorrow or whenever you are able to return. The more help you give, the sooner we arrive and cheerfully. My mother is preparing some food and we will have a system for keeping watch. It is not safe if one person is too tired."

She had dark circles under her eyes. Her skin was stretched tight across her bones and her cheeks were hollow. The word haggard came into Luke's mind. He saw the bruise which discoloured one side of her face.

He didn't feel sorry for her at all.

She didn't care what he noticed or what he thought. This was a mission: he'd been press ganged.

"My mother is making pottage," she told him "It is for everyone. There will also be bread. You will carry a portion to the Kapitein together with her full glass of geneva – carefully so it does not spill – and then you will take the helm so she can eat. You are now on her watch and you will be wise if you obey. I have Mijnheer Vandervelde with me from six pm and Engel will assist my mother with her general duties. It may be she can sleep. At ten pm we all will change and then again at two."

The captured crew ate their pottage in silence. It was so thick you could stand your spoon up in it. No chance that it would slop. You could probably have turned the bowls upside down and made little mounds like pea-green sandcastles. It was tasteless, but who cared? It could have been the winning entry from a TV celebrity chef and they'd have had trouble getting it down – except that they were all so desperately hungry. And frightened about the night ahead.

Then Helen gave Luke an oilskin jacket and sent him on deck with Elsevier's meal and a glass of clear liquid poured from a large stone bottle. The Kapitein accepted the food and drink without a word or smile and jerked her head to indicate that he should take the tiller.

"Course 030 degrees," she said. "You understand how to steer? I am watching you like an eagle of the sea."

She looked like something out of a black-and-white pirate film in that hat and boots and cloak. Or a faked-up musketeer. It was humiliating to be so scared of someone who was dressed in such stupid clothes.

It was the gun that did it for him. Like it obviously did for Ants. Sent him completely shaky. The gun that he couldn't see but which he knew would be there, pointing out from within the heavy cloak, ready to blast him if he made one wrong move. He could almost feel the bullet ripping into his body. The heat, the pain and then…the blood. He wouldn't be playing war adventures any more.

Elsevier had seated herself in the corner of the cockpit. She stared as he shivered. The cabin had been warmed by the working of the engine. He hadn't brought his jacket or any of his spare clothes on board and the oilskin that Helen had lent him was just that – old-fashioned oilskin: solidly black and waterproof with no soft lining or modern thermal layers.

Drie Vrouwen's tiller was cold to the touch. It was metal and was bolted to the high black-painted rudder by a pair of thick metal plates. There was no chance he could pull it out and use it as a weapon – even if he'd had the nerve.

You had to stand to steer *Drie Vrouwen*. There was a rigid canvas awning that provided some protection from the weather. It had large clear plastic inserts but these didn't give very good visibility especially when they were being dashed constantly by drizzle and salt-spray. If you really wanted to see clearly you had to look round it or move outside. It was even wetter and colder there.

Inside there was an illuminated compass and a garishly bright chart-plotter. It showed their track as a moving pink line following the north-east curve of the coast.

The daylight was already fading. When Luke looked out over the port side of the barge towards the shore he couldn't properly see the beach and the sandy cliffs where he and Liam had played all summer.

The last time he'd been at sea heading north along this coast he'd been on board *Strong Winds*. He'd been in primary school then and still living with Rev. Wendy. He'd been ten years old. Almost a different person! He remembered when he'd come on deck in his pyjamas, playing at being a hostage, rubbing the sleep out of his eyes and grumbling when he heard that they were 'only' going to Lowestoft. It had been one of the best days of his life. He'd been with Donny then and Skye. And Gold Dragon, who was dead.

Strong Winds had pulled along with her sails full, racing the following waves. Even when the tide turned and it got rough she'd felt as if she was leaping in the water. That she was joyful.

Drie Vrouwen didn't leap or surge. The wind was against her and she was battering her way through, demolishing each sharp-peaked wave and flinging spray to either side. She was sort of like angry and determined. Fighting the sea, not riding it.

Lift and bang, lift and bang. You couldn't imagine *Drie Vrouwen* playing in the water, not ever.

They'd all be with his dad at the hospital by now. Would Anna have guessed that the message wasn't from him? What would they say to Bill when Luke didn't show up? Would they tell him that Luke had gone wandering up the coast with unknown people on an unknown boat or would they make some excuse?

Except that his dad did know *Drie Vrouwen*. They'd been neighbours for months, though not friends. What had his dad said about demons when he was on the morphine? Revenge? Blood gelt? He must have guessed something: Luke should have listened better.

Elsevier had finished her food and was drinking her geneva. She struck a match and held it curved in her hand so that her face was illuminated from beneath. He guessed she was doing it on purpose; that she knew how spooky she looked. It was such a put-on.

Elsie. He was going to call her Elsie. Cut her down a bit. Call it in his head even if he didn't have the guts to say it aloud. Not Elsevier and definitely not the Kapitein.

Her face returned to shadow, touched occasionally with orange. She had lit herself a cigar. Luke didn't like tobacco. It gave him asthma if he was indoors but he guessed that wasn't something that would bother Elsie.

Gold Dragon had smoked a pipe. Donny said he really missed the smell.

Luke looked again at the chart-plotter. The pale pink line crept steadily north-east, taking him further from his home and the people he loved. The sea stretched ahead and so did the night. There was a lighthouse in the distance, its whiter beam intermittently lighting up the sky. He knew that one. It was Orfordness – another familiar mark.

It was almost dark now and the rain was coming down. Everything was blurry from inside *Drie Vrouwen*'s spray hood. Elsie had turned a windscreen wiper on but it didn't seem very effective. Was he just supposed to follow her compass course and watch the pink line on the electronic chart? His dad had set lobster pots off the beach in the summer. They were marked with black flags but you wouldn't have been able to see them on a night like this. It was a pity the barge hadn't got tangled in one.

"You. Go and look out for the buoy."

Elsie had stood up and was jabbing her finger at a small flashing dot on the plotter. She took the tiller from him and gestured that he should go out onto the side deck to confirm they were on the right side of the buoy that marked the beginning of the next long shoal.

Luke didn't have a safety harness or a life jacket. It was cold and exposed on the narrow deck and it felt slippery, even though it had metal ridges. *Drie Vrouwen* had started to roll as well as to lift and bang. He remembered how easily Mike had gone overboard. He got down and crawled.

The fronts of his jeans were sopping from the knees down and his gloveless hands were frozen by the time he found a secure lookout place. It was next to the bundle that was the crimson king. What had Mike said – that it was something off of a warship? That made sense with all the bad feelings he'd got from it.

Helen's knots looked a mess and the bashing of the barge against the waves was putting them under strain. The edge of the material was stretching and one of the eyelets had already come out. Luke hesitated. He wondered whether there was anything he could do to loosen the knots or fray the material faster? The thing was a monster but he didn't want those women to have it. No reason – except the fact that they wanted it.

Elsie was shouting at him. He was glad he couldn't hear what she was saying. His fingers were too cold to make any headway with the knots. Next time he came up here he'd try to bring a knife.

Luke looked ahead and to starboard across the tossing water. There were white waves breaking in the distance and before them, quite close really, a pinprick of flashing light. He counted the seconds as Donny had once explained.

"One thousand, two thousand, three thousand …"

It wasn't all that easy. He got to fifteen thousand before the flashes began again. Had he missed some? He should have asked how many there should be. Or Elsie should have told him. From their top floor apartment at Bawdsey you could see about twenty different navigation marks on a clear night and they all had different patterns when they were flashing. Different colours too. You needed to know which one you were meant to be looking for if you wanted to find it quickly.

Luke tried again.

The stolen figurehead slid and tugged beside him. Was the lion writhing in its bonds or was the motion getting rougher? Luke looked across towards the shore on the other side of the boat. There was a distant green light showing between the waves. And now the lighthouse beam had turned red instead of white. It was like some wild quasar game that they were playing as they struggled through the dark

Elsie was yelling again. Gesturing him to come back. Luke

sighed. He crouched onto the wet side deck again and crawled.

He felt *Drie Vrouwen* alter course. Elsie had turned her sharply to port across the waves and she was beginning to roll violently. Luke found the single low guard rail, lay down flat and hung on as best he could. He could so easily go over.

The deck plunged towards the sea and up again. Down – and Luke could see the bubbles of white foam that the barge was making as she motored away from the quick flashing buoy. Up – and he was thrown against the cabin side.

Small streams of water cascaded along the deck with each down-roll, seeping up inside the bottoms of his jeans and down into his socks and trainers. The up-rolls were the ones he could use. It took him three before he made it back to the cockpit and the relative shelter of the spray hood.

The lighthouse beam was white again. Elsie had returned *Drie Vrouwen* to her course and was gesturing furiously at the plotter.

"Stupid, ignorant son of a creek-crawler. You almost ran us on that sand."

Luke looked where she was pointing. He could see the light-house beam segmented on the display into green and white and red. And if they had continued in the red section they would have gone into shallow water, very shallow water, a shoal. That's where the waves had been breaking.

Okay, they'd obviously had a narrow escape. But it hadn't been him on the helm. His emotions began churning round like deeper layers of the sea. Scraps of anger and resentment and the residue of fear came tossing up like flecks of shell.

Luke knew that there were long, thin, shallow banks of sand and shingle all along this coast. Some were close inshore: some miles out to sea. They'd been there for centuries, growing and shifting. That's what made the fishing grounds. It made danger too, and wrecks. He hadn't totally connected this knowledge with coloured lights and flashing navigation buoys.

He felt stupid. She was right about that.

Luke looked more closely at the chart-plotter. This sand was called the Whiting Bank. It even had his name on it! That was what the flashing light was marking.

"My dad's never a creek-crawler," he told Elsie. "My dad's a fisherman and the son and the grandson of fishermen. And that means I am too."

"Well, who'd have guessed?" she sneered. "Now take the helm again, mud-spawn, while I re-plot."

"Maybe you should an' all. Maybe it was following your course that put us too close to the shoal in the first place. Maybe you ain't much better as a navigator than I am as a fisherman's son."

She'd been wearing heavy leather gloves and had taken one off to adjust the instrument settings. Two strides across the cockpit and she'd hit him with it before he could protect himself.

"I am your Kapitein. I endure no insolence."

Luke's left eye watered and his cheek burned. He turned them into the night air and the rain to cool them. He'd felt pain worse than this from primary school bullies. It was her contempt that hurt. Plus he deserved it for his ignorance and weakness.

She was checking calculations now and tapping in new numbers. He couldn't see the compass or the plotter because she was blocking them. He couldn't steer the course she'd ordered and he didn't care. He gazed starboard across the waves. How many miles to Holland?

Drie Vrouwen wasn't showing any navigation lights and those thick cabin curtains meant that there was nothing from the portholes either. Her hull was black, her upper-works dull red. She would be very hard for any other ship to see.

Not like the night when she'd been full of candles for all those people who had died. Where had they died, he wondered now?

The breaking waves were still visible, catching the lighthouse beam in the near-darkness. White water on the Whiting bank. A whiting was a sort of fish. He'd seen people sitting on the beach at night time trying to catch them when they came in to feed in the shallows. Maybe there'd be fish there now.

Should he drive *Drie Vrouwen* onto the Whiting Bank on purpose? Stick her there like he should have let her stick on the Deben Bar?

The waves were rough. They'd bang her on the hard sand. Maybe she'd start to leak. She was metal but even metal had to be joined together somewhere. Would she float when the tide came up? Or would she fill – like that other metal container that Luke didn't never think about – except in nightmares.

Luke didn't want to drown. Not if he didn't have to.

"A fisherman fills his boots and goes straight down," his dad had said.

But he'd also said that drowning was a horrible death. Luke guessed that Mike and Ants wouldn't want to drown any more than he did.

The quick flashing light had gone astern. Luke peered round the edge of the spray hood. He could see another pinpoint of white light in the distance.

"One thousand, two thousand, three thousand…"

The beam of the lighthouse was closer and stronger. It kept getting in the way of his concentration. Would he ever get the hang of counting seconds? If this was a proper electronic adventure, he'd have Powers he could use.

"Press the OFF switch."

That was funny. He could hear Anna in his head. Or maybe it was Lottie? She was telling him to turn off his Nintendo and not even to carry on playing until he reached the 'Save Game' point.

Maybe he was getting delirious. People did at sea. It was the salt. Or the motion. Or your brain hitting the sides of your skull.

"PRESS THE OFF SWITCH!"

The voice was getting louder. It was definitely Anna – his ratty big sister who always knew best.

"Put it down and walk away then."

That's what she'd say when she knew he simply couldn't press OFF in the middle of a game. When his Nintendo was warm in his hand and magnetically full of life.

"PUT IT DOWN AND WALK AWAY!"

Oh. Okay. Thanks Anna. He'd got the message now.

"I'm not playing any more. I'm going back to my friends," he said, as quick and as clear as he could, to Elsie. "You can take your own tiller." And he was past her before she properly heard what he'd said.

"I'm not helping any more and you can have your oilskin back," he told Helen, as he arrived cold and wet in the cabin.

"You know she told you that you'd be going on watch with her?" he said to Mike, jerking his head towards Helen. "Well, you shouldn't. And you shouldn't either," he said to Ants. "We shouldn't never have helped them get off the Deben Bar. We're prisoners and that's what we ought to behave like. I don't care if we took their pills or ate their foul food. We're not their crew. We shouldn't help them."

"The *Royal Katherine* even …" said Mike, pushing his hands behind his back and turning to face Helen. "I'm sorry, Mejuffrow de Witt, but Luke's right. Policy of non-cooperation from now on. Non-collaboration even."

Luke didn't get the difference but Helen obviously did. Especially when Mike repeated it in Dutch. 'Collaboration' – that must be a really bad word.

Elsevier came storming down the steps. She ordered Helen to take over the steering and then she hit Luke again. She used her fist, this time, not her glove. Punched him on the jaw.

He reeled back.

Mike stepped towards her, shocked and objecting, but rather uncertain and surprised. She punched him in the stomach.

Mike doubled up gasping for breath.

Angel flung herself at Elsevier, teeth and claws, and then Hendrike came bellowing from nowhere. She full-on charged Angel, knocking her over, then plonking her heavy weight on top.

"I'm obliged, mijn lieve koe," said Elsevier, kicking the small girl with her leather riding boot.

"Oh no you don't," she said to Luke, who was coming at her as bravely as he dared.

And there was that gun again, pointing at Angel. "You are keen to behave like prisoners? You go into prison then. NOW!!!" she screamed. "This is your child, Van der Traitor. Filthy turn-coat. English kiss-arse. Get into the side cabin. And you too, mud-spawn."

She was screeching and waving her arms. Striding around and swirling her cloak. Out of her skull hysterical, you'd have thought. Except that her gun stayed pointing rock-steady at Angel's head.

Angel's eyes had gone weird again. They'd sort of rolled back so you could only see the whites.

"Oh my god, she's having another episode."

Completely not noticing any danger Mike hurled himself at Hendrike. She didn't topple though, she was far too heavy. He knelt beside his daughter.

"Angela, sweetheart, Daddy's here."

"Please," he said to Hendrike. "Please will you get off? How can I possibly move her with you sitting there?"

"Okay," said Elsevier. "Help him shift her to the side cabin. My gun's on the boy."

"I have reached the North-East Whiting, Kapitein. I need to change course." Helen shouted from outside.

Hendrike shoved them into in a cramped bare room. There was a cupboard, a patch of floor and the rest of it was bunk.

Angel wasn't floppy this time, she was rigid. Mike got her onto the bunk and was struggling to roll to her side and keep her there in a recovery position. They could hear Hendrike grunting as she locked the door.

Then it all went black. They felt *Drie Vrouwen* change direction. It was like she was trying to bounce them off her metal walls. Luke was struggling to find somewhere to brace himself so he didn't fall on Mike and Ants. It was impossible. Another wild, disorientating plunge and he landed on the bunk beside them.

"It's Orfordness," he said to Mike "We're going round the

bit that sticks out into the sea. That's where the lighthouse is. My dad says it's always rough between the Whiting Bank and Orfordness."

Bill could have told him – or Donny could have – or Gold Dragon who had let him be such a happy first-time hostage – that it was about to get a whole lot worse.

CHAPTER THIRTEEN

Sole Bay I
Thursday 6 November, dark of the moon

Luke, Helen, Angel.

The tide was on the turn again. By the time the flood had started running north to south they would be away from Orfordness and the shelter of the curving coast. The tide would be in the same direction as the northerly wind and the waves would be smooth and huge instead of spiky and unpredictable. As soon as Elsevier set their course east or north-east for Holland they would be broadside to the swell. They would go sideways up and sideways down, rolling between the mountains and valleys.

"What's broach?" asked Angel.

The word had sort of come to Luke as *Drie Vrouwen* seemed to be sliding uphill sideways and trying to flip right over before lurching down again. It was like she was some sick-making, gravity-defying gyroscope and no-one who had tried her in a theme-park would ever be persuaded to get on more than once.

Luke and Mike and Angel were all lying together on the bunk, arms round each other and holding tight, trying not to be hurled up onto the low ceiling or sideways against the walls. They could only feel each other's bodies: not see.

He'd tried the word because it felt like talking would be a good idea. There'd been silence for a moment then Ants had tried to ask about what he'd said. That was good that she could manage that. She must be getting better.

"Getting stuck and turning over. It's not…the right word."

It was hard to think coherently let alone find words when your brain seemed to be bashing about inside your skull like a ball in a bucket. "It means…they're…completely mad," he said. "You can't…argue…with the sea. Whoever you think you are."

He guessed their cabin was somewhere under the cabin roof where they'd tied the stolen figurehead. There were thuds and sounds of sliding as well as the struggling roar of the engine and the slap of solid water when they hit the crest of a wave. He remembered how the bundle had been working loose – as if the lion inside was attempting to escape.

Then a new noise joined the din above their heads. It was *Drie Vrouwen*'s ship's bell swinging wildly through more than 180 degrees, clanging against the wind as it tried to loop the loop.

"Kapitein, we cannot keep this course."

Helen's foot slipped in the slick of her mother's vomit. The only light in *Drie Vrouwen*'s cockpit came from the chart-plotter display. The pale pink line that marked their current course ran left to right across the screen. It looked so simple – and so flat! There was nothing to indicate the lurching upwards and the tipping sideways; the terrifying hesitancy near the top before the beginning of the downward slide and the fitful instants of peace in the trough between the waves before the whole sequence began again, though never quite the same each time.

Her mind was running slow. The ship's bell was a tocsin, an alarm call. If the barge rolled over there would be nothing she could do. They would all die but the prisoners would die locked in. She had lured them on board. Their deaths would be her fault.

Helen and her mother had both been sick. The Stugeron she'd taken hadn't been enough. Her mother hadn't taken anything at all. She had been too distracted by whatever was happening in her head. There would be lumps of pease pottage scattered in the slime.

Helen knew she should find a bucket, fill it with saltwater and sluice the sick away, then pass it to her retching mother. But she wasn't going to do that. The other thing was more important. She was going to be sick again but first, in these few moments before she heaved, she had to make the Kapitein listen.

"We must point her bow to the waves."

"Why so? I wish to return to my country. I do not choose to travel to the Pole."

How was it that Elsevier had not been sick? Was that the stone bottle of geneva that she was always lifting to her mouth?

The ship's bell rang once more. A flat, metallic noise.

Helen felt the bile rising in her throat. She gulped it down. The deck on the downhill side was under water.

"I have a faster way. I have learned from my rowing."

She must persuade Elsevier to round into the up-slope of the waves. Find a better angle and their leeway would keep them on their eastwards course. They could sidle crab-wise home. Alter later if they had to.

She couldn't give in. Must gain control of the tiller.

"Please, Kapitein, allow me."

The older woman surprised them both as she relinquished the helm and moved aside. She needed her other hand to light the next cigar. It was wearing having to do so much for lesser folk. The girl could take a turn before she fetched a second bottle.

Luke felt *Drie Vrouwen* begin rearing up and plunging down. Rearing up and plunging down. Not rolling.

He and Mike and Angel were feet first to the boat's direction. Lying on a blanket on some sort of hard and shiny mattress. They carried on holding their arms around each other as they slid rhythmically forwards and back along the bunk.

It wasn't pleasant but it was easier. The bell went quiet. The lion thumped but didn't grind.

They didn't try to talk any more. It was sufficient to believe that they might live. Perhaps they even slept a while?

Angel couldn't stay asleep for long, even when she'd had seizures. She woke and it was dark and the boat was still going up and down, up and down. Luke and her father were lucky to be out of it. She mustn't fidget or she'd wake them.

This cabin was so small. She couldn't see the walls and ceiling but she felt them pressing on her.

The three of them slid backwards down the bunk. Their heads were jammed against the end. She tried to ride the boat's rhythm – like she was pumping her knees to skate a half pipe.

The tickly feelings racing round her legs and arms: the fireflies of light …

"Dad!"

Mr Vandervelde stirred and mumbled. Knocked his head and remembered where they were. Groaned.

She knew he'd rather sleep but she couldn't wait. "Have you got my fitting pills?" No reason why he should have. "Cos I haven't had them since before yesterday. I think I need them urgent."

That woke him.

"Your pills! I hadn't even thought."

"But have you got 'em?"

"Mum usually keeps them. She knows I'm so forgetful."

"Only about some things."

"I'll tell those women. If they know you're getting multiple seizures, that you need medication, they'll surely have to take you home."

Mike knocked his head in a different place as he sat up. The ceiling was so low above this bunk.

Luke woke. His hand went groping for his Nintendo. His knuckles hit the bunk-end, then tangled in Ants's spiky hair.

She mustn't hit him.

"I can't see."

This hateful dark. *Lowestoft Lass* had electric light. Never mind you had to save it because of the battery, it was there, with switches. Hendrike and Helen couldn't live with candles all the time.

"Stay still," he said. "I'll try and find a light."

"Can't stay still," said Angel. *Drie Vrouwen* plunged deeply. They all slid downhill and Luke's stomach hit his throat.

"Think theme-park," he told them. "Let yourself go with it. Try roller-coaster ride."

"Never," said Mike.

"Even boarding wasn't doing it for me."

"Well, I dunno, talk or something. But I need to climb over both of you because I reckon we'll all feel better if we can see."

"I think so too." Her tickly feelings were like twenty million insects running sprints with all their tiny feet but she was going to try again what Luke said. She tried to breathe more slowly, wished she was in that kayak with the paddle.

"Can I hold you, Dad? Like you're my safety bar. You can talk about your work if you want. Say your papers even. We don't mind."

Luke climbed over with nothing much worse than a knee in Angel's stomach and an elbow toppling him onto Mike's chest. Then he began to move about on the tiny patch of floor, struggling to keep his balance, groping to find a switch.

"Okay," said Mike. "Let's have the *Royal Katherine*. Battle of Sole Bay, May 28th 1672, afternoon. It's my Lecture Number 3 'The Prize'. I know all of them by heart."

Mum probably does as well, thought Angel. But she doesn't let on because she loves him. Her mum and dad seemed as funny and endearing as if they were garden gnomes unexpectedly brought to life. How could she have doubted them?

"So which one's the *Royal Katherine*, Dad? Was that the one that got blown up?"

She was breathing a bit fast and she gripped Mike's arm with both hands. Maybe she could do that channelling again. Focus her feelings into a stream. Use that gold and red.

"Good heavens no! That was the *Royal James*. She burned for hours. No-one whoever saw her could forget the sight. The *Royal Katherine* was the one that got captured by the Dutch. The English prisoners started shouting that she was going to sink so the Dutch let them back on deck. Then they fought them and won and sailed her back to Harwich."

Luke turned on the light.

"Will those women see it," Mike wondered anxiously. "Will someone come and hit us again? I'm so sorry children. I'm a useless protector. You'd better let me stand near the door. I'll explain about your condition, Angela."

There was only one tiny porthole and it was covered by a sort of blackout curtain.

"Don't do that, Dad. I need you talking. I'm trying to do what Luke said. Trying to ride it."

"Start talking, Mike," said Luke. "I'll try and find something to hit them back."

"If you're sure. Well, here goes…The *Stavoren* was captured between four and five o'clock in the afternoon of May 28th 1672. Ever since the tide had turned and they'd put about, the English and the Dutch fleets had been sailing roughly south-east in two long lines, firing at each other. There was still very little wind and the tide was against them."

Luke settled himself on the heaving floor and began to search inside the cupboard. There wasn't much there: no clothes or personal things. Just files and boxes. The files were all full of paper so he didn't bother with them. Began looking through the boxes. The drum was in one of them and another had a folded cloth with a big circle and coloured symbols that he didn't understand. They looked sort of astrological.

"…When the tide had turned at noon Dutch admiral Van Nes had captured the *Royal Katherine*, an 82-gun second-rate English 'great ship'. He'd taken her captain and officers on board his own vessel and put some of his men onto the *Royal Katherine* to sail her back to Holland. The English crew were imprisoned below decks…"

"What's the time now?" Luke asked. Without his mobile the answer could be anything.

"Nine o'clock," Mike broke off, briefly. Angel took a quick extra breath and carried on clinging to his arm.

"They'll all be home, our families. Not knowing where we are." Even Anna couldn't get a mobile traced that had been chucked into the sea several hours ago.

"Please, don't stop Dad talking."

"Sorry."

Luke pulled out the next box. It was full of part-used nightlights and the stumps of tiny candles. Had Helen and her mum been having a vigil for them dead sailors?

Maybe he would listen to Mike's talking for a bit.

Mike finished describing the recapture of the *Royal Katherine* and went back to the beginning of his series. He reached Lecture Number 2 'The Butcher's Bill'.

"…even the foam was tinged with blood…"

Luke had heard that before. All those different ways to die and the people watching from the shore who couldn't help even though they might have been their families. It was all horrible.

"Do you think these women really care?" he interrupted.

The heist would be sort of understandable if they wanted the lion for some real reason. Like a memorial or something.

He could also maybe understand how thinking of so many dead people could have driven Hendrike crazy – especially if some might have been her and Helen's ancestors. Was Mike saying that their ancestors were the brothers who got torn to pieces? That bit was gross.

Mike wasn't stopping for questions so Luke opened another box.

There was the poppet that had been dressed to look exactly like his dad and there was the heavy runestone that had been used to smash it from behind.

He felt the blood drain from his face and a lurch in his stomach that was nothing to do with fly agaric poisoning or with the motion of the sea. Mike was still reciting and Angel was gripping onto his arm.

Luke sat on the floor of the tiny cabin stroking the lifeless doll. It was as if this broken doll was real and the figure in the hospital had been a dream. As if Hendrike had really killed his dad.

"Not everyone died," said Mike. He'd reached the place where he usually paused. "Not even off the *Royal James*."

"The *Royal James* is the painting we had in the living room, isn't it, Dad?" asked Angel. "The one Mum made you take down."

"It was just a poster, from the National Maritime Museum. I've got a collection. Postcards too. Nelly says all the ships look the same to her. And the battle scenes are too upsetting, she says. She's right of course – about the battles, not the ships. There's a lot to see in those drawings if you take the time to look. She's promised to come…"

"Dad…if you don't mind. I'd rather not think about Mum at the moment. I know I said it first but I shouldn't have."

Mike gulped. As if he could have been gulping back tears.

"No. Sorry. I'll carry on. Try to…"

He cleared his throat, shifted about on the bunk, then got caught out by an extra-huge leap from *Drie Vrouwen*. The sort that leaves your stomach floating somewhere twenty metres above your head and you can't believe you'll ever get back together again.

"I think I'm going to be sick. Those pills don't last…"

"No, you're not, Dad. Don't go all cold on me. You just talk and I'll do the concentrating."

Mike sort of panted a bit, cleared his throat again and had another try.

"Now that I've reached this point in the series I want to say that I'm happy to take any other questions you may have. There's no need to save them until the end. After all, we don't at the moment know that there'll be an end, do we? I mean, not the sort of end where the chairman gives a vote of thanks. We know that there'll be other ends – the end of this night: the end of this trip: the end of our lives. Even the survivors from the Battle of Sole Bay didn't go on for ever. Not the human ones.

"I'm sorry Luke. I'm sorry Angela. I'm rubbish if I lose my script.

"You've been an exceptional audience. Both of you. I have to admit that there have been occasions when I've found myself in an empty hall. I usually give the talks anyway – as long as the caretaker doesn't mind. It's all so vivid in my head. There's always a chance that someone might come in if there's heating available and a cup of tea afterwards.

"That brings me back to the Dutch prisoners. In July 1672 there were one hundred and eighty Dutch prisoners starving in Harwich. They'd been given 2d each for food to last four days. That's all we know. You can see why thinking of a cup of tea helped recall them to my mind. I've often wished I knew what had happened to them, any of them. Just recently – and this isn't yet incorporated in my talks – I've discovered evidence that some of them…"

"STOP! Mr Vandervelde, please STOP!"

Mike had been speaking for two hours…three? It could be past midnight and into next day. And all this time *Drie Vrouwen* had been taking them away from England and their families.

Luke had replaced the broken doll in its box and put the rune-stone in the pocket of his fleece. It was awkward and it made his jacket sag but it was the nearest to a weapon he could find.

"I need you both to move. I've searched everywhere else in this cabin. Now I want to look under the mattress."

CHAPTER FOURTEEN

Sole Bay II
Friday 7 November, first of the waxing crescent

Luke

They looked surprised, confused and similar: Ants with her
hennaed mane tamed and crumpled by her cramped position
on the bunk, Mike with his fly-away grey hair stiffened into
salty peaks by his soaking earlier. They were both white-faced,
both with charcoal shadows beneath their eyes. He remembered
Helen's exhausted face.

Hateful Helen. Enemy.

"On *Lowestoft Lass* there's storage under the bunks.
There's sometimes even space to crawl through. Me and Liam
discovered it."

They still looked bewildered. They didn't move, as if they
didn't know where they should move to.

"Put the mattress onto the floor. No room? Roll it up then
and shove it across to the side. And move yourselves. I'm having
those panels off."

"We're gonna like re-enact the *Royal Katherine* and escape?"
This was Ants.

"Huh?"

"She was the prize that was taken by the Dutch and then
the English crew fought back," explained Mike. "She was a big
second-rater but poorly designed. She'd been damaged. The

206

English overpowered their captors and sailed her for Harwich."

"Yeah. Okay. Whatever."

He had got the panels out and pushed them to one side. As he'd expected there was a big space underneath the bunk. Trouble was that it was nearly filled by some large tank. Sealed off. Not storage. There was a gap about a foot or so between the tank and *Drie Vrouwen*'s metal hull.

Luke could hear water. Twice. Water outside the rearing, plunging hull and water sloshing next to him as well.

Needn't be water. It could be fuel. *Lowestoft Lass* had tanks for both. Point was that it was a tank and it was in his way and he didn't think that he'd be able to break it. Or even that he should if he wasn't certain what was inside.

Could he get round the tank? Luke tried to bend his body, feet first, into the gap between the tank and the hull. It felt well tight. So then he tried the other way. He sucked his stomach in, leaned down next to the tank and stretched his arm as far forward as he could.

He almost dislocated his shoulder but his fingertips touched a bulkhead – a partition between this space and whatever came next. The bulkhead didn't feel that solid. It could be his way out to…somewhere, if he could smash it.

The problem was that his arm wasn't long enough to get any force behind a blow but his shoulders and chest were slightly too big to let him squeeze any further in. Luke pulled back to think.

What if he got into the gap feet first and used the length of his leg? He could probably kick out the bulkhead. But what was the point if he couldn't then fit his body through?

"Ants…?"

"Yeah?"

"You know you're small…?"

"…mmm."

"Well there's a gap between this tank and the hull. Then there's a partition but I think we might be able to kick it out. If I made a hole, would you be on for trying to get through?"

"Course I would. I do get quite bad claustrophobia."

Oh.

"The stress could trigger another seizure." This was Mike sounding parental. "And who knows what's on the other side. She could be going straight into the Kapitein's bedroom."

"Otherwise known as the lion's den. What if I try the kicking bit anyway and then we see what happens next? If I go first and there's anyone there, then it'll be my foot that gets used for target practice."

It was odd how even thinking such a thought made the bottom of his foot feel like a mass of soft, warm flesh, a delicate net of nerve and bone. A bullet smashing into that! The pain would be terrible. And there'd be no help on board *Drie Vrouwen*. He might get gangrene. Have to have the whole leg off. Crippled for life – if he didn't die.

"I'll do it," said Mike. "My legs are longer."

But Mike's pelvis was much broader and he was so awkward and so stiff. He couldn't even touch the partition with his leg. It turned out that it had to be Luke.

"It was my idea anyway."

The runestone in his pocket jammed against the narrow opening so he took it out and passed it to Ants to hold.

"What is it?"

"Whatever that bitch-witch used to club the doll she'd dressed up as my dad."

"She what?"

"She didn't like my dad so she made this doll and I think she'd been sticking pins in or something and then she got this stone and tried beating him to bits. No wonder he had an accident. I told you. She's evil."

"You think," breathed Mike, "A genuine survival of seventeenth-century dark arts?"

"But …that was me and the lads what knocked out the chock and made the boat fall on your dad. You know that …"

Ants's voice could make you think of the smallest lost kitten abandoned in the cold.

"Maybe you were in Hendrike's power. It was Halloween, remember. You could have been Possessed. Or maybe it was an accident. But if you take a look at the doll inside that box – like I've been doing for the past hour – you'll find it pretty clear what she meant to happen to Dad. That accident was exactly what she wanted. BITCH-WITCH!"

Luke pushed himself deep into the gap and began pounding the bulkhead at the end with more strength than he'd known he had.

"BITCH-WITCH! BITCH-WITCH!"

He timed his blows with the motion of the barge: each thud of his foot on the thin wood coinciding with *Drie Vrouwen* plummeting down some unseen wave. A half dozen hefty kicks and he felt the partition start to sag. He felt no fear that there might be someone on the other side. It splintered and he was glad.

"BITCH-WITCH! BITCH-WITCH!"

He needed to make a really good-sized hole so there wouldn't be any problem for Ants getting though. Then she'd have to find her way back round and unlock the cabin door to let them out. He kicked a few more times, his anger draining as he felt the opening increase.

What sort of key had the bitch-witch used? Whatever it was she probably hadn't left it hanging neatly on a hook outside. Much more likely to be in some pocket deep inside her horrible baggy clothes.

Tackling Hendrike would be like tackling some human hippo. They were supposed to be the most dangerous animal in the wild. Worse than lions, weren't they? He couldn't ask Ants to do that.

Luke stopped kicking: the hole was big enough. He tried to remember what sort of sound the lock had made when she had shut them into the cabin. Was there a bolt or had Hendrike used a key? He'd wriggle back and ask the others.

But he couldn't. Couldn't move at all. As he'd kicked – violently, repeatedly – with his right leg, using the forward surge of the boat each time, he hadn't noticed how he'd slipped further and further along the narrow gap. His hands were still either side of the opening, gripping awkwardly onto the frame, but his left leg was doubled underneath him and his pelvis was completely wedged around the far corner of the tank.

"Mike! Ants! Can you give us a pull please?"

He heard some sort of exclamation from Mike and then he felt Ants's small hands gripping one of his and heard her telling her father that he needed to get hold of Luke's wrist. They began to pull.

"Not like that, Dad. Pull with the boat. When she goes up in the air."

The place he was caught by was just completely wrong and the pain was suddenly excruciating.

"Stop it! Please!"

"What's the matter?" Mike's head was peering into the space, blocking the light.

"I've gone too far. My…bum's stuck around the end of the tank. I can't get back."

He could hear the panic in his own voice.

Mike was worse. "Oh good heavens what shall we do? I shouldn't have let you go down there. I should have known better."

Now it seemed like Mike was trying to climb into the gap with him. "Can you give me space, Mike? I feel like I might suffocate."

"Sit up, Dad. You're blocking out all the light. Luke, you need to hold my hand and slow your breathing. Don't think about anything except that. We're not going to leave you and you're going to be okay. Try to relax."

Was that Ants? Must be. He could feel her holding one of his hands with both of hers. Feel her sort of beaming reassurance into him.

He did as she said and tried to slow his breathing. Relaxed his body bit by bit. Understood that there was no reason for his shoulders to be hunched up around his ears. That wasn't the part he was caught by.

"If I try to kick again, could you try and push this time? See if we can get me through into wherever it is that I've made the hole?"

Ants and Mike both tried but by now he was kicking empty

air. As much as he tried to jerk himself forwards with every wave-slide he knew he wasn't getting anywhere. That same bit of tank was sticking into the same bit of him and he hadn't progressed a millimetre.

Then he felt someone grab his leg and begin pulling. Pulling from through the hole. Pulling really strongly.

His left leg was doubled underneath him, the edge of the tank was pressing hard into his groin. This person had muscles.

Luke couldn't help it. He screamed.

Everything stopped. He was panting, trembling, covered in sweat.

"I'm sorry," came a voice from beyond the opening. "I had changed sides. I've been watching you and now I was trying to help."

He needed to wait for the pain to stop. Those small hands of Ants's were still there, holding his clammy one.

"Are you…?"

"I am Helen. I am very sorry."

"Are you Helen on her own or Helen with her bitch-witch mother and her mother's murdering friend?"

"Only Helen. Helen who loves her country and thought that she would do anything to get home but discovers that she can't."

"Can't which? Can't get home. Or can't… whatever it is."

"Can't either, I don't think. May I try to pull you through?"

"Not like you just did. How could your ancestors have been torn to pieces? That was agony."

"I don't know. I hate the seventeenth century. I hate everything about it. I hate violence, oppression of women, religious mania, power politics and poverty. I hate state-operated torture and if there was truly witchcraft in the seventeenth century then I hate that too. What exactly is preventing you?"

It was a good question. He couldn't quite think how to explain that he was somehow straddling the corner of an unyielding water tank and that every time she pulled – or Ants and her father pushed – his balls got crushed against it.

"Not sure. Possibly my other leg. It's hooked up underneath me and I can't get it out."

"Okay. I'll fetch a torch to take a proper look. Don't move."

"Can't move!"

"Are you okay?" That was Ants.

"I'm good. But don't stop hanging onto me. I've got Helen at the other end."

"Oh."

"Please, Ants." He squeezed her small hot hand. It was maybe like a paw. "Stay with me."

He thought he heard her sniff. "Ain't got no choice. You don't want to trust her though."

"I'm not seeing a lot of choice about that either."

There was a light by his feet. Helen had a torch and she was reaching in and feeling round the corner of the tank (that was nearly embarrassing) and then she was getting hold of his doubled-up left leg.

"It's not broken?"

"No. It's stuck."

"Okay. Wait a minute while I make it straight. Then I give you soap."

Which she did. She sorted his left leg, gently but firmly so that it was lying alongside his right leg. Both of them now pointing into some unknown place where he trusted that there was only her.

Then she passed him a large damp block of old-fashioned soap.

"You rub this everywhere," she said. "On all the surfaces that are stuck. Mainly on your trousers."

Luke had started this holiday – however long ago – determined to stop dreaming and be practical. He'd never dreamed he would meet anyone as practical as Helen.

"Sorry, Ants," he said. "I need both my hands for this bit."

She let him go without a word. He knew she wasn't happy. He wasn't happy either.

"Rub it on thick," said Helen. "And tell me when you're done. Then I pull again."

It was pretty bad. He used the soap as thickly as she said and also managed to rearrange himself so the rigid corner missed his private parts and went scraping up the inside of his hip and over his flat stomach.

She stopped pulling when he got stuck again with the corner of the tank half way up his chest.

"Okay," she said. "We don't panic here. You lie still and you breathe. Then you stretch your arms behind you and you make your shoulders loose. Who has the soap now?"

"Me."

"That's you, Engel, is it?"

"Is."

"Then you must use the soap all over his chest where it is stuck and also his shoulders and the tank. The head will be okay."

Angel did as Helen instructed, hating her more furiously every moment. Then *Drie Vrouwen* plunged, Helen pulled, Luke twisted and suddenly he shot out through the opening as fast if he'd ridden down a flume.

Angel was right behind him. He'd knocked Helen backwards when he came out and the small girl was straightaway on top of her, pinning her arms to the floor, blazing with fury.

There was some muffled shouting coming from behind them. That must be Mike, trapped in the cabin and calling after his daughter. No one took any notice.

"Cool it off, Ants. Helen's okay. She's sorry and she's on our side. I think …"

"Don't call her by that name." Helen wasn't fighting back though she easily could have done. "She hates it. It's what the bullies call her at school."

"You should know. All about bullies!" Angel wanted to sob that she'd ever trusted this nice girl. Looking at her now, she remembered – she'd liked her so much.

"Is that right, Ants? I mean Angela? Do you really hate your name? I thought you said it was okay."

Angel couldn't never lie directly. (Not except to her parents, possibly.) "Well yeah. At school I hate it. Always have. And there's a reason – which I told her. And which I'll TOTALLY NEVER FORGIVE if you tell anyone else," she said to Helen, sort of bashing her arms back against the floor and banging her chest with her head. "But you're my friend, Luke. My only ever friend and you can call me what name you like."

"But" Luke wasn't especially quick but he was getting there. "If I'm your friend…(which I so am) of course I can't call you a name that you don't like. What name do you like?"

"Doesn't matter." Angel felt awkward now, as if it was she who'd made the fuss.

"She likes Engel."

"I so do NOT! Stupid Dutch girl."

"My dad said you were his angel. Is that the name you like? Angel, short for Angela?"

Angel nodded but she didn't say anything because she couldn't. Not quite.

"Sorry," she muttered to Helen.

"No. I'm sorry. In Dutch they are almost the same word. I think I mixed them. One means English and the other is angel. I have been trying to think of you only as English because that makes you my enemy. It made it easier for me to betray."

"Luke says you're sorry. He says you're on our side now."

"Yes. If there must be sides then I am on your side – if you'll have me."

"Of course we will. Come on Angel. Let her get up. We have to make plans."

"Then we'll get my dad out too."

Helen rolled up into a sitting position as soon as Angel got off and the two girls looked at each other. Luke checked out where they were and then he called back through the gap to Mike.

"It's okay, Mike. Angel's fine and Helen's on our side. I think we're in her cabin. She'll come and get you in a moment."

"Excuse me," said Helen. She had straightened her clothes and she was twisting her pony-tail back into position. "It may be better for Mr Vandervelde if we leave him where he is."

"Huh?" Angel went tense and suspicious again.

"Please listen to what I have to say. I am almost fifteen years old. Both of you are younger, I think?"

"So?"

"So we are children and – if things go wrong – we cannot be so badly blamed. Your father is an adult. They will say he is responsible."

"Who will?"

"The police."

"Yeah, but if we're going to use your phone to ring for help, maybe that's good from Mike's point of view. He's the adult: he gets the credit. He could talk to them even."

"But my mother and the Kapitein, they are crazy tonight. They won't give up so easily. Elsevier is drunk and she has given my mother some more powder that she should not have. Once I had put the ship on her course and found the root of ginger that stops my mother being sick they sent me down here to be out of their way."

"Is that why you decided to change sides? Fed up with being gooseberry."

He saw that she didn't understand.

"Are you jealous of Elsie with your mother?"

"Yes, of course I am, but that wasn't why I changed my side."

"What was it then? You've been helping them all along. You tricked us on board and it must have been you who helped to steal the red lion."

"And started the fire at the moorings," Angel added.

"No it was not. The fire was my mother. We needed a diversion and an excuse for the electricity to fail. I didn't know she would try to make a fireship. And, before you ask, I didn't know either that she would try to poison you. It was meant to be only a sleeping drug in the mushroom soup."

"Soup!" said Luke. "Not Lottie's sausages?"

"Stop," said Angel. "We need to know that my dad is hearing this."

They all moved closer to the opening.

"Dad," said Angel. "Are you listening to what she said?"

"I'm listening," came Mike's voice. "I'm not sure yet that I'm agreeing. You're an extremely clever girl, Mejuffrow de Witt. I don't think it would be easy to fool you."

"I am my mother's daughter. That is all. I have no other relatives. I agree I helped to steal the *Stavoren* lion from the pub and I rowed it down the stream and there are other things that I have helped to steal. I tricked you all on board and I maybe didn't stop long enough with the old man."

"I don't know that bit," said Angel.

"I do," said Luke. "It was Peter and he'd been lost somewhere along by the sluice and you were trying to get him over the gap and I met you and I wasn't much use because I was so wobbly."

"But you phoned the farmer. And then I think you went back with him? It was convenient for me to leave you once he was in the Land Rover."

"I went up the track through the woods with Miss Grace and I opened the gates and I went and fed his cat while she put him to bed at the farm. I don't know what you did."

"I returned to my ship and I helped the Kapitein and my mother to pull the figurehead on board. I wasn't sure you'd gone to the farm and I was afraid you might have seen. That's why I wanted you on board. So you couldn't talk. I still thought that we were only thieves and seventeenth-century freaks. Wreken de Dame is politics."

"But you knew that your mother's … a witch. You knew that she attacked my dad."

"No. She isn't. That bit I'm sure about. She takes stupid drugs and she thinks that she has powers but they are not – I may need help for the words – powers beyond nature. She can make bad medicine but she can't do more than that. I was there when she attacked the figure with the stone and I know exactly what time it was. Then I asked you and the accident to your father had already happened. I would have stopped them if that had not been so. I swear it. I wanted to love and obey my mother but not that much."

"That accident was completely all my fault." Angel didn't know whether she was glad or sorry. Better not to have been Possessed probably.

"What's made you change?"

"It's the gun. All along I have allowed myself to think that it was fake. But it's real. The Kapitein is truly dangerous. I thought it would be all right if we could just get home. Now – I'm not sure."

"You must let me protect you all." Mike's invisible voice was anguished. Luke could imagine him twisting his hands around each other.

"I'm sorry, Mr Vandervelde, but you are a weakness. You heard what the Kapitein said about hostages. She has only to threaten your daughter and you are defeated. If we ring the police she won't stop at anything. And my mother … is not sane. They will use your love. It doesn't matter about me because I am on the wrong side anyway."

"I don't agree," said Mike. "And if you won't allow me to join you yet, can you promise me at least that your cabin door is locked? And can you also tell me what you did with my wet clothes? I think Angela's pills are in the top pocket. I was thinking of my wife Nelly and I remembered that she'd put them there befire we left. They're important and they're in foil."

"My door is locked securely from the inside. I will pass the clothes and pills – you should all take more Stugeron – and then we will make our plans together. I am not dictating."

"You are in such bad trouble, Helen." Angel spoke as one who knew. "Let me have your phone. Before you ring the police I want to send my mum another text. Just to tell her Dad and I're okay and we haven't forgotten the pills."

"Me too," said Luke.

But the texts wouldn't send.

Helen's shoulders slumped. "Then we have drifted too far out to sea. I hoped my course would keep us closer to the land. The barge is slow and flat and she goes sideways. Elsevier won't steer properly."

"It means you can't call the police," said Angel.

"It means we're out here in bad weather in the middle of the night with a couple of lunatics and a stolen lion and there's no way we're going to get help," her father added.

"We think *Royal Katherine* then," said Luke. "Because we're not going to give up and let them take us all the way to Holland."

"This *Royal Katherine* I don't understand."

"Tell her, Dad. Tell her in Dutch. Anything to make it quick."

CHAPTER FIFTEEN

Sole Bay III

Friday 7 November, first of the waxing crescent

Helen

It was so dark. When she had last been up on deck there had been the loom of lighthouses to remind her of the comforting existence of the land. After Orfordness had come Southwold. The little town that she and her mother had visited when they first came over to England.

It had been August. There had been a holiday feeling about the small streets full of visitors and the people actually queuing for entrance to the white-painted lighthouse and the unobtrusive museum. Helen had felt not uncheerful. She hadn't understood, then, how long they would be staying in England nor precisely why they had come. All Hendrike had said that they were on a mission to bring back something that was so important that the Rijksmuseum would beg her to work for them again.

Helen had never liked being in England. Of course not. But she wasn't missing school on the day they went to Southwold and she was glad to be away from Amsterdam and have her mother to herself for a while, without Elsevier. This day out by train and bus to visit the site of the battle was something that almost any mother and daughter might have done if one of them had such an overwhelming interest. She knew her mother was a dedicated researcher. Admired her skill and single-mindedness.

She only didn't like most of the things her mother found.

They'd walked across a small bridge and along to the sand dunes at the mouth of the river until they could see the length of Sole Bay and gloat over the complacency of the English and French who had allowed themselves to be caught so unprepared. The horizon had been hazy in the summer heat, the sea almost viscous in its lapping calm. The few yachts that were attempting to sail drifted slackly with the tide.

Helen had looked carefully at the maps in the museum which showed how this coast had filled and flattened over time. She had thought about shoals and sea drift as she stood on the beach in the sun and she had tried not to listen to her mother as she conjured up the smoke and the guns and the killing.

It had been such a beautiful day. The sea like milk. It was impossible not to imagine the early morning of the battle. The alarm bells ringing in the little town, the sailors being hurried back to their ships. Away to kill and be killed.

"And even the foam was tinged with blood," Hendrike kept repeating, as they stood together on the summer beach. Helen thought her mother should have been sad about this but it was more as if she was excited.

That was the moment she had begun to feel frightened. Her friends would be packing tents and picnics, spending whole days in Amstelveen beside their favourite lake. She had gazed towards the horizon and wondered how long it would take her to row across to Holland.

Southwold had struggled in the months after the Battle of Sole Bay. There'd been eight hundred wounded sailors in a town where there were only one hundred and fifty-three households.

In the museum she'd read a copy of a notice from the Southwold town clerk, after the battle in 1672. He'd offered one shilling to anyone who found and buried the body of a dead sailor. Helen wondered how much he'd had to pay out? She shrank back from the water lapping gently against the sand. It felt tainted.

This November night was completely overcast. No moon nor stars, no cloud shapes nor streaks of grey against the black. No twinkling navigation marks.

It was cold too. Nothing had hindered or diverted this north wind as it had come blowing down from – the Arctic? It drove the rain against *Drie Vrouwen*'s spray hood as relentlessly if it were generated by a machine. The swell was unremitting and the barge was struggling as she laboured up one side of each rolling wave-mound and slid ungracefully down the next.

It was two in the morning. They had left the creek more than half a day ago. Fourteen hours motoring in tough conditions. She wondered whether the Kapitein had remembered to switch the diesel tanks. She doubted it.

There was no automatic steering on *Drie Vrouwen*. The tiller had been lashed in position and Elsevier slouched in the corner with her hat pulled down over her face and a velvet cushion behind her. Two stone geneva bottles rolled empty at her feet and only the glow of the constant cigar warned Helen that she was still awake.

Helen looked at their track on the chart-plotter. Their progress was painfully slow but they would soon be approaching the first of the deep water shipping lanes. She needed to act – for all their sakes.

"Where is my mother please?" she asked.

"The cow is on the cabin roof. The covers have blown from the lion and she rides it like a Valkyrie."

The long line which she'd stolen to lash the trophy to the roof had disappeared on the night of the fire. Helen had attached the bundle to the rails as securely she could by tying knots directly from the eyelets round the edge of the tarpaulin. If the tarpaulin had come off, how was the prize secured?

"I have a problem, Kapitein. There is water over the cabin floor. A leak perhaps from the moment that we struck the shoal? I have pumped, of course, but I can't keep up any more. The man would help if we threaten his daughter. They are sleeping now. They will be shocked to submission if we wake them."

It had seemed like such a simple plan when the four of them had been talking. Make holes in the fresh water tank to flood the floor and get either of the lunatics down to enforce obedience. Then jump them. Hit them on the head. Slam them in the side cabin and lock the door.

Luke was waiting with the runestone. He had promised that if it was her mother he had to cosh, he'd try not to remember what she'd wanted to do to his dad. There were no restrictions if Elsevier was the likely victim.

Up here in the wet and wind-blown night the plan was juvenile. Adventure story stuff.

Elsevier took a long drag on her cigar. "Why should I care? So the carpets get spoiled. So the mutineers get wet feet. So they catch cold and die? What's it to me."

"The extra water slows the ship. At best it will delay our arrival. At worst she may sink."

Elsevier pulled out the gun and shot a hole in the spray hood.

"Get the cow to deal with it," she said. Her voice was slurred. She was very drunk and therefore dangerous.

Helen wished she'd never got involved in anything so idiotic. She could hear scraps of wild singing coming from the cabin top. Her mother was up there with the *Stavoren* lion that she'd identified and traced and stolen. She was bringing it home to the country where it had been made. It meant so much to her, this old relic. She wouldn't feel the weather. She'd be way back in the seventeenth century, returning with her prize, restoring the glory days.

And now her dutiful daughter was going to try and lure her below so that Luke, who hated her, could hit her on the head.

Hendrike would be safer if she was shut away. They'd used the side cabin before when she'd been out of her mind.

They'd all be safer.

Luke wouldn't hit hard. If she and the others could get control of the barge and take the carving back to England, she could explain to the authorities that the heist was a gesture that went too far. She could help them understand her mother's obsession – and her illness. She'd point to Elsevier as the criminal master mind.

Mike and the others would back her up. She wasn't on her own anymore.

Elsevier would be taken away and her mother would be sent to a hospital. Helen didn't know where she would live or go to school. Nothing could be worse than these last months when the cockerel had been her only friend.

Reluctantly she eased herself round the edge of the spray hood and onto the narrow side deck. She did as Luke had done.

She got down and crawled. The waves were growing wilder and less predictable. Maybe the tide had turned again or there could already be wash from the big ships travelling fast along the deep water lanes. Visibility was minimal in this rain-soaked air.

Helen had good balance. She was at ease with water from her rowing and she'd lived on *Drie Vrouwen* all summer. She'd already done this crossing once.

Her own fear shocked her as she inched forward.

The barge was at an angle to the swell. They couldn't risk her getting across the waves again – as she had when Elsevier turned her eastwards.

Helen's instinct had told her that they could make the most of her length, weight and comparative lack of resistance by skilful hand-steering. But the Kapitein had lashed the tiller and chosen to get drunk.

Drie Vrouwen's sliding motion was becoming uncontrolled. It wouldn't be long before she'd swivel broadside and lie trapped in a wave trough waiting for capsize.

There was the single guard wire on the seaward side of the deck, no sheets or jackstays lying along the flat surface and nothing to hold onto beyond the spray hood or the cabin structure. They had no life jackets, no harnesses and nothing to assist a rescue if anyone went over the side. The inflatable dinghy was hidden in the forepeak: Luke's elderly kayak was wedged underneath the forward bulwarks. She'd pulled it on board to avoid leaving it abandoned in the Deben but it wouldn't work as any sort of life raft. Not in these seas.

She had to reach her mother. She got down onto her stomach and wriggled.

The wind hit harder as she reached the low cabin top. There was some light here, leaking from the thick glass panels in the roof of the saloon. They'd been concealed beneath the tarpaulin but the tarpaulin had gone. The light gleamed crimson on the gloss paint of the carving and diffused upwards until it was lost in the night.

There was a low metal rail welded to the roof. Helen ran her hands along the rail as far as she could reach. The only cords she could feel had snapped or had been cut. They were attached to nothing.

She was glad of that rail. She gripped it tightly with her left hand while she pulled herself up and felt for the prize.

The barge lurched. The lion crashed across the cabin top. Helen whipped her fingers out of the way and flattened herself to the deck again. As she glanced upwards to check that it wasn't coming all the way over, the light shone fleetingly on its strong, dark breastplate and the curve of its crimson tail where it tapered into sea-creature.

It looked alive and ready to attack.

Helen lay where she was until the barge plunged downwards once again and the monster slid in the opposite direction. She refused to believe that it had snarled.

Safe to sit up again? Hold onto the rail again and take another look?

The red lion had shifted from its crosswise position. It was working its way round to lie parallel to the ship's movement. Once it reached that point it would have the freedom to roll instead of slide.

There was her mother's leg in her clog and knitted sock

and long wet dress. Further up and the light reflected off her mother's stiff, black oilskin. She was, as Elsevier had said, riding the lion.

It was clear that there was nothing connecting the trophy to the barge except its own weight and that of her mother. Plus those low metal rails which it hit every time it slid sideways. Helen could see that the one closest to her was already buckled.

The cabin top started to tip in her direction once again as *Drie Vrouwen* heaved herself up the next big wave. Helen lay flat and wriggled forward as swiftly as she dared. Then she sat up again and gazed back at her mother.

Hendrike hadn't noticed her. She was gripping the lion between her legs and holding out her arms like wings. Her white hair must surely be drenched yet, as the light caught it streaming in the wind and rain, it gleamed as pale as spindrift.

And she was singing. Helen had never heard her mother sing before. Chanting, drumming, wailing yes – but this sounded like something very old…and beautiful.

"Probably believes she's been transformed into some kind of mythical water-creature," thought Helen bitterly. It hurt to see her mother so blissful. There was so much to worry about. So many practical things: fuel levels, steering every wave correctly, crossing the shipping lanes in poor visibility with no navigation lights, the fate of their prisoners. Yet her mother was away with the sea-nymphs, riding the storm and singing.

Those tears again. Hot, angry tears that no-one would ever know she'd shed. Tears of impotence and rejection and despair. Tears of hatred, even. Her mother had forgotten that she was a woman with a teenage daughter who had loved her. She saw

Helen, when she saw her at all, merely as an assistant. She had transferred her devotion to Elsevier, who fed her drugs and despised her. Elsevier, who had stolen Hendrike's meticulous, misguided, historical research and was going to dump her as soon as they were back within range of a press conference.

Singing!

Te deum laudamus. Her mother was in ecstasy. She loved the lion of the *Stavoren* and all it represented. She was happier in this moment than she'd ever been in her life, probably. Happier, certainly, than she'd ever be again.

A huge wave hit them. Bigger than anything they'd felt yet.

They were near the deep water route. Some gigantic vessel must have passed unseen. This was its wash, first of the twin lines of cresting waves that had fanned out in its wake.

The lion slid backwards and hit the raised area of the cabin top, twisting with the force of its recoil.

Hendrike leaned forward and flung her arms around its neck. The figurehead swung parallel with the line of the boat. The low rails wouldn't impede it any longer.

Drie Vrouwen hung on the brow of the wave.

Helen pulled herself as far out of the way as she could. Her eyes met her mother's. They locked. There was recognition.

"Mother!" shouted Helen.

"Goodbye my daughter! May the Great God always bless you!" Hendrike shouted back.

Then she wrapped herself more tightly to the lion and stared out into the pit of the waves.

The barge plunged down the precipice. The lion and Hendrike flew off on a course of their own. Deep into the lightless ocean.

Drie Vrouwen's bow hit the water as hard as if as if it were solid. There was spray cascading everywhere. Helen could only cling, white-knuckled. She couldn't see at all.

There were crashes and dim screams from below deck.

Then she felt *Drie Vrouwen* climb the second wave. She didn't think they could survive another.

There was water pooling everywhere. It had surged over the cabin top and down the side decks and was cascading back into the sea.

Helen dragged herself up and sprinted for the cockpit, her trainers splashing in the stream. She couldn't be bothered with handholds. The hammering rain was no more that an irritant. She'd lost her fear.

The spray hood had been wrenched half-off by the force of the water pouring over the barge but there was Elsevier still. She was balanced on the aft deck using both hands to pull her ridiculous hat back on. She had made no effort to unlash the helm or turn the ship. Probably hadn't even pressed the Man Overboard button.

"God damn the bloody cow," she shouted when she saw Helen. "She's lost my prize."

Helen stopped. She remembered her mother as she'd last seen her.

In ecstasy.

She remembered that she'd been recognised and blessed.

If that freak wave had been a big ship's wash they would hit the far side in a moment. There'd be another huge, destabilising lurch. Even through the rain and the night she could see it coming, white water foaming along its crest.

Elsevier stood on the exposed aft deck shaking her fist after Hendrike. She was oblivious to danger. Helen stepped forward and pressed the Man Overboard button on the plotter. Then she turned to face the Kapitein.

There would be a body overboard – though it wouldn't be a man's.

✦ ✦ ✦

The rain had stopped before sunrise. The wet sun struggled through torn clouds staining them blood red. There was a mast coming over the horizon – two masts, three masts with cream sails reefed from this night of heavy weather.

The people on board the sailing vessel were anxious. Where in the wide sea would they find a single motor barge? How fast would she be travelling? How far could she have gone?

The harbourmaster at the mouth of the River Deben had noticed a Dutch barge in trouble on the bar. He'd been about to go out in his launch and investigate when she'd freed herself and had set off northwards. The heaped shingle on the Bawdsey side made it impossible for him to see any more once she'd changed course by the Woodbridge Haven so he'd phoned a fisherman who lived further up the coast and asked him to keep an eye out to sea. People who were that reckless to set out over the Deben bar on a spring ebb, with the forecast as bad as it was, might, in the harbourmaster's opinion, be so pig-ignorant that they'd try entering the River Ore against the tide – once they'd discovered how rough it were going to be around the corner there.

The fisherman rang back almost two hours later. The barge

had come inside the Whiting Bank but had carried on past Orfordness despite the fading light and worsening conditions. The harbourmaster informed the coastguard who tried to make contact with the vessel using VHF. There was no response.

Enquiries at Fynn Creek, where there was now a police investigation, had established that the barge, *Drie Vrouwen*, had originally come from Amsterdam and was likely to be returning there. A confused old man had been trying to tell officers a story about something or somewhere named *Stavoren*. Police established that Stavoren was a small town off the IJsselmeer in northern Holland. The farmer who was caring for the old man expressed surprise that he'd managed to remember this single word. He wasn't usually good on names.

If the barge was going north up the coast to Lowestoft she'd probably be all right unless she got herself into trouble on the shoals. If she was attempting to cross eastwards – either to Amsterdam or, indeed, further north towards the IJsselmeer – she was going to find conditions extremely challenging. The coastguard agreed to stand a listening watch and put out an alert to any other vessels in the area. No search operation was thought practicable before first light – especially as no request for help had been received.

The people on the sailing vessel couldn't wait that long. They blamed themselves for not phoning ahead. They'd been planning to surprise their friend but they'd arrived too late to get into Fynn Creek. They'd anchored further down the river then had been shocked by a text message from his sister to tell them he was missing.

They'd seen the black Dutch barge, they realised. Waved to it even.

Donny, Maggi, Xanthe and Skye knew that they were trapped inside the River Deben for the rest of that tide but they sailed for Bawdsey anyway and talked to the harbourmaster.

It was easy to reef a sea-going junk and there were enough experienced sailors on board for them to organise a watch system. It was equally easy to shake some of the reefs out again and press ahead when they saw the barge they'd been searching for. She was lying head to wind and stationary. Or she could have been moving ahead very, very slowly.

After that single moment of relief, the anxiety was almost worse for the length of time it was taking them to reach her. They failed to get any response either by radio or phone. They wanted to shout or blow a foghorn but of course they were too far away.

The whole situation made them jumpy. Luke wouldn't have set off for Holland on a whim, however much he wanted adventure. Or would he?

"He's only twelve."

"And a boy."

"I resent that," said Donny. "And anyway," he added quickly, "Anna was certain he hadn't written the text himself. Too coherent, she said."

Xanthe and Maggi exchanged glances.

"We could maybe run up some flags? Use the dragon to get attention. If Luke's on board he'll understand."

"And if he can't? If he's … some sort of prisoner?"

"Anyone else will simply think that we're eccentric."

"Eccentric?" exclaimed Xanthe, looking at their sturdy

bamboo masts and the three broad battened sails, close-hauled to the morning breeze. "Doesn't everyone sail pirate-built Chinese junks off the coast of Suffolk in November?"

"The person we saw earlier didn't look like she'd have given us the time of day if we were the front page feature in *Classic Boat*."

"Did you see her hat! And I think she might even have been wearing some sort of cloak. She was far worse than eccentric – she was skulduggerous!"

None of them really want to talk or make jokes. They were desperate to reach the barge and discover for themselves what had happened. Skye, Donny's mother, had fetched an armful of flags from the cabin locker and was spreading them wordlessly on the bridge deck.

"Here's the dragon," said Maggi. "We'll use that. Do we want add anything? Like a message?"

"Threaten them with U? Red and white quarters? 'You are running into danger.' What about X? Blue cross, white background? 'Stop carrying out your intentions and wait for my signals.'"

"Yeah, brill, Xanthe, 100% guaranteed to make them push the throttle down if they've anything to hide. I don't know why they're dawdling atm but we deffo want them to stay that way."

"Okay, okay, point taken. No need to go on. We'll use K – yellow and blue vertical stripes – 'I wish to communicate with you.' Happy now? The International Code hasn't got a flag for 'pretty please'."

They were all of them tense and trying not to snap. It was seven o'clock in the morning. The tide had turned an hour ago and the waves were large but smooth and regular again. The air felt wet and the sky was full of clouds.

Skye had the best eyesight of them all so she was concentrating on the barge. Donny was steering and the two girls were scanning the surface of the sea. It had become a habit. You never knew what you might come across; a baulk of timber, a breakaway length of net, a metal container …

They didn't admit their fears. Not even to each other. Just kept that extra lookout.

Maggi moved towards her sister. She touched her arm and pointed. There was something in the distance being lifted up and over the swell. Something that disturbed the surface of the water but only rarely broke it.

Then Skye began signing. She was too fast for the girls to understand so Donny translated.

"She says there's a kayak being launched from the barge. A child getting in."

CHAPTER SIXTEEN

Sole Bay IV
Friday 7 November, first of the waxing crescent

Angel, Luke

Angel would never forget Helen's call for help in the lightless early morning.

"Come quickly please. I need friends. They haf all gone."

The three of them were hidden, waiting for Elsevier or Hendrike to come down the companion way. They were ready to jump them, hit them, push them into the side cabin and lock the door.

They were frightened. There'd been those two gut-wrenching leaps when lockers had burst open and plates had flown spinning from their racks. Then, just as they were picking themselves up and getting back into their positions, there'd been a third destabilising crash.

Helen shouted again, desperation in her voice. "No more *Royal Katherine*. Help me. Please."

The barge was surrounded by the deepest darkness Angel had ever known. Not even a hint of dawn visible through the driving rain. The spray hood had gone so there was no shelter. Nothing but the surging water either side and the thick rain pouring down.

Helen had switched on *Drie Vrouwen*'s navigation lights. They made puddles in the dark: red to port and green to starboard. There was some light from the open door of the cabin, some light from the compass and the chart-plotter. Enough to show them Helen's blonde hair loose and whipping in the wind and her face so gaunt that Angel could see every bone of her skull.

"My mother and the lion. They haf flown into the sea. The Kapitein went after."

It seemed terrible that she should have to say such things in a language that wasn't her own.

"Gone overboard! We should be searching! Where are your torches?"

"I don't think so. It's too dark. And you look at the sea. We can't come round in it."

"Oh Helen!"

"You will help me?"

"That's such a no-brainer," rushed Angel.

"Of course we will," said her father. "You can rely on us completely."

Then Mike switched language and began to speak in Dutch and Helen began to cry. It was extraordinary how she stood there sobbing in the windy darkness, helming carefully into each oncoming wave – mainly by feel as she couldn't see them until *Drie Vrouwen*'s bow was already reaching skywards. She'd slowed the engine revs right down, but those big waves kept coming and the cockpit was so open without the canvas cover.

Angel hung on to the nearest bit of solid boat and looked around her. She was trying to understand. There were two people out there in the cold sea. They must be dying or dead.

Her dad was still talking but she sensed he was probably repeating himself. What could anyone say that would be right in this situation?

"Helen," said Luke. "I think I can steer. Just show me what you want."

She stopped crying for a moment and looked at him, surprised.

"I've been on boats before, with my friends. I mean they usually did everything but I had a go. My friend Donny showed me how. And I helmed this one before for a while with…Elsevier."

He couldn't pretend he was sorry that Elsie was gone. He didn't understand exactly what Helen said had happened but he'd save asking her for later.

"My friends had a VHF radio to call for help. We could send a Mayday. Don't you have one?"

"We d-did. The K-kapitein tore out the wires when she f-found they were c-connected to the s-satellite."

Helen had controlled her tears but she was shaking with cold – or maybe it was shock. Same thing probably. Angel really wanted her to come down to the cabin. She was going to make them all drinks and help Helen get warm. She'd zipped her own jacket right up to the top and had shoved her free hand deep into her pocket. She could feel the other going blue but she needed it to hang on with.

Luke was listening intently as Helen told him about the speed and the course and not getting near the section of the chartplotter that showed the navigation lanes. She'd recorded their position at the time of the tragedy and was trying to explain, through her chattering teeth, that their only hope of finding the bodies was to continue to motor, very slowly, in the direction of the tide.

"It w-will be t-taking them a-w-way to the n-north. But

at w-what speed I am n-not sure. I am only w-waiting for the l-light. Perhaps a c-couple hours?"

They found Luke an oilskin and gloves and a waterproof hat and Helen tied a rope around his waist and found somewhere to fix it. She was shaking all the time she did these things.

"I haf no f-family at all," she kept saying. "There is n-no-one." She showed them the point on the chart where she'd pressed the MOB button. "It l-looks as if we are l-leaving them b-but I am t-t-trying to stay c-close."

Angel made the drinks then and her dad did his best to help. They weren't neither of them good in the kitchen at the best of times and when it kept on heaving up and down and swinging sideways as this one did, even four cups half full of tea felt like a big success.

"More tea!" said Luke, swigging it back. He seemed to have got his balance really well. Her dad had found a waterproof and was offering to join him though to be honest, it wasn't clear what he would be able to do.

She asked Helen where there were dry clothes and blankets and persuaded her to get changed out of her wet things. Then, very daring, she asked whether she'd like her to hold her hand while she settled in her bunk to sleep.

Helen carried on auto-crying for a while and Angel sat next to her. She'd never exactly seen the point of sleep. Now it seemed the best and kindest thing. She hoped that Helen would sleep undisturbed for weeks.

When there were no more hiccuppy sobs, Angel found as many layers of clothing as she could for herself and went to keep Luke company. She told her dad he could go back into the cabin.

She'd even put on the buoyancy aid that she'd used in the kayak though she could see that would be useless in such heavy seas.

Mike tried not to look relieved. He promised that he'd keep checking on Helen. Then he started rummaging in the cupboard where Luke had found the boxes and all those files. He pulled out a stack of papers and said he'd keep himself busy looking through them. He was interested in Hendrike's research.

"Talk about obsessive!" Angel thought.

The new day dawned so slowly. There was a paleness in the sky to their right – which Luke said was the east – and then, gradually, each individual wave seemed to take shape again. The rain had drizzled to a halt but the sun, when it finally appeared, was big and red and still partly covered by thick grey cloud.

Angel realised that, if there was anything close enough to see, they would now be able to see it. Helen told them to wake her as soon as it was light. It wasn't a moment Angel was looking forward to.

Luke was looking ahead all the time, and at the compass and the chart-plotter, fixated on keeping his course. He had no idea that there was a boat with masts quite a long way behind them. Or that there was something…floating…over to their left.

"There's something over there," she said, feeling queasy for the first time. "I think it could be…Can you go that way?"

"Yeah, probably, but it's right off Helen's course. I s'pose we ought to fetch her. Or your dad?"

"But what if it's…you know…her mum? I think we should check it out first ourselves."

"She'll feel it if I change direction. It'll wake her anyway."

He knew that he desperately didn't want to see…whatever it was. That the nightmares would begin again.

Angel was on tiptoe, really staring. The thing was mainly under the water. It couldn't be alive. And it wasn't that far off.

"We could call Dad but he'll fuss."

"Well, yeah. I mean, why not? Anyone would."

"And that'll wake Helen. Think about it Luke, your mum's dead body. It's got to be everyone's worst nightmare."

She didn't notice that he couldn't answer. She was completely fired up.

"I'm going to get in the kayak and check it out. It's really near and we could be worrying about nothing."

"You can't! You absolutely can't! It's dangerous. And what if it's Elsie?"

"It's not alive whatever. And I was only scared when she had that gun."

"Well, what if you, you know, start fitting again?"

"Helen found my pills and they weren't even wet. I'm going and you can't stop me. The waves are way better now and if the floater's nothing to do with us, then think how we've saved Helen's feelings."

Luke didn't know what to think. Bodies. His mum and his dad in those tip-up hospital beds. That container that he and the others had found, caught on the sand off the Desolate Shores. Mike's description of the Sole Bay Battle. He'd caught himself wondering whether any of that blood could still be there in the water washing round them – diluted hundreds of thousands of times. They weren't that far away from the site.

Angel didn't wait to wonder why he didn't speak. She'd gone

running up to the foredeck and had the kayak over the side and streaming beside them before he could find a word.

"Look how easily it moves. I'm really going to be cool," she said climbing so nimbly over the guard rail and taking the paddle with her.

Drie Vrouwen was going up: the kayak dropping down. How did she do it? She was amazing but she was completely stupid. No wonder her parents panicked about her. That fiery red hair and her gold-brown eyes blazing with delight.

"Angel, no," he began.

But she had gone.

And then *Drie Vrouwen*'s engine stopped.

+ + +

"I've called the coastguard. I've told them that we've seen the barge. And I've told them about the kayak as well."

"And the Thing?"

"That too."

"I'm putting her about now. We should be going for the kid."

"They wanted to scramble the helicopter but it won't come close until we tell them that he's safe."

"He?" Donny queried as the three sails swung across and *Strong Winds* settled to her new course.

"Only one person I ever knew stupid enough to go over the side in cold water and a heavy sea and he was male, Donny-man."

Donny shut up. He wished he could coax a few more knots of speed out of the junk but the tide was running hard against her. It would be pushing the kayak and the Thing in their direction.

He hoped his boat-handling was going to be accurate enough to pick them up without swamping or collision.

"Will the coastguard get in touch with Lottie and Anna? Tell them at least that we're in sight of the barge?"

"Yup. And they're in contact with the mum of the other one as well."

"You mean the girl Anna mentioned – called Angela or something? The one with the dad?"

"That's who I mean."

"And there was another girl on board – Grace Everson said – a Dutch one.

"A Dutch GIRL. Do you hear what you're saying, Maggi?"

"Oh okay. So you double-xs might not have a monopoly on crazy stunts. Now shut up and sail. I'm going to fetch some binoculars."

"You know," she said after a while. "That is a girl. And she's totally awesome. She's like surfing the waves. I'm not sure we're going to reach the Thing before she does."

"Or it's going to reach us." The older sister's voice had none of its usual warmth.

"What is it, Mum?" Donny had developed a way of steering the junk with the crook of his leg so he could use both hands to talk. "Can you see it yet? Do you think the Thing could be a body?"

Skye, who'd been watching without speaking, signed back to him and he passed her answer to the others.

"Mum's not sure. She doesn't think that it's human. It may be only a large lump of wood but there's something strange about it. It keeps turning in the waves."

"Not the sort of thing you'd want to hit if you were in a plastic kayak then." It was a statement not a question.

"So why isn't the barge going after her?"

✦ ✦ ✦

Angel had always been rubbish at assessing Risk. Everyone who'd ever written a report on her said that. This time what she hadn't worked out was how difficult it was going to be to see the floater once she was down at the level of the waves herself.

The paddling was sensational; powering up and over the big smooth waves. She wished she could do this for ever. The difficulty was the floater being up on the top of a wave at the same time she was. Because usually it wasn't.

And as she got further away from the barge it began to be hard to see that either, not reliably. Especially when she could only twist and glance behind her.

She realised that she'd made another of her terrible mistakes. Should she try to turn back? Would Luke follow?

All the same it was brilliant fun. She discovered she could flatten her paddle behind her and use it to steer the kayak and control its speed down the sides of the waves. Then it took all her strength and all her concentration to climb the next slope. She worked out her technique: exactly how she should be stretching forward from her hips to place one blade in the water and drive it backwards along the side of the boat while she rotated her body and stretched again for the other blade to follow in a smooth continuous flow.

She savoured each magic moment poised on top of the

water-mountains, looking urgently ahead to spot the floater or glancing backwards over her shoulder to check on the barge before accelerating again down the steep slopes ahead of her, like the surfers she'd seen in films.

She'd pulled the skirt thing round her waist so there wasn't any water coming in and if she'd only known where she was headed, or what she'd find if she got there – she'd have been completely happy.

Angel vanished in a wave trough and Luke had lost power. For a moment he thought of Reepicheep, the mad Narnian mouse who set off to paddle for the end of the world.

What had happened to *Drie Vrouwen*'s engine? Since they'd all come on board at the Fynn Creek moorings – it felt like a lifetime ago but wasn't quite a day – its noise had been a constant part of their existence. Chugging steadily as they'd motored down the Deben, roaring when the barge was stuck on the bar, labouring as it drove her into the wind and rain and up the massive waves. Now there was nothing.

Luke couldn't hold the barge on her course, her head was slipping round. In a moment she would begin to roll.

Why didn't someone come and help? Maybe Helen was so traumatised she couldn't wake but Mike must surely wonder what had happened? Luke was still attached to Helen's make-shift harness but he got as close as he could to the top of the companionway and shouted down.

There wasn't any answer.

So it was up to him to work out what had happened and to fix it. But he couldn't.

But he had to.

The silence was bizarre. Nothing but the slap of the waves against the barge's sides and the sound of objects sliding in new ways. *Drie Vrouwen* was worse than rolling, she was wallowing.

It was odd how this silence made him think of cars. Car engines when you turned them off: Lottie's car which was so quiet that you hardly knew when it was on. Was there any chance that *Drie Vrouwen*'s engine could still be on without making any noise? Luke went back to the tiller and pushed it, experimentally.

There was no feeling of leverage and no response from the barge. The swell was big but smooth. The light was good. The wind and rain had died. Luke didn't think he was in imminent danger. He was well away from any shoals and the barge didn't feel like she was going to roll three-sixty. Not like before.

He wasn't in danger but Angel could be. Crazy lion-mouse Angel.

Cars. Fuel. Lottie's car was quiet because it was a hybrid. It had an electric battery as well as petrol.

The boats Luke knew didn't work like that. He guessed *Drie Vrouwen* would have diesel. *Lowestoft Lass* did. And *Strong Winds*. She'd have lots of diesel if they were going all the way to Holland.

But if you were playing a game and you hadn't been checking your scores you could unexpectedly lose power. A light would have come on or something, wouldn't it? Like in a car?

Luke looked hard at the row of gauges that were mounted on the side of the cabin opposite the chart-plotter and the compass. There was a red light. But that was next to the ignition key so it was most likely telling him that the engine had stopped.

Well, duh! he reckoned he knew that.

A splosh of cold wave slopped over the side and slapped him on the side of his head.

There were two round black gauges with simple white needles that had probably been luminous in the dark – except that he been so busy staring at the plotter that he hadn't bothered to look at them. One needle was far over towards the right, 'vol': the other flat down into a red zone, 'leeg'.

Luke didn't need a translator. He was looking at one thing that was empty and another full: 'dagtank' and 'hoofdtank'. Someone had used one of those machines that did raised lettering on sticky plastic strips. Luke felt a moment of pure love for the person who had made those labels.

Drie Vrouwen did another hundred and something degree roll. Luke's stomach heaved and he remembered that terrible time in the night when her ship's bell had started to ring like a tocsin.

Angel! Crazy lion-mouse, wild-cat Angel! He needed to get after her.

If there were two tanks and one was empty and the other one full, you must be able to switch between them. Luke clicked on a small metal lever about half an inch long, sited above the two gauges. There was a sort of distant hydraulic noise and the needle in the 'dagtank' began lifting itself slowly out from the red zone.

He had never seen anything so beautiful.

He waited until the needle was almost up to 'vol' and then he switched off. Scarcely daring to breathe he pushed the throttle forward as Helen had shown him and turned the ignition key.

Tgg – tgg – tgg. Please *Drie Vrouwen*, please!

Oh yes! And he was back at the helm and turning her into the waves. Angel!

Where was she? She been gone…it felt like hours. Disorientation. The empty sea. Which way should he go?

And then he saw the three masts of *Strong Winds* and her streaming dragon flag.

✦ ✦ ✦

The lion looked up at Angel as she swung the kayak through 90 degrees to lie alongside it. This was the first time they'd been close.

The lion's eyes were blank and its mouth was full of the cloudy seawater. Its red paint, dull beneath the surface, made her think of blood and she realised how horrible this moment would have been if she had discovered a human body.

There were two human bodies, she remembered. Probably somewhere close by. She hadn't thought at all what she'd been doing when she set off. She was an idiot – just like everyone always said she was.

Angel feathered her blade to hold the kayak steady as she and the lion were lifted up towards the summit of another wave. She could see its wooden teeth and claws and flaring nostrils … but then they were over the top and it rolled exhaustedly away.

"Old and tired and ready to die." She could hear her father saying that in one of his talks. The lion's magnificent mane had come up from the sea as it turned over. Then it was gone and the next thing that she saw was the plain, flat surface where it would have been bolted to the front end of a warship – or to the outside wall of a pub.

Angel and the lion were floating together with the tide. The carving moved more heavily than the kayak so she didn't find it at all difficult to avoid collision.

She wasn't going to beat herself up anymore for being stupid. There'd always be someone else to do that. She was going to stay beside the Lion of Sole Bay for however long it took. It wouldn't be alone any more.

Strong Winds took the lion under tow and Angel said goodbye. Once Luke had arrived, steering *Drie Vrouwen*, she agreed to go back to the barge in case Helen might wake and need her.

Xanthe rigged the Mirror dinghy, Lively Lady, and came across to join them. She brought a portable VHF with her and used it to transmit the MOB reading to the search and rescue team. The Southwold lifeboat passed the two boats as they headed west and they could hear the noise of approaching helicopters

In fact Helen never stirred and it was Luke who took *Drie Vrouwen* into his own home port of Lowestoft.

"Harwich might have been neater. That's where the *Stavoren* was taken and the *Royal Katherine* and all those Dutch prisoners."

"Possibly a good reason to be somewhere else," suggested Mike.

"Yeah, Luke," said Angel. "Helen's our friend, not our prisoner."

"S'pose so." Luke had been thinking about Helen; what precisely she'd said and when.

"As it happens," said Mike. "The figurehead's been here before. Helen's mother's notes document the *Stavoren* being present at the Battle of Lowestoft in 1665 – although that was a Dutch defeat. Fascinating stuff in those boxes. Primary source material."

"So while Luke and your daughter were battling the high seas, you were checking source material?" said Xanthe, trying to keep the amazement out of her voice. "I mean I do think history's totally awesome but …"

Mike pulled his straggly beard and looked awkward. "I hoped that I was doing something that might be useful to Mejuffrow de Witt. I was only occasionally distracted. I'm sorry, Luke, that I didn't hear you when you called."

"Am I getting this or not?" Xanthe wasn't easily put off. "This Helen – who I haven't met – is about fourteen years old. She's lost her mother and her mother's friend in a single night. She'll probably be charged with involvement in criminal activity and she has no known family to help her. I'm sure she'll be well-chuffed to know the away match score from the Battle of Lowestoft, 1665 – particularly when her side lost!"

"I wasn't searching for those reasons." Mike's professional pride was hurt. "Her mother claimed to have traced their direct descent from Johan de Witt (d.1672), who was the Grand Pensionary of the United Provinces from 1652. It's an axiom of family research that you must start with the known facts – the evidence of the generations closest to you – before working backwards to the unknown. Hendrike de Witt was a good researcher. I was looking for her starting points."

"I'm sorry," said Xanthe. "I was out of order."

"So come on, Dad, what did you find?"

"I found names, birth dates and contact details for Hendrike's birth family. I also found letters which her parents had continued to write to her during all the years since she left home to study art history in Amsterdam and fell pregnant with Helen."

"Do they know then, her parents – about Helen?"

"Hendrike had kept her daughter's existence secret until this year. It seems her parents are conventional farming folk of strict views and she was too ashamed to confess. Finally, when she was about to leave for England to pull off this nationalistic… stunt, she found the courage to tell them."

"And?"

"It seems their views are not so rigid after all. They are longing to meet their granddaughter. They live near the town of Stavoren which is on the IJsselmeer. It seems Hendrike had planned the reconciliation as part of her triumphal return."

"But she never said anything to Helen?"

"No. Her infatuation with Elsevier had a most unfortunate effect. The notes over the most recent period became quite markedly disordered."

"Elsevier!" said Xanthe, "You don't mean the bully on TV who always wears that unbelievable hat and cloak? I knew I'd seen her somewhere! She's the one who wants to be the new Dutch dictator – Wreken de Dame?"

"A disgrace to her name and tradition," said Mike. "The world was a better place when she went over the side."

"We'll never know whether she was trying to rescue the lion or Helen's mother," said Angel.

"No," thought Luke, "We won't."

He remembered precisely what Helen had said in her suddenly shaky English. "My mother and the lion. They haf flown into the sea. The Kapitein went after."

The Kapitein went 'after'. Did Elsie follow *after* Hendrike and the carving – sacrificing herself for them, as Angel so sweetly assumed? It didn't exactly seem in character.

Or did she go 'after' as in *afterwards*, later on in time, in a separate incident?

The MOB button had only been pressed once, by Helen. Helen would know exactly what had happened – and when – but somehow Luke didn't think he was going to ask her.

The death of Elsevier had been the practical answer to all their problems.

And Helen was outstandingly practical.

CHAPTER SEVENTEEN

Remembrance Day

Sunday 9 November, third of the waxing crescent

Luke

"Mike," Luke asked a few days later, when *Drie Vrouwen* and the lion had been left in Lowestoft and he'd sailed home to the River Deben with Donny. "How did you know so much? I mean, you work at Suffolk Archives, which isn't exactly the Maritime Museum, and you've never been to sea in your life."

"No," Mike agreed. "Not in this life I haven't. And probably not in any other but I've always been obsessed with the Van der Veldes. They were seventeenth-century Dutch artists – a father and two sons. The father was there at the Battle of Sole Bay, sketching. He was the official Dutch war artist. Earlier in the 1650s he'd sailed in the *Stavoren* when she was quite a new ship – all the way to the Baltic and the Battle of the Sound.."

"Was he captured at Sole Bay? Was he one of those prisoners in Harwich?"

"No. He wasn't on board the *Stavoren* then. He was in a little boat, a galjoot, dodging about between the great ships as the bombarded each other. But the Battle of Sole Bay did, indirectly, change his life. I suppose I should have mentioned it. It makes me feel awkward."

"Why?"

"After the battle you must remember – the French had

THE LION OF SOLE BAY

invaded, the land was flooded and there was chaos in the United Provinces. It was the beginning of the end of their greatness. Willem III was shrewd and successful but he had to drain the country of money to help him fight the French. The Golden Age was gone."

"Ye-es?"

"Well, the Van der Veldes left the United Provinces later in 1672, after the Battle of Sole Bay and moved to England. King Charles II gave them a really generous salary and good living and working conditions. They had rooms in Greenwich Palace even. Next time there was a battle (in 1673) and old VV went out to sea, he was in a ketch not a galjoot – and he was drawing for the English side."

"You feel bad about that? That's why Elsie shouted at you?"

Mike adjusted his specs and pulled his beard and hid his twisting hands.

"It wasn't only us. In June 1672 King Charles offered an invitation to any Dutch citizen to live and work in England. Lots of artists and craftsmen accepted. They couldn't function in Holland anymore. It had been flooded. It was a war zone. You English gained from us. We brought you so much expertise. For instance, I'm currently researching the whole history of Dutch prisoners. Large numbers of them moved up into Cambridgeshire and helped to drain the Fens. We're good at that sort of thing."

Luke noticed that Mike hadn't answered his question. "You called Helen a collaborator when you were really angry with her. Maybe she should have called you one?"

Mike looked shocked. "Oh no! That would mean I helped the

invader. And that would have been the French. I'd never do that. I mean my ancestor wouldn't. Not that he was really my ancestor."

"Have you done family research as well – like Hendrike?"

"And I can't trace any direct connection. None at all. Except I've always felt I understood old Van der Velde. All he did, all his life, was draw boats. Hundreds and hundreds and hundreds of boats – all sizes. He must have been an obsessive. So when he couldn't draw boats at home anymore, he moved to a country where he could. He drew boats for King Charles, boats for King James and when Dutch Willem came over to England and was crowned King William III, he drew boats for him as well."

"Dad," said Luke, later still on that same Sunday, when it was visiting time again and he was back in the plastic hospital chair beside Bill's bed. "I might be getting interested in family history. I know a bit about the Whitings because they were fishermen and Mr Vandervelde says there were loads of Whitings in Suffolk in the 1670s. There were even some of them living in Southwold when there was the Battle of Sole Bay. Also there's the Whiting Bank and all that. But that's only half of me. I don't know anything about my mum."

Bill looked a bit knocked back. Maybe Luke should have waited a bit until his dad was stronger. Bill kept saying he was all right but the doctors had told Lottie that it would take a long time. Lottie and Anna were already planning how to install special equipment in Bawdsey Manor to make it accessible for Bill.

His dad was shifting himself, trying to get comfortable.

"Not surprising that you want to know. Not that you really need t' ask. You an' your mum! Course I could always see where you got your thinking skills from but it's more than that, since you've grown up a bit. Seems to me, when I look at you sometimes – or I listen to the things you say – that she ain't really dead at all."

Bill's last words came out in a rush and he turned his head away from Luke and into the thin white hospital pillow. There was a bit of a gap before he sorted himself out to carry on.

"She weren't overly practical, your mum, but she did love an adventure and she had such a way with words. Always got some little story for you when you was a baby. Liam too of course, but you was her first."

Luke was getting a bit choked up now. All those words of his mum's must still be inside him somewhere but he couldn't seem to lay a hand on them. Sunk into his memory like water into sand. Maybe he needed a few more facts to fix her with. Things a researcher would ask.

"Where'd she come from Dad and what about her family? Did they live in Suffolk like the Whitings?"

"Hers was an old Dutch family from the Fens. Refugees or prisoners or something but she'd moved down to Suffolk when I met her."

"Where Dad? Where did you two meet?"

"I first met your mum in the Red Lion pub. She was standing outside. Looking up at that sign… "

"Anna, what do you think? Should that Lion of Sole Bay be given back to Holland or go in some museum somewhere?"

"Only if the pub-owner wants it to."

"I just wondered. What would be right? It is really historical."

"Okay, since you're asking – that figurehead was made to show off and look powerful and bully people into fighting each other but, from what you've said, it wasn't all that good at it. The *Stavoren* got damaged, got captured, got damaged again, got broken up. So what the lion's actually spent its lifetime doing – since it stopped being part of a warship – is mark out a place where people come and have a drink together. In the early days, when the Red Lion was a coaching inn, people on long journeys would have been pleased to see that sign because it meant they'd arrived so they and their horses could have a rest. People would have met at the Red Lion to do business: parish business, private business. They probably still do. Or they go and have a beer, eat a meal, meet their friends. Fall in love. Sing shanties. I mean, I'm no fan of shanties, but if it's a choice between them and cannonballs …"

Luke heaved a sigh of relief.

"That's okay then. So now can you give me my Nintendo back?"

The Stavoren, *detail from*
The Dutch Fleet tacking off the North Frisian Islands,
9 October 1658, Willem Van der Velde the Elder,
© *National Maritime Museum, Greenwich, UK.*

Van der Velde was sailing on the *Stavoren* as part of the
Dutch Northern Expedition which led to their victory
at the Battle of the Sound, 29 October 1658.

THE SOLE BAY LECTURES
BY MW VANDERVELDE
NUMBER ONE: ONE FINE SUMMER'S DAY

28 May 1672, Sole Bay, Suffolk

An east wind was a Dutch wind. A light breeze in the early morning haze of a fine summer's day. A wind that would die fitfully throughout the morning leaving the sea 'smooth as a bowl of milk…the fairest day we have seen all this summer before'. This east wind brought Admiral Michiel de Ruyter and seventy-five ships of the United Provinces reaching across the North Sea to Suffolk.

Our Suffolk coast is a lee shore with an east wind blowing. The ninety-three ships of the combined English and French fleets had last seen Admiral de Ruyter more than a week ago dodging in and out of the channels around Oostende and Nieuwpoort, off the coast of Flanders where they couldn't follow him. He'd done his best to use false lights to lure them in but they were wary of the wrecking shoals. And rightly so: their ships were deeper than his and they didn't have the local knowledge.

Now they were lying at anchor in Sole Bay taking on fresh water and provisions. This was a job that took time when you'd 34,000 men to feed.

The French were anchored furthest south – off Dunwich and Aldeburgh – the two English squadrons were off the town of Southwold. Many of the men had spent the night in the alehouses or were busy ferrying supplies. The *Prince*, flagship of the Red squadron, with the King's brother, the Lord High Admiral, James, Duke of York on board, was heeled over onto her side being cleaned. The Lord High Admiral and his entourage had enjoyed a good dinner and a comfortable night ashore.

A fresh breath of east wind in the early hours of the morning brought a scout ship running in, her top-gallant sails flying and her guns firing to sound the alarm. Behind her the horizon was a-prickle with the masts and sails of the Dutch fleet, smugly to windward in the morning light.

The French set off south-east, with the tide but against the wind, struggling to comply with a plan that they would lead the fleet. Meanwhile the Lord High Admiral decided to reverse the order of battle. Both squadrons of English ships set sail north-wards, clawing away from the coast with the wind on their starboard side. Somehow the French didn't get the message. The English were quick to accuse them of treachery and cowardice: the French admiral wrote afterwards that James's orders were unclear because he'd been partying in Southwold. It was the day before his brother, King Charles's, birthday.

The Blue squadron was already the furthest north. It should have brought up the rear but now it was in the vanguard. Admiral of the Blue, the Earl of Sandwich, on board the 100-gun *Royal James,* was old and tired and ready to die. His captain, Richard Haddock, set the headsails, ordered the anchors weighed and set off as briskly as the breeze would allow. The *Royal James* had been anchored in the deeper water furthest from the coast. She was therefore the first to be surrounded by the Dutch.

It was 7 a.m. and the *Royal James* was under heavy attack. She was fighting off two of the three Dutch admirals, their seconds and two fireships. The *Groot Hollandia* was rammed under her bows, struggling to board. The sea around the *Royal James* began to boil with musket shot. More than 250 of the 800 men on board were killed or wounded in the first hour and a half.

The sound of gunfire reverberated across the smooth water and the morning air was dirty with smoke. There was so little wind to blow it away that each ship became its own shrouded island of death and killing. It was hard to tell friend from enemy. Sir John Kempthorne, second in command of the Blue squadron, saw the *Groot Hollandia* grappled against the *Royal James* but thought she was an English ship. 'By reason of the great smoke we could not discern the contrary.' He sailed past.

The Earl of Sandwich sent a message to his next in command, Sir Joseph Jordan, ordering him to come and help. Sometime after ten o'clock that morning the desperate men of the *Royal James* saw Sir Joseph and several smaller ships passing by to windward 'very unkindly'. (Sir Joseph said later that he was under fierce attack himself and that he couldn't properly see what was happening.) They realised that there would be no rescue. They were on their own.

At last, at about twelve o'clock, the tide turned. Captain Haddock had been shot in the foot. His shoe was full of blood and he was going below for treatment when he spotted an opportunity to use the tide to separate the *Royal James* from the *Groot Hollandia*. He ordered a stern anchor to be dropped and told his men to begin cutting the tangle of boarding lines and rigging that bound them to their enemy. The *Royal James* stayed anchored where she was and the *Groot Hollandia* drifted away on the ebb, her decks heaped with dead men.

Captain Haddock carried on giving orders as the surgeons

hacked away at his shattered flesh and tendons. The crew were to hoist the mainsail, pull the anchor up again, get the ship sailing.

There was, however, no final escape for the *Royal James*. A Dutch fireship grappled from the stern and she was set ablaze. Most of the rest of the crew were burned or drowned. No-one who saw the last hours of the *Royal James* ever forgot the sight.

In the centre of the battle the Dutch were attacking the *Prince*, flagship of the Red squadron, with the Lord High Admiral, James Duke of York, on board. Seven ships surrounded her, led by Admiral de Ruyter in his flagship *De Zeven Provinciën*. No help came to the *Prince* as she kept them at bay hour after hour with her heavy guns. Her captain was killed, the main topmast crashed down, the deck was a chaos of rigging and broken spars.

It was impossible to manoeuvre such a badly damaged vessel. The Duke of York shifted himself and his admiral's flag to the *St Michael* and the Dutch attack soon shifted with him. The new captain of the *Prince* ordered rowing boats to begin towing her closer to the rest of the squadron.

Once the tide had turned, around midday, all the combatants were being carried northwards with the ebb. The Duke of York's pilot, who had moved with him to the *St Michael*, warned that they were in danger of running aground on the sands off Lowestoft, 'which were the last words that he spoke for he was immediately slain'. The wind was backing north-east, so both fleets, laboriously, put about and continued to batter each other throughout the afternoon as they sailed slowly south again.

The sound of their guns could be heard for miles; doors and windows shook in their frames but the watchers along the coast could see nothing except smoke and dim shapes. Only the veteran

Dutch war artist, Willem van der Velde, had any wider perspective on the action as he shifted through the fleets in his small galjoot.

By now the *St Michael* had six feet of water in her hold and looked likely to sink. James Duke of York moved once again to the 96-gun HMS *London*.

The battle continued through the long afternoon and into the summer's evening until at last, the sun set and the wind and waves began to rise and Admiral de Ruyter took his fleet back across the North Sea. The English and French followed him, hoping to fight again on the next day or the day after that.

But first there was fog and then the wind blew so strongly that the big ships couldn't use their topsails or roll out their lower tier of guns. They spent a third day at sea, anchored off the Galloper Sand 'in the gusty, cloudy, blowing weather' until their scouts reported that the Dutch were tucked away behind the Oosterbank, one of de Ruyter's favourite 'lurking holes'.

There was nothing more they could do. The wind was blowing north north-east 'a stout gale'. Finally the Duke of York admitted defeat and gave the order to sail back to Sole Bay and the coast of Suffolk.

The Sole Bay Lectures
By MWVandervelde
Number Two: The Butcher's Bill

The most likely estimate of dead and wounded from both sides at the Battle of Sole Bay is about 5,000 men. They would have been all ages and from every social class – from ships' boys to admirals. There' would have been several different nationalities as well. Although the English used the press gang system to man their ships from their own coastal areas, the Dutch recruited seamen from the German ports or from Scandinavia and way up into the Baltic.

Most of the battle had taken place within sight of land. There were bodies washed up on the beaches or found drifting at sea with the tide. The people of Southwold were forbidden to leave the town in case the Dutch were victorious and decided to invade. Clearing the beaches and caring for the wounded was a major problem for weeks afterwards. Suffolk people claimed that even the foam was tinged with blood.

The wreck of the *Royal James* had carried on burning for hours. After the other ships had changed tack and were sailing south, most of them had to sail round her. Admiral de Ruyter picked up a few survivors and when James Duke of York passed by, he saw that the water was full of men swimming around clinging to whatever pieces of timber they could find. He ordered one of the smaller ships in his division to stop and try to rescue them. He couldn't do it himself as whichever ship he was in – the *Prince*, the *St Michael*, the *London* – attracted attackers like iron filings to a magnet.

Captain Haddock of the *Royal James* survived but Admiral the Earl of Sandwich, didn't. He and his son-in-law had climbed into one of the smaller boats which was then capsized by the weight of desperate sailors jumping after them. The admiral's body was discovered ten days later, floating miles out to sea close to the Long Sand Head. It was surrounded by nibbling fish and would have been unrecognisable except for the medals he'd been wearing.

The total casualties after a battle used to be called the Butcher's Bill. The bill for the Battle of Sole Bay was high in terms of money as well as in human life. These 'great ships' were ruinously expensive.

The Dutch hadn't built any new warships for several years and the French were only beginning to develop their fleet. But the English Kings had an addiction to ship-building. The *Royal James* had been the newest in a series of grand and deadly warships. Ironically it had been because King Charles II had spent so much money on his fleet that he'd been forced to go to war.

These 'great ships' were designed to impress – though I can't help thinking how wasteful it was to build such beautifully decorated wooden objects then send them out to sea to smash or burn or sink each other.

The most extravagant ship of all (in my opinion) wasn't at the battle of Sole Bay though she was back in action the following year. She was called the *Sovereign of the Seas* and she'd been built by King Charles I of England – the father of King Charles II. Charles I believed he was appointed by God to rule over land and sea and had demanded a flagship to express this. Every exterior surface of the *Sovereign of the Seas* was smothered in decoration. Charles had employed his court painter, his theatre designer and dozens of artists and craftsmen to make her magnificent.

The *Sovereign of the Seas* wasn't just a floating showcase: she was deadly. She had one hundred and six guns, more than twice as many as the next biggest ship of her time. The previously most expensive ship had cost £10,000. Normal ships cost £6,000–£7,000. The *Sovereign of the Seas* cost £65,000. When Charles demanded a special tax called Ship Money to help pay for her, people were outraged. Finally Parliament was so angry that it declared war against the King. This was the English Civil War. Charles lost his throne and then his life. It was a high price to pay for a ship.

When Charles II became King in 1660 he appeared to have learned little from his father's mistakes. He too wanted enormous floating gun platforms with splendid ornamental carvings and big cabins so that he and his brother and their courtiers and servants could stay on board in comfort. He rebuilt his father's *Sovereign of the Seas* and about six others weighing over one thousand tons. Then he built the *Prince* and the *Royal James* which were even bigger. The *Royal James* was less than a year old when she burned to death at Sole Bay.

Charles II spent so much money on his navy that he couldn't ask Parliament to give him any more. By 1670 he was a million pounds in debt and became so desperate that he entered into an alliance with his official enemy King Louis XIV of France. Louis offered Charles more money to spend on ships if he would use them to attack the Dutch. (He offered even more money if Charles would change his religion from Protestant to Catholic but this had to be kept a secret.)

In the spring of 1672 Charles II made an excuse to declare war on the United Provinces and sent his fleet and his brother out to sea to join up with the French and attack Admiral de Ruyter while the weather was good.

If you think of these maritime battles as deadly strategy games, you'll realise that de Ruyter was a master. His ships were not as large as the English ships and less money had been spent decorating them. It was his seamanship and his knowledge of the North Sea that won him so many victories. That – and his ability to take the English by surprise.

Before the Battle of Sole Bay the United Provinces was a republic. De Ruyter's ships were provided by separate admiral-ties for each of the seven provinces and they weren't particularly co-operative. There were no kings demanding great ships as status symbols but most of Admiral de Ruyter's vessels were sponsored by a particular town and they naturally wanted to look good. The provincial guilds paid extra for carved figure-heads and elaborately decorated sterns on which they could show off their coats of arms and locally significant symbols – rather like personalised number plates on cars and the rear window stickers which boast 'If you can see this then I'm in front of you!'

Captured ships were financially valuable. During the Battle of Sole Bay the Dutch came close to taking two of the big, 1000-ton English ships (the *Royal Katherine* and the *Henry*) but both of them escaped. The English gained the *Stavoren*, a 48-gun ship which was sailing with the Amsterdam admiralty. She took her name from the town of Stavoren in the province of Friesland. It had once been a rich and important trading port but had declined as its harbour silted up. Some people said there had been witchcraft involved. They blamed a greedy woman – the Lady of Stavoren.

The ship *Stavoren* had been built in Edam. In the past she'd carried one of the Dutch admirals. She'd sailed as far as Scandinavia and fought at the Battle of the Sound against Sweden in 1658. Now she was one of the oldest and smallest of the Dutch great ships. She had a painting of her home town on her stern. Her other main item of decoration was her figurehead, a carved red lion.

THE SOLE BAY LECTURES
BY MWVANDERVELDE
NUMBER THREE: 'THE PRIZE'

The *Stavoren* was captured between four and five o'clock in the afternoon of May 28th 1672. Ever since the tide had turned and the fleets had put about, the English and the Dutch had been sailing roughly south-east in two long lines, firing at each other. There was still very little wind and the tide was against them. It must have been immensely slow.

The Dutch ships were to windward where the English would like to have been. If you were to windward, you had 'the weather gage' and if you hammered your opposing ship so hard that she had to stop firing or could no longer sail properly you could use the wind to bear down on her, then come alongside and capture her. The captain and crew who took a ship earned a generous financial reward.

It looked as if the Dutch were going to be lucky. When the

tide had turned at noon Dutch admiral Van Nes had captured the *Royal Katherine*, an 82-gun second-rate English 'great ship'. He'd taken her captain and officers on board his own vessel and put some of his men onto the *Royal Katherine* to sail her back to Holland. The English crew were imprisoned below decks.

Unfortunately for Admiral Van Nes he'd done the first part of his job too well. The *Royal Katherine* was an awkward ship at the best of times and she was now so badly damaged that she wouldn't go to windward at all. She couldn't point in the right direction for Holland.

And she was leaking. So, when the English crew locked down below began yelling, 'The ship sinks! The ship sinks!' the Dutch allowed them back on deck to help save her. Instead the English prisoners attacked the Dutch, locked them below, and headed the *Royal Katherine* for Harwich with those few precious breaths of wind comfortably on her quarter.

This line-of-battle fighting was toughest on the smaller ships. They couldn't use their qualities of nimbleness to get out of the way and might be trapped into a long duel with an enemy who might have twice as many guns. Once they were too badly damaged to keep their place in the line, they would have to fall back, easy prey for enemies. It makes me think of those TV documentaries where some weaker animal is separated from the main herd and the predators close in.

That's what happened to the Dutch 54-gun ship, the *Josua*. She'd been battered by the 96 guns of Sir John Kempthorne's *St Andrew* until she could sail no more. She was so badly damaged that the last survivors of her crew took to their boats and abandoned her. She wasn't even worth taking as a prize so the English ship, the Edgar, carried on firing at her until she sank.

The 48-gun *Stavoren* had suffered badly during that long slogging match that lasted the full length of the ebb tide. Eventually she could no longer keep up with the rest of her countrymen. She drifted helplessly to leeward until she found herself in the midst of the English line-of battle – easy prey for the *Greenwich*, a slightly larger ship of 60 guns. 'Between four and five o'clock I saw the *Greenwich* board a disabled Dutch ship which had fallen among our ships. The *Greenwich* took her and carried her away.'

But where was she taken? Harwich was the nearest port with ship-building and repair facilities and that was where most of the damaged English ships headed when they could no longer continue fighting. The wind was fair for Harwich but fair for the Thames as well.

In July 1672 there were 180 Dutch prisoners close to starvation in Harwich. They'd been given 2d each to last four days. Some of these men could have come from the crew who'd attempted to take the *Royal Katherine* and had then been overpowered – but I'm guessing that most of them were sailors from the *Stavoren*. She had a crew of 200 and there must have been many casualties before she was sufficiently weakened to be captured. It's likely that her captain, Daniel Elsevier, and his officers were removed separately, perhaps in hope of a ransom. They could even have been exchanged later for the captain and officers of the *Royal Katherine*. So my best guess is that the 180 Dutch prisoners struggling to survive in Harwich were from both of the two ships, the *Stavoren* and Dutch prize crew who had been put aboard the *Royal Katherine*.

What happened to them? No-one knows. There doesn't seem to have been any system in place for ordinary prisoners. I have some suggestions but my research is at an early stage.

What's certain is that the *Stavoren* herself was repaired and sent out again the next year as part of the English fleet, fighting against her own countrymen at the battles of Schoonvelde and the Texel. The English scarcely bothered to change her name. They wanted the Netherlanders to see their own vessel turned against them, their own figurehead sailing to attack, their own guns rolled out against them. She was now His Majesty's Ship *Stavoreen*.

The *Stavoreen* had to be sent home again for repairs after the Battle of the Texel in August 1673 and then the war against the Dutch was over. She was used for a while in the Channel to protect merchant men or the fishing fleet but the years from 1674 until 1689 (when England went to war with the French) were years of great reduction in the size of the English navy. In 1682, ten years after she'd been captured at Sole Bay, HMS *Stavoreen* was officially declared useless and sent to be broken up.

THE SOLE BAY LECTURES
BY MW VANDERVELDE
NUMBER FOUR: 'THE WATER LINE'

June 1672, the United Provinces

Admiral de Ruyter's battered fleet, anchored safely behind the Oosterbank, must have been pleased with their surprise attack at Sole Bay. The *Royal James*, a first-rate ship had been destroyed, the *Prince*, the *St Michael*, the *Royal Katherine*, the *Henry*, the *Resolution*, the *Cambridge* – all first- and second-rate ships – had been so badly damaged that they'd been forced to withdraw. It was a pity that they had not gained any prizes themselves and they had lost the Josua and the *Stavoren* but their strategy had been successful. They'd made sure that King Charles II of England would earn nothing from his treacherous French alliance.

On land however it was a different story. While de Ruyter and the navy had been away, the French army had invaded the United Provinces. The warm, dry weather made it all too easy for King Louis XIV and his troops to cross the shrunken rivers on the landward side. There were only the local militiamen and peasants to resist them. Most were too shocked even to try.

Within weeks the French had crossed the River IJssel and Louis XIV had installed himself in the heart of the seven provinces. Johan de Witt's republican government was in chaos. His rival, twenty-two year old Willem III of Orange, was ready to take command.

The French had thought young Willem might play their power games with them but they were wrong. He was Protestant: they were Catholic. He'd been Stadtholder-in-waiting all his life.

He knew that his moment had finally arrived.

Willem III had just 12,000 men to help him defend Holland and Zeeland, the last two provinces: Louis XIV had 100,000 trained professionals.

Guns and sailors were taken from de Ruyter's ships and hurried to the final line of defence – the Water Line. One in every two able-bodied men was required to join up and all the strongpoints along the dykes were fortified. Then Willem convinced his countrymen to use their ultimate weapon: they opened the sluices and flooded their own country.

It was a slow process in a dry year – but it worked. Homes and villages, years of patient farming were ruined. South Holland became a vast network of water and marsh from the River Maas to the Zuider Zee. Better to lose everything than give it to the Catholic French. Holland was now an island and Louis XIV could advance no further. He left an army to occupy the other captured provinces and returned to Paris.

The Hollanders were angry though, dangerously angry. They needed scapegoats. First there was an attempt to assassinate their former leader, the shrewd, peace-loving Johan de Witt. Then, in August, his brother Cornelis was arrested and tortured on a faked-up charge.

Only five years earlier Cornelis had been a national hero for masterminding a daring raid on the English ships lying undefended in the river Medway. Johan had organised the survey work – discovering how the Dutch could navigate safely through the English shallows – and Cornelis, with Admiral Van Ghent, had captured the English flagship, the *Royal Charles*. Together they had sunk or burned another half dozen of the English 'great ships'.

Cornelis had been present at the Battle of Sole Bay. He had remained on the deck of Admiral de Ruyter's *De Zeven Provinciën* throughout the fighting, refusing to take shelter even as those around him were killed and wounded. His loyalty to the United Provinces was absolute. He had nothing to confess so confessed nothing.

Cornelis de Witt was sentenced to banishment. He was weak from torture with both his legs broken. Johan arrived in a carriage to collect him from prison and the crowd went berserk. The brothers had led their country into its Golden Age. Now they were savaged. Then the militia, who should have protected them, joined in to finish them off. Their bodies were bound together and hoisted on a gibbet, then dragged down again and torn to pieces: parts of them were eaten or sold – a finger joint for six stivers, an ear for twenty.

Willem III didn't grieve for the dead de Witts and made no attempt to punish their murderers. He put some of the cannon and the sailors back in the ships and ordered de Ruyter to stand guard against an English invasion from the sea. Then he set his mind to getting rid of the French.

The question that I'm surprised that you haven't asked is what difference the Battle of Sole Bay made – the money spent, the lives lost. So what? Where's the bigger picture?

Obviously the battle must have made about 55,234 differences. That's the number of men and boys in the English, French and Dutch fleets who were directly involved during that long summer day in 1672. And you might want to multiply that by their families, the people emotionally close to them, or financially dependent.

For some of those people the battle made the ultimate difference – between life and death – or between health and disability; freedom and captivity. Sole Bay was the battle, remember, that Admiral de Ruyter recalled as the longest and hardest fought of his entire career. You were in as much danger at the Battle of Sole Bay if you were a cabin boy or an admiral.

(And just in case you're sufficiently interested in the great de Ruyter to wonder what happened to him, I can tell you that he was fatally wounded by a cannonball in 1676, just four years later, when the Dutch and Spanish fleets had joined together to fight the French.)

When historians ask what difference a battle made, however, they're not usually asking about the 55,234 differences. They're more likely to be thinking about issues such as the balance of power between countries or the effects on an economy.

Initially the Battle of Sole Bay looked like bad news for the

English. They'd only taken that single prize, the *Stavoren*, and many of their larger ships had suffered too much damage to go out again soon. James Duke of York spent the next two months trying unsuccessfully to find and capture some of the rich Dutch merchant ships.

Charles II had been given the money for this war by the Catholic King Louis XIV. England was a Protestant country and it wasn't too long after the battle that people began to grumble about taking Catholic money to fight another Protestant country. Maybe the ordinary people in London and the East Coast ports had watched too many boatloads of wounded being brought home. There was no system of care for the ordinary seaman. They were dumped 'on the parish'. In Southwold they were left looking after 800 sick and wounded crewmen. There were only 157 households in the town.

James, Duke of York, who was already not-very-secretly a Catholic, couldn't continue as Lord High Admiral. When the English fought the Dutch in 1673 James had been replaced by his protestant cousin, Prince Rupert.

This time de Ruyter stayed close to home. He knew the English were frightened of running aground on the shoals off the Dutch and Flemish coasts and he played on this. 'They will fight with me when I please but I won't when they please,' he said, removing the channel marks and putting small boats in place so his own ships knew where to go.

The English lost again and finally made peace with the Dutch. This was bad for the ship-builders and the gun-powder factories and the officers who made fighting their career, but good for the economy of the whole country once the King stopped getting into debt for the sake of his staggeringly expensive warships.

What about the Dutch? What happened to them once the English gave up fighting? After the Battle of Sole Bay they'd been invaded by the French; they'd had to flood a large part of their country; the de Witt brothers had been murdered; 22 year old Willem III was in charge.

It's almost another story – but not quite. The events of 1672 kick-started Dutch Willem's career in a way that no-one could have expected. The royal families of Europe were closely inter-married. Willem was already Charles and James's nephew as his mother had been their sister. After the war, in 1677, he made the relationship even closer by marrying James's oldest daughter, Mary, who was his first cousin.

Mary cried all day when she heard she'd got to marry Willem and live in the United Provinces but politically it was a shrewd move. Neither Charles nor James had any legitimate sons – which meant that Mary was heir to the English throne after her father. And she'd been brought up as a Protestant...

When Catholic James had become King James II and had a baby Catholic son, Willem crossed the North Sea and invaded England with his own ships and army. He was greeted by a political sigh of relief. James fled. Willem and Mary became joint King and Queen. Now he was William III of England as well as Willem III of the United Provinces. It was almost as small a name-change as when the Dutch *Stavoren* had become the English *Stavoreen*.

King William III was soon re-building the English navy to help him fight the French but the new war came too late for HMS *Stavoreen*. She'd already been sold to a ship-breaker. This could have been in Harwich; it could have been in Ipswich. Her masts and cannon would have been taken out of her: all her rigging and equipment sold in some massive boat jumble. Her timbers might have been used in other ships or even in people's houses. The only thing we do know is that her carved wooden figurehead ended up at the Red Lion pub in Martlesham.

We don't know why. The Red Lion was a coaching inn. Its owner would have been quite well off. Maybe his family had a connection with the sea or maybe he just fancied it. The carving became locally famous. 'That's as red as the lion of Martlesham,' Suffolk people used to tell each other. Gradually they forgot to remember that the red lion of Martlesham, a local landmark for more three hundred years, is also the last known survivor of the Battle of Sole Bay.

The Lady of Stavoren

There is little direct reference to the *Swallows and Amazons* series in this story – though expert readers may detect some trace of *The Picts and the Martyrs*. The obvious borrowing is from Arthur Ransome's *Old Peter's Russian Tales* where the storyteller lives in the woods with his grandchildren, Vanya and Maroosia, and their dog Bayan. The folk tales surrounding the Lady of Stavoren are not in Ransome's collection as they are Dutch not Russian.

Stavoren is the oldest city in Friesland and was an important trading port until a sandbar developed across the harbour entrance and eventually blocked access to all but the smallest vessels. A story was told that a rich and spoiled lady merchant had instructed her captain to bring her the most precious thing in the world. When he returned home with a cargo of wheat – food being the most precious thing in the world – she was so angry that she ordered him to tip it into the sea. She refused even to allow it to be given to the hungry. According to the story the wheat swelled and began to send out shoots and that was when the harbour silted up.

Some versions of the story go on to say that the Lady herself was so arrogant that she threw a ring into the water, boasting that she would never be poor or hungry until that ring returned to her. The very next day she found her ring in the mouth of the fish that was served for her dinner.

The town of Stavoren was on the Zuider Zee, which has now

been enclosed into the IJsselmeer. In 1657, a few years after the warship Stavoren had been built, it suffered a devastating flood and was almost destroyed. Today it's an attractive small town, mainly focussed on holiday-makers, with a marina, camping and access to both the the Ijsselmeer and the Frisian lakes. If my character Helen decides to settle in Stavoren with her grandparents I think she'll be very happy.

GLOSSARY OF DUTCH WORDS AND PHRASES

dagtank	daytank	*mijn lieve koe*	my dear cow
Drie Vrouwen	three women	*mejuffrow*	Miss (title)
engel	angel	*mijnheer*	Mr (title)
Engel	English	*moedertje*	mother
heilige vlammen	holy flames	*pompiert*	pumpkin
hoofdtank	main tank	*stivers*	seventeenth century coins
kapitein	captain		
koe	cow	*woote*	wheat
kracht van de leeuw	power of the lion	*wreken de dame*	revenge of the lady
leeg	empty	*vol*	full

Van der Velde sketching in his galjoot
In the days before cameras, you had to be
good at drawing – imagine doing it in
the middle of a roaring battle in
rough seas!

From the Wheelhouse

I think that the first time that I passed the Red Lion of Martlesham must have been late in April 1954. I was less than two weeks old and I was visiting my grandmother who lived in Waldringfield. Our home was in Woodbridge and the quickest way to drive from one place to the other was to take the turning opposite the Red Lion pub. "Red wo-wo, red wo-wo!" my brothers and I used to shout as we made that same journey almost every weekend throughout our childhoods. Somehow it was always an exciting moment when we turned off the (then) main road and onto the narrow, twisting lanes. It wasn't just Granny and our uncle Jack Jones who lived in Waldringfield – from 1957 the most important resident, as far as we were concerned, was our family yacht, *Peter Duck*.

But for most of the next half century that was all the red lion meant to me – a welcome signpost on a favourite journey. Then two things happened. The first was that my youngest brother, Ned, moored his sailing boat *Gingerbread Man* at the top end of Martlesham Creek for a few months. I was immediately attracted by *Gingerbread Man*'s new location, full of eccentricity and atmosphere and with all those wonderful walks over the hill and onwards to the Deben but my mother, in her late eighties, declared that it was "too spooky".

Then, at about the same time, I happened to read *Swatchway Magic* by Paul Antrobus and Charles Scoones. Their identification of our "red wo-wo" as a seventeenth-century ship's figurehead from the Battle of Sole Bay came as a shock. I'd been born in Woodbridge, educated in Ipswich and in Southwold – studied A level history even – yet I knew almost nothing about the Anglo-Dutch wars that had been fought so near our coast. I have since spent happy hours pouring over the National Maritime Museum's catalogue of the Van der Velde drawings and reading the different first hand accounts of the battle that have been collected with the Journals of John Narborough by the Naval Records Society. These provide most of the quotes in the Sole Bay Lectures. I feel doubly fortunate that my friend Richard Woodman has not only checked my facts with his usual generous stringency but has also recently written his own seventeenth-century trilogy. Richard's Kit Faulkner novels take the adult reader from the reign of King Charles I, through the Civil War and the Restoration of King Charles II to the end of hostilities with the Dutch in 1674.

My partner Francis owns *Goldenray*. She's a former fishing boat, now a houseboat, and is moored in the Ferry Dock, Woodbridge, next to the Dutch barge *Cromarty*. They've been neighbours for several years and heaven know what they whisper to each other when the humans aren't around. Both of them are work boats: *Cromarty* transported eels in her past life, *Goldenray* fished the turbulent waters off the Scottish coast. They have loaned some of their outer attributes to this story but not their personalities or even their interiors. *Goldenray* has been transformed since Claudia Myatt has been living on board: *Cromarty* is a warm and glowing family home – as unlike *Drie Vrouwen* as she could possibly be.

Ever since *Peter Duck* has been my responsibility I've taken comfort from the fact that whenever I'm uncertain about something I've only to take a couple of walks up and down the Woodbridge river wall and I'll find someone who'll give me their advice. Add the Facebook messaging system and the same is true of book research. Thanks to Art Butler (Deben Marine), Julie Cochrane (National Maritime Museum), Gill and Tim (Twee Gebroeders), Roland Mann (Cromarty), Rob Lusher (Red Lion, Martlesham), Polly Robinson (Food Safari), James Wheen and everyone else who has shared their knowledge so generously. Conversations with children at Alton Park Junior School, Frobisher Primary School and Kessingland CE Primary School have also been most helpful. I'm especially grateful to my friend Fiona Freeth who talked about the problems of families with ADHD (attention deficit hyperactivity disorder) and epilepsy.

I couldn't put a book together without the professional expertise of Megan Trudell (book design), Matti Gardner (ebook conversion), Nicky Prentis (Berforts printers), Jim Sheehan (Signature book reps) and the friendship of the Authors Electric group. Particular thanks to Heidi Carhart, Peter Dowden, Ruth Elias Jones, Frank Thorogood, Peter Willis, Richard Woodman and Francis Wheen for reading, advising, fault-spotting (especially Peter Dowden!) and encouraging.
Claudia Myatt, you are a wonderful illustrator and friend.

Lowestoft Lass

kayak

Drie Vrouwen

Strong Winds

Lively Lady

rowing skiff

Ra'

Look out for more titles in the *Strong Winds* series

Books by Julia Jones

The *Strong Winds* Trilogy:
Volume One: *The Salt-Stained Book*
Volume Two: *A Ravelled Flag*
Volume Three: *Ghosting Home*

The Allingham Biography series:
The Adventures of Margery Allingham
Cheapjack by Philip Allingham (edited with Francis Wheen)
The Oaken Heart by Margery Allingham (edited with Lesley Simpson)
Fifty Years in the Fiction Factory

Books by Claudia Myatt

RYA Go Sailing: a practical guide for young people
RYA Go Sailing Activity Book
RYA Go Cruising: a young crew's guide to sailing and motor cruisers
RYA Go Cruising Activity Book
RYA Go Inland: a young person's guide to
Inland Waterways
RYA Go Green: a young person's guide to
the blue planet
RYA Go Windsurfing
Log Book for Children (new edition)
Buttercup's Diary and other tales
Claudia is an illustrator, an author and an artist. Visit her website
www.claudiamyatt.co.uk to discover more about her work.

Richard Woodman Kit Faulkner novels

Volume One: *A Ship for the King*
Volume Two: *King or Commonwealth*
Volume Three: *The King's Chameleon*